The Newcomer

Books by Suzanne Woods Fisher

Amish Peace: Simple Wisdom for a Complicated World

Amish Proverbs: Words of Wisdom from the Simple Life

Amish Values for Your Family: What We Can Learn from the Simple Life

A Lancaster County Christmas

Christmas at Rose Hill Farm

The Heart of the Amish

LANCASTER COUNTY SECRETS

The Choice

The Waiting

The Search

SEASONS OF STONEY RIDGE

The Keeper

The Haven

The Lesson

THE INN AT EAGLE HILL

The Letters

The Calling

The Revealing

THE BISHOP'S FAMILY

The Imposter

The Quieting

The Devoted

AMISH BEGINNINGS

Anna's Crossing

The Newcomer

The Return (Summer 2017)

AN AMISH BEGINNINGS NOVEL

The Newcomer

SUZANNE WOODS FISHER

Revell
a division of Baker Publishing Group
Grand Rapids, Michigan

Published by Revell
a division of Baker Publishing Group
P.O. Box 6287, Grand Rapids, MI 49516-6287
www.revellbooks.com

Printed in the United States of America

Library of Congress Cataloging-in-Publication Data is on file at the Library of Congress, Washington, DC.

ISBN 978-0-8007-2749-9 (paper)
ISBN 978-0-8007-2863-2 (print on demand)

Scripture quotations are taken from the King James Version of the Bible.

This book is a work of fiction. Names, characters, places, and incidents are the product of the author's imagination or are used fictitiously. Any resemblance to actual events, locales, or persons, living or dead, is coincidental.

Published in association with Joyce Hart of the Hartline Literary Agency, LLC.

17 18 19 20 21 22 23 7 6 5 4 3 2 1

To those pioneers in our life,
grandparents and great-grandparents (and so on),
who forged a trail through uncharted wilderness
for the rest of us to follow.

All the wilderness seems to be
full of tricks and plans to drive
and draw us up into God's light.

—John Muir

Cast of Characters

Bairn (Hans) Bauer—ship carpenter on the *Charming Nancy*, son of Jacob and Dorothea, had been separated from family as a boy and raised by Scottish sea captains. Recently reunited with family

Anna König—childhood sweetheart of Bairn who emigrated with her church from Ixheim, Germany, on the *Charming Nancy*

Jacob Bauer—Amish bishop of church of Ixheim; emigrated one year prior (1736) to claim land for church to settle

Dorothea Bauer—wife of Jacob Bauer, mother of Bairn and Felix

Felix Bauer—eight-year-old son of Dorothea and Jacob, brother to Bairn

*Benjamin Franklin (and wife Deborah)—printer in Philadelphia

Christian Müller—Amish minister of church of Ixheim; emigrated on *Charming Nancy* (1737)

Maria Müller—wife of Christian Müller

Catrina Müller—ten-year-old daughter of Christian and Maria

Isaac Mast—church member, widowed father of Peter

Peter Mast—sixteen-year-old son of Isaac

Josef and Barbara Gerber and twin toddler boys—church members

Simon Miller—church member, elderly bachelor, on the lazy side of lazy

Henrik Newman (The Newcomer)—immigrant from Germany who arrived on another ship (1737) and joined the church of Ixheim

Captain Charles Stedman—captain of the *Charming Nancy*, the ship that carried the church of Ixheim across the Atlantic

Captain Angus Berwick—captain of the *Lady Luck*

Countess Magdalena von Hesse—German noblewoman who came to the New World to find her missing husband

*Maria Saur (Sister Marcella)—wife of printer Christoph Saur

*Peter Miller (Brother Agrippa)—one of the brothers at

Ephrata Cloister who, after Father Friedsam's death, ran the Cloister

*Conrad Beissel (Father Friedsam)—a charismatic preacher who, along with his faithful following, started Ephrata Cloister

*nonfiction

Glossary of Historical Terms

anchor home means the anchor is secured for sea. It usually rests on the outer side of the hull, at the bow of the ship.

barque is a three-masted, square-rigged sailing ship designed to haul cargo.

binnacle is built-in housing for a ship's compass.

boatswain, pronounced 'bō-sən, is the ship's officer in charge of equipment and the crew.

bollard is a large ball on a short pedestal.

bowsprit is a spar extending forward from a ship's bow to which the forestays are fastened.

cleat is a low fastener with a horn on each side.

coaming is a raised border around the hatch of a ship to keep out water.

companionway is a set of steps leading from a ship's upper deck down to the lower deck.

fo'c'sle deck is a raised deck at the bow of a ship.

forecastle or *fo'c'sle* is the forward part of a ship below the deck, traditionally used as the crew's living quarters.

Fraktur is both a German style of lettering and a highly artistic folk art created by the Pennsylvania Dutch in the 18th and 19th centuries.

galley is the ship's kitchen.

Great Cabin is the captain's quarters.

halyard is a rope used for raising or lowering sails, spars, or yards.

land warrants were official documents (though, in the 1700s, they were often scraps of paper) authorizing a person to assume possession of a specific plot of land.

larboard was the historical term for the left-handed side of the ship, looking forward. In early times merchant ships were loaded from the left side. *Lade* meant "load" and *bord* meant "side."

leeward is the side sheltered or away from the wind.

Mutza is a traditional coat worn by Amish men to church and other formal occasions. The coat has no collar, pockets, or lapels. Normally black, some coats from 18th- and 19th-century Europe were red.

oakum, from the word *off-combing*, is loose fiber obtained by untwisting old ropes, used to caulk wooden ships.

Oath of Allegiance was created in 1727 by the Provincial Council of Pennsylvania and administered to all immigrating male Germans in the Philadelphia Court House. The Oath required an immigrant to disavow ties to his former monarch and pledge allegiance to King George of Great Britain.

round house is the chartroom where the ship's progress was planned and plotted.

spar is a thick, strong pole used for a yard.

starboard comes from *steor* meaning "helm" or "rudder" and *bord* meaning "side." At one time, a boat or ship had rudders tied to its side. The modern word, starboard, refers to the right-handed side of a vessel, looking forward.

stern is the rearmost part of the ship.

trammel is a hook in a fireplace to hold a kettle.

triangle trade is an historical term indicating trade among three ports. Sugar (often in the liquid form of molasses) from the Caribbean was traded to New England, where it was distilled into rum. Profits from the sale of sugar were used to purchase goods; those goods were sold or bartered in West Africa for slaves, who were then brought to the Caribbean to be sold to sugar planters. The profits from the sale of the slaves were then used to buy more sugar.

upper deck or *waist* was the middle part of a British ship. This large area, lower than both the raised forecastle deck toward the bow and the even higher quarterdeck toward the stern, was where passengers could congregate if there was no maneuver requiring the area to be cleared for action.

yard is a horizontal spar on a ship's mast for a sail to hang from.

1

Philadelphia
October 15, 1737

Bairn was suffocating. Not literally, mayhap, but as close as a man could get. Hardly a week had passed since he had been joyfully reunited with his father, and then, with each passing day, joy slipped away, and in its place swept anxiety, disappointment, frustration, even panic. He felt a jumble of feelings for his father—part of him loved Jacob Bauer as a son ought to love his father, part of him resented him mightily.

The first night they were all together in Port Philadelphia, Bairn had told his parents the story of how he had been snatched from the ship as a boy, sold off as an indentured servant to an evil man, and his father informed he was dead. He had been treated brutally by his master, tried to escape, and was sold off in a gambling game. He ended up as a cabin boy for Captain John Stedman, the first man in the New World to treat him well. The captain educated him and taught him ship-faring skills, and he learned quickly. He was given more responsibility, and eventually promoted to ship's carpenter. Anna König helped him translate the story to his parents, because his German dialect was rusty from disuse.

For the rest of his life, Bairn would remember standing in the carpenter's shop of the docked *Charming Nancy* ship, waiting for his father's reaction. He would remember how quiet it was. He would remember dust dancing in shafts of light filtering through the door left open to let air circulate. He would remember how tired his father looked, how old he'd grown. Streaks of gray now colored his beard; his skin bore fine white lines in the squint wrinkles that creased his eyes.

And he would never forget what happened next.

Jacob Bauer listened to his son's story one time—only *one* time—and when Bairn had finished, his father smoothed the long beard at his chin and calmly said they would speak of it no more. As if those years had not occurred! His father insisted on calling him Hans, his birth name. Bairn felt such detachment from his childhood that he didn't even realize his own mother was speaking to him when she called him Hans. That boy was gone for good.

Bairn had lived an entire life that his parents didn't want to know about, or hear about, or think about. They wanted him to be the son they remembered, the boy they had lost. They wanted to pretend his disappearance had never happened, to pick right up where everyone left off as if he had been away on a lengthy visit to a grandparent. But such thinking was impossible. He wasn't that boy any longer. He was a grown man, a seaman, shaped by a thousand different influences. Most all of them considered, by the church, to be the devil's influence.

How would Bairn ever be able to stand a farmer's life in

the wilderness of Penn's Woods, under the narrow constraints of the Amish church, with his even more narrow-minded father as bishop?

Jacob Bauer had chosen the farthest place under British boundaries to claim for land warrants—right up against the Blue Mountain range. A metaphor, Bairn realized, for how his father planned for the church to live—separate, isolated. Cut off from the rest of the world.

Bairn's dialect was inadequate to express his concerns. English was best. So tonight, before supper, with his darling Anna's help as translator, he gathered his courage to question his father's wisdom to choose land so far north, near the frontier, rather than west on the trade route. The group had to remain in the *Charming Nancy*, docked, until the men went through the process of getting naturalized. Normally, it was a swift procedure but the portico at the Philadelphia Court House had been crowded with late arrivals. Soon, though, they would be cleared. And that's what concerned Bairn. "Why did y' choose land so far from civilization?"

Jacob's eyes stayed on Bairn as Anna interpreted. "Most of the land around Philadelphia has been claimed, but the area northwest of the city is unsettled."

"Aye, 'tis unsettled for a reason. Y'll spend years clearin' land in the wilderness. It will require hard, physical labor."

"We are not afraid of hard work." Jacob's fingers tapped on the wooden chest, a mannerism Bairn had forgotten, a sign of growing irritation. His father did not like to be challenged. "The land up north is made for farming. Soil, rich in limestone. Spring-fed creeks. The trees provide good building material for the cabins." He narrowed his eyes. "I chose well. It's an ideal place to settle. You'll see that for yourself, soon enough."

"But why not buy land closer to Germantown?" The earliest immigrants had developed the settlement into a prosperous place for Germans, including a town square like the ones in Europe. "Why must y' settle such a distance from the main colony?"

"Germantown is a hodgepodge. Lutheran, Reformed, Mennonites, Dunkers. They will work their wiles and take our children from us. And those settlers aren't farmers. They're weavers or carpenters or ironworkers, that sort."

That *sort*? Jacob Bauer spoke as if plying a trade was right up there with the devil's handiwork. Farming, in his mind, was the only vocation blessed by God. "Y' should be grateful that there are craftsmen who can make wagons and iron tools t' purchase. And y'll need a market to sell yer produce."

"We will produce all that we need to survive."

"'Tis no way the church can be entirely self-sufficient." Bairn's frustration was growing. "At the very least, consider letting the women and children winter in Germantown while the men survey the land and build shelters."

"No," Jacob said in that firm, dismissive tone. "We won't be separated. That time is done."

"Think of the winter cold," Bairn said.

"It's been a dry summer and fall, which augurs a mild winter. I've built a snug cabin that will provide shelter."

Bairn looked at him. "What of the natives?"

"Oh dear." His father sighed. "Not that old chestnut."

Bairn had brought that worry up before. "'Tis not to be trivialized. Yer heading into the heart of Indian territory.

They've lived there far longer than William Penn and his land agents."

Anna's brows rose at that. She hesitated before she translated that last bit, and when she did, her voice, always soft, became even quieter. But the words spoken were not without impact. The room went utterly still, no one breathed. Bairn's mother was the first to speak, saying aloud what everyone else was thinking.

"Into the *heart* of Indian territory?" Dorothea said. "Jacob—you never said anything about that. You said you had met only one."

"He was friendly," Jacob said, his voice rising momentarily. "He helped me build the log cabin. All summer, he worked alongside me."

"Y've seen only one Indian?" Bairn said. "Trust me, plenty have seen you. They're everywhere y' fail t' look. Y' have to be on guard all the time. Yer heading right into their hunting grounds." That was when Anna looked Bairn in the eye, a warning, and dropped her voice again as she translated for Jacob.

"They're *friendly*," Jacob insisted. "William Penn took care to treat them fairly."

"Was this one who helped y' a Delaware or an Iroquois?" The two groups were bitter enemies.

"Delaware."

That was good to hear, as the Delaware were not as aggressive toward Europeans as the Iroquois. Still, Bairn knew it was wrong to use fear to make his point. His mother feared her own shadow. He changed his tactics. "Most of the Mennonites trade blankets and baskets and other goods for skins and furs from the Indians. Someone will have t' learn the languages. 'Tis a way t' show y' mean t' be good neighbors."

"Not necessary." Jacob's features hardened in a look of disapproval. "We will be self-sufficient. Separate from those influences that have gone west."

"Aye, they've all gone west for good reason, those Mennonites and Dunkers. They know they need the trade route to survive, t' buy and sell supplies. The roads are good, goin' west. If y' go north, yer headin' into uncharted territory. Y'll be having to clear Indian trails as y' go, assumin' you can find them." His voice became more forceful and he tried to moderate it judiciously, but he could feel a flush starting up his cheekbones. *Say it*, he thought. Someone had to say it to him. "The Mennonites and Dunkers know that the British border is not a secure one. They know the French want to claim those borders. They know the French have the Indians in their circle. The French are able to negotiate treaties with Indians. The British only antagonize the natives."

His father rose without warning, startling the group who'd been watching the quarrel escalate between father and son, wide-eyed and open-mouthed. "Enough!" Jacob thundered, but Bairn saw his hands were trembling. "You're frightening your mother with your talk."

Jacob's gaze swept the room, locking eyes with each church member. You could see the calm come over him as he slipped back into his role as bishop. Cool again, he said, "Let us thank God for bringing us here and ask Him to bless our choice of land." The group circled Jacob and bowed their heads in prayer.

All but Bairn. He quietly slipped out the door to walk down by the Delaware River.

He could not join in on such a prayer. These people were

naïve in the ways of the world and put themselves in jeopardy, then expected God to have mercy on their foolishness.

He couldn't see himself living a life of such foolishness. He felt a growing, desperate panic rise within him, something he couldn't even tell Anna, though he knew she sensed his troubled spirit. He loved her, yet she would not understand why he was suffocating. And then there was Felix, his brother. He loved that laddie as well. Where did his obligations lie? To himself or to his family? To his dreams or to their dreams? That was the swirl of emotions that he couldn't seem to untangle from his gut.

Bairn had gone down the rabbit hole of doubt and he couldn't climb back up—he wasn't sure he wanted to. Not with the choices his father had made.

He could always walk away from a sea captain. But he could not walk away from a father.

Philadelphia
October 16, 1737

The tension that hung in the air last night lingered still.

Anna was on the upper deck of the *Charming Nancy*, spreading freshly washed laundry on a ship's yard to dry in the sun.

Bairn lowered his voice. "Is something wrong?"

"You tell me." Anna hung the last shirt over a rigging and leaned her back against the railing. "You seemed different after supper." She tilted her head. "Did your mood have anything to do with the quarrel you had with your father?" The afternoon sun caught Bairn full on the face.

"Y' think I was to blame for the quarrel, dinnae y'?"

"Truly, I don't know." Who was to blame for the quarrel seemed far less important to her than the anger that flared between them. In that moment they were no longer father and son, but strangers.

How could a man and son be reunited after years apart with such rejoicing . . . yet scarcely a week later, they had stood glaring, hands on their hips, legs stiff, thoroughly frustrated and exasperated with each other?

"Then am I mistaken in my thinkin'?"

"The land your father chose, he described it differently than you did." For the last week, Jacob Bauer waxed eloquent as he filled everyone's minds with images of pristine wilderness. A man could see a long way from anywhere, he said, the sky was *that* big, the horizon *that* far. He spoke of the clear, cold creeks and streams that crisscrossed the land and teemed with fish, the plentiful virgin timber for houses and fences and firewood, the wild game that was there for the taking, the untouched soil that was ripe to plow.

"'Tis true what he said, I dinnae disagree. We are in the Land of Penn and Plenty. But there's good reason the vast wilderness remains unsettled."

"I heard your father refuse to consider your suggestion to go west to Lancaster." Everyone heard. "He seems determined to see this through."

"This thing Jacob Bauer has set out to do—he encourages at great risk." He sat on the ship's railing and looked out toward the mighty Delaware, at the wooded islands that dotted the river.

"You speak of him as if you don't belong to him. As if he is another man's father."

"When I left the ship as a boy, I stopped being my father's son."

It isn't true, Anna thought. *A man is always and forever his father's son*. But what was true was that Jacob Bauer was not the kind of father, or bishop, that Bairn wanted him to be.

The initial excitement of arriving in the New World had disappeared quickly for everyone. They all had such high expectations, unrealistic and unfounded ones. Everyone assumed their troubles were behind them, left in the Old World.

Port Philadelphia was so young compared to ancient Rotterdam, the only other city she'd been to. From the docks rose a well-planned grid of wide streets, a few paved with cobblestones but most remained unpaved, lined with brick houses. Building was going on everywhere. Meant-to-last kind of buildings. The State House was half built, the steeple of Christ Church stood tall and proud. The young city was in a state of flux, with horses pulling carts filled with bricks to building sites or farm wagons filled with vegetables for sale at market.

And the sounds of industry that carried in the air! Steady hammers that sounded like woodpeckers, the rackety sound of metal wagon wheels on the cobblestones, the clip-clop of the horses. A riot of languages too. Swedish, Dutch, Norwegian, Russian—languages she'd never heard spoken. Anna had an ear for languages, a gift from her professorial grandfather, but the variety of tongues overwhelmed and bemused her. Accents too. So many variations of the King's English—Irish, Scottish, and now she had learned to recognize a new accent, the American one, where it added *r*'s in some places and dropped them in others. A confluence of influences.

This New World was an exciting place to be and Philadelphia was at the center of it. A few days ago, Felix had brought a newspaper to her, the *Pennsylvania Gazette*. The headline reported Philadelphia as the fastest-growing city in the colonies, surpassing New York and Boston.

But travel due north or west a short distance and the roads were primitive, dirty, filled with ruts. And beyond that, toward the top of the Schuylkill River, a person would be face-to-face with wilderness.

And wasn't that the crux of last night's quarrel between Jacob and Bairn?

She watched Bairn for a while; his eyes did not leave the busy port. "The last few days, you've been so quiet . . . so removed," she said softly. "I'm beginning to think you wish yourself back at sea."

He turned to her. "But if that were so, then the girl I have loved since childhood would not be beside me."

"*Do* you love me, Bairn?"

He lifted his hand to touch her cheek, and creases angled at the corners of his gray eyes as he smiled. "How could I have ever stopped?"

But what she should have asked: Was love enough?

2

Philadelphia
October 16, 1737

Eight-year-old Felix Bauer was having the best day of his life.

In just one week, he had explored every single corner of young Philadelphia and declared it the most beautiful city in all the world over. The only other city he'd ever seen was Rotterdam, which was old and crowded and smelled like rotting fish, which was why, Felix decided, it must have been given its name. In Rotterdam, the cobbled paths toward the shops were narrow and winding; he had to cover his nose with his sleeve to stomach the stench of rubbish in the lanes. The streets of Philadelphia did not smell, other than of horses and fresh-cut wood. And here the roads were wide, big enough for two wagons to pass.

Anna had told him that William Penn had witnessed the Great Fire of London, so that was why he designed the streets of Philadelphia to be wide, lined with trees. If there were a fire in Philadelphia, and no doubt there would be, the damage would be minimized. She had also pointed out that William

Penn named the streets after trees: Chester and Oak, for example, which was impressive to Felix. Very easy to remember.

Everything was new in Philadelphia. Each day, while his father and Christian Müller and Josef Gerber and Simon Miller and Isaac Mast gathered in a circle to pray and to wring their hands and pray some more (Who should stand in the portico at the Court House today to keep their place in line? Who should go into Germantown to buy supplies?), Felix would wait until the discussions began, and then he would quietly slip down the gangplank, taking care to remain unnoticed by his mother, who constantly hovered over him. And if it wasn't his mother who hovered, it would be Maria Müller and Catrina, her walleyed daughter. They treated him as if he was nothing but a child. And here he was, nearly nine!

Worst of all hoverers was the dead sailor Squinty Eye's awful dog, who tracked Felix like he was a fox. Anywhere he went, the awful dog found him, looking so pleased, with its pink tongue hanging out.

Felix had found a favorite route, a long walk through Philadelphia that gave him time to observe craftsmen at work. He made his way down Church Street toward the waterfront, dodging horses pulling heavy carts of bricks. *Bricks.*

The wind rustled the yellow and red leaves in the trees lining the front of Christ Church. He stopped to count the bricks lining the enormous walls, built in the shape of a cross with beautiful arched windows, but he quickly lost track of brick rows and got bored. Still, the church was something special, something made to last.

Someday, he would build himself a brick house. Another for his parents. Maybe one for Anna and Bairn too, if they ever married. No more flimsy wood houses, cold in the winter and hot in the summer. Wood houses burned like dry hay. He wondered where this busy brickmaker worked and if he could apprentice to him. He might keep a lookout for a horse pulling an empty cart and follow it back home.

Other livelihoods interested him too. He walked past the ship chandler's shop, then the cobbler's shop, admiring displays propped in open doorways to lure patrons in. On a street corner, he watched a blacksmith pound nails with his mallet on a broad anvil, then spent too long watching workers in a candle and soap shop—skimming rendered tallow from boiling cauldrons of stinky beef fat. It was particularly smelly. Cutting wicks and filling molds looked to be endless work. Cross "candle making" off the possible apprenticeship list.

An old woman tried to sell him a withered apple from her fruit basket, but he had no coins to pay her. He was hungry, though. He was always hungry. Anna said he was growing so tall that one day he would be as tall as Bairn and his father. He hoped so. They were the tallest men he'd ever seen, taller than any in Philadelphia. Catrina didn't want him to be tall, as if it was something he could control. She made no secret that she planned to marry Felix, which was a terrible thought, a truly terrible thought. He had no plans to marry her or anyone else. Girls were nothing but a nuisance and a headache. Other than Anna. Other than the Sally Lunn bun girl.

She was his current favorite. On the first day he spent exploring Philadelphia, he followed the aroma of freshly baked bread. He peeked in the windows of the City Tavern and saw a group of men around a table, lifting their glasses and shouting "Salute!"

A servant girl spotted him through the window and waved

to him. She motioned to the door and tossed him a Sally Lunn bun, and he fell in love. He'd never tasted anything so delicious. Each day after that, he walked by the City Tavern and waved to the Sally Lunn bun girl, and each day she would come to the door and toss him a bun. She laughed at his attempts to say "thank you" in English, and said he was a cute little boy. If Catrina had called him a cute little boy, he would have slugged her. But the Sally Lunn bun girl could call him anything she wanted, as long as she gave him a bun.

He thought he'd go by City Tavern in hopes the Sally Lunn bun girl was working, so he turned onto Second Street, then to Market, and passed The Printing Office and Bindery. A bespectacled man in a leather apron stood at the open door, cheerfully chatting with those who walked past his shop. He spotted Felix watching him and pointed to him. "You there, young boy. You look German. Are you? A Deutschmann?"

Felix stopped, nodded, and crossed the street toward the man.

"Do you speak English?"

"Yes. A little." He understood more than he could speak.

"Your English is better than my German. Would you try to translate a letter for me?"

Felix followed the man into the print shop—struck at once by the smell of ink, fascinated by the large wooden machines that looked a little like the looms of the weaver in Ixheim, but these held thin sheets of paper and tiny metal letters. Large windows brought light in, yet there were lit candles everywhere. The man's eyebrows lifted at Felix's curiosity. "Every good German should know about movable type. Haven't you heard of Johannes Gutenberg?"

Felix shook his head.

The man reached behind Felix to pull a metal piece of lead out of the wooden printing press. "See this? Type is cast into molten metal and poured into a carved mold. I can change the letters and reuse them. That's the beauty of a printing press."

"So Johannes Gutenberg, he lives in Germantown?" Felix had heard a lot of talk about Germantown among the men in his church. If it were up to him, he would move to Germantown and leave Penn's Woods as nature intended it. It would save everyone a lot of work.

The printer laughed, and when he laughed, his stomach jiggled and shook. "That would be rather difficult, as Gutenberg passed on to his glory in, uh, let's see . . ." He lifted his eyes to the ceiling as if the answer were written up there. "Deborah, when did Johannes Gutenburg die?"

A red-faced, plain-looking woman barely looked up from her desk, where she was setting type into wooden boxes. "1478."

The man burst out with a laugh, as if she had told a great joke. "There's a reason a woman is called a man's better half. Anyway, this letter is from a fellow named Christoph Saur. In fact, he has a son about your age. They visited my shop last month to learn about my printing press. So he said, anyway." He lifted Saur's letter. "What does *Saur* mean in German?"

Felix squinted. Was he jesting? "Sour."

"Aha! I'm not at all surprised. You know, his wife left him to go to Ephrata Cloister." He gave Felix a knowing look, though Felix had no idea what he was talking about. Before he could ask, the printer waved off the comment. "Never mind. You're too young to know of such things." He handed him the letter, written in German. "Look at that dramatic handwriting. How can anyone make sense of it?"

"It's German. It's the way we make letters." Felix wiggled his hand in the air. "Fancy letters."

"And Christoph Saur wants German to be the official language of Pennsylvania. I simply cannot abide that man." He peered at Felix. "So can you translate for me?"

Felix read the letter. "He says that the Poor Richard's Al . . . Alma—"

"Almanack. *Poor Richard's Almanack.*"

"What is it?"

The man looked surprised. "You don't know? Of course not. How could you know? You're fresh off the ship." He hurried to his desk and returned with a pamphlet. He thrust it in Felix's hands. "This is the *Poor Richard's Almanack*. Tells you everything you need to know about life. Household hints, postal rates, sunrise, sunset, weather forecasts. Farmers can set their clocks by the time of the rising of the sun in this calendar."

"Are you Poor Richard?"

"No."

"Yes." The woman with the red face spoke up. "Everyone thinks so, anyway."

"Well, I suppose you could call him my alter ego. Poor Richard Saunders is an unschooled philosopher with a carping wife. Pure fiction." He winked and tipped his head toward the red-faced woman. "But not really," he whispered.

Before Felix could open his mouth to ask another question, the man pointed to the letter from Christoph Saur. "So what are his complaints about *Poor Richard's Almanack*?"

"He says you are using German proverbs and passing them off as English proverbs. He wants you to credit them as German proverbs."

The printer's mouth sagged to an O. "I have freely admitted that Poor Richard's sayings are not original. They contain the wisdom of countless ages. They belong to everyone. They're in the general vernacular. I have merely sharpened their point." He huffed with offense. He reached over to pick up the *Almanack*, then went to the open door for better lighting and motioned for Felix to join him. "Son, have you ever heard of these? 'An ounce of prevention is worth a pound of cure.' 'A stitch in time saves nine.' 'Rather go to bed supperless than rise in debt.' Here's one of my favorites: 'When the cat's away, the mice will play.'"

"Wann die Katz fatt is, schpele die Meis."

The printer looked at Felix out of the corner of his eye. "A miss is as good as a mile."

"Net gschosse is aa verfehlt."

"Well begun is half done."

"Gut aagfange is halwer gschafft."

The man frowned. "The apple doesn't roll far from its tree."

"Der appel rollt weit vum Schtamm."

"Interesting. So you've heard that in your dialect. In Germany."

Felix nodded. "And there's an extra part too. Der appel rollt weit vum Schtamm ecksept der Baam schteht am Barig."

"What does that mean?"

"The apple doesn't roll far from its tree unless the tree stands on a hillside."

The man's eyebrows shot up in surprise, then his face crinkled up and he laughed like he was a boy. "I suppose I've been spending too much time in German taverns." He broke up again, wiping tears from his eyes. "I certainly believe in giving credit where credit is due, but proverbs come from many sources. Most of them are anonymous and difficult to trace. Even King Solomon borrowed from the Egyptians. They belong to everyone, even Poor Richard Saunders." He pointed at Felix. "I like you, young man. And I don't believe I've properly introduced myself. I'm the youngest son of the youngest son." He lifted his hand and spread his fingers wide. "Five generations."

Felix took off his hat and scratched his forehead. "I'm the youngest son too."

"That is a salient feature of a man. The last of the litter. It often means we have to make our own way in this world. Those older brothers have taken the first of everything." He reached out his hand to shake Felix's. "My name is Benjamin Franklin." He peered at Felix. "And who might you be?"

"Felix Bauer."

"Well, Felix Bauer, it's not every day that a man meets a literate young fellow in this town. Not just literate, but bilingual!" He lifted a finger in the air. "No. Wait. Trilingual! You read Saur's letter in German, you speak your own dialect, and you can understand English. You, sir, are an anomaly in Philadelphia. Few are the readers in Philadelphia. As a printer, I am sorely aware of that sad fact."

"Felix!"

Felix whipped his head around to see his brother Bairn striding across the street. "Uh-oh."

"I take it you are acquainted with that tower of a man."

"My brother." He turned back to Mr. Franklin. "I must go." He started across the street, but in two short strides, mid-street, Bairn reached him and grabbed his shoulder to stop him.

"Did y' let yer mother know where y've gone?"

"I was helping the printer with German!"

Bairn gave him a look as if he was telling a tall tale. "Yer to get t' the ship right now and stop wanderin' around. Yer apt to give yer poor mother another dose of the sea devils."

3

Philadelphia
October 16, 1737

Dorothea Bauer felt the stares of others when they thought she wasn't looking. She knew how they perceived her—as fragile as spun glass. Even her husband had sharp words for her this morning. "Why can't you be happier?" Jacob said. "Our boy has returned to us, like Lazarus risen from the dead."

Of course she was happy to have her eldest son reunited with them. Of course she was! It was a miracle.

But why wasn't her son happier to be reunited with his family?

When she had first walked down the gangplank of the *Charming Nancy* over a week ago now, she thought that at long last, hardship and suffering lay behind her. And there had been such suffering, both from outside the church and within her home. She had left behind a grave in Ixheim, of her second son, Johann. She and Jacob and Felix were reunited, and then . . . behind her came the ship's carpenter with their Anna. He held out the red Mutza to Jacob and announced the most shocking words she'd ever heard in her life: he was their missing son, her firstborn, Hans.

How did she feel, watching her son stride toward her? She wanted to weep, rejoice, fall upon her face and thank the God of heaven that her missing son had returned to her. Anna reached out and grabbed the infant held in Dorothea's arms as Bairn, this tall ship's carpenter whom she didn't know at all yet felt she always knew, grasped her and held her close to him.

Dorothea could not release him, not for the longest while. Her boy! He was not dead but alive. Bairn pulled himself back, holding her hands in his. Then he straightened to his full height—oh my, he was taller than Jacob! The two men looked at each other, Jacob with tears streaming down his face, down his beard, down to the dock. Jacob held up the red Mutza, whispering over and over, "Meiner Sohn. Meiner Sohn." Then they embraced, father and son.

Dorothea's heart had never been so full. Never.

But today, it felt empty again.

Their son seemed to want to remain a stranger to them. He insisted they call him Bairn, not his birth name of Hans. He stumbled over their language. He seemed cautious of their beliefs and customs. She noticed how he held himself back during morning and evening devotions. She heard Felix ask him why he didn't pray, and he said that Jacob said enough prayers for everyone.

The comment struck like an arrow through her heart. Why did her son feel so isolated from them?

He couldn't seem to find his place among them. He lived among them, but he had not truly accepted them. They had welcomed him in every way she knew, yet still he kept himself aloof.

And he had yet to call her his mother. He avoided the words. Last evening, he had told Felix to "take an extra blanket to your mother." Not "*our* mother." She heard that slight yet significant choice of words. She heard.

The wind gusted and she shivered, feeling the cold surround her. She gripped her arms tighter, as if she were trying to hold herself together, to keep the wind from pulling her apart. Maria often warned her that if she wasn't careful, melancholy would do her in, she would reach that terrible place where she no longer cared about anything. She believed that of herself. Melancholy was always hovering nearby, eager to claim her, to exaggerate her fears.

It was true that Dorothea was frightened about what lay ahead in the wilderness. She recognized the logic of her son's rationale—they would be utterly vulnerable in the frontier. But Jacob had told her the Indians caused little concern. Just the opposite, he said. One Indian, in particular, had become his friend and helper. "One morning," he said, "I spotted a deer in the forest. Before I could get a clear shot with my rifle, the deer fell down. Just collapsed! When I investigated, I found an arrow was imbedded in its side. I looked up and saw an Indian. He offered the deer to me."

The Indian remained with him over the summer, helping him build the cabin that would house the church for the winter. He was always alone, that Indian, Jacob said. He did not speak English and Jacob did not speak his language, but somehow they communicated.

Where was the tribe of that Indian? Dorothea wondered. Why was he alone? Would they come looking for him?

She wanted to accept her husband's bold assurances, but the thought of encountering natives terrified her. On the ship,

Felix had relayed horrific stories of scalpings and raids and kidnappings from talk among the sailors. When she tried to tell Jacob about her concerns, he dismissed them with a wave of his hand. He thought she was overprotective in the best of times, but now he felt she insulted him by implying that he hadn't planned and provided well for the church. For his family.

Tonight, despite the brisk wind, she had told Jacob she was going to walk the baby to sleep outside where it was quiet. The truth was she needed to get out of the *Charming Nancy* and its stale air, away from him, from everyone. She walked down the docks, gently rocking the baby in her arms, watching anchored ships loll to and fro on the river.

This sweet little babe's mother had died in childbirth on the ocean voyage and Dorothea had adopted him, without Jacob's knowledge. It was the only time in life she had done something of her own accord, not caring whether he would bless her choice or not.

She walked a distance along the docks, then turned to find the ship's carpenter, her son, Hans, standing a few feet away. He had come to find her and it made her heart soar.

"That babe you hold so tenderly. You see him as your own, don't you?"

He spoke haltingly, thinking carefully about his words, but he did attempt to use his first language with her. She liked hearing it from him much better than the clipped, cultured tones of his Scottish English.

"You love him as you loved Johann. As you love Felix."

Her eyes hungrily absorbed the details of his face. She could not get enough of him. "And you, Hans. You are loved. Do you doubt that?" How do you explain maternal love to a man who has never married or loved a child?

He looked at her with a slightly perplexed expression. "You say you loved me, yet you let your husband take a mere boy to the New World. I was not much older than Felix is now."

She lowered her gaze; the question needed a thoughtful answer. How could she make him understand? "Your father promised me he would take care of you. I trusted him."

"And yet you were wrong. He was wrong." He bent down and yanked off his boot, then his sock, and lifted his pant leg over his ankle. There were scars, horrible scars.

Dorothea's legs suddenly turned to mush. She could feel her heartbeat pounding in her ears and looked for a place to sit down, but there was none.

Her precious son. What had happened to him?

She looked down at the sleeping babe in her arms. This tall man standing in front of her had once been like this babe. She remembered the first time she had held her firstborn, when he was only minutes old, placed gently in her arms by the midwife. She remembered examining those little feet and tiny toes, astounded at the miracle of life. Those feet were once so small, so beautiful, so perfect. And now those same ankles were riddled with hideous red scars.

"They're from shackles." He was talking in a raw, hoarse voice now. "They're from the man I was sold to, off the ship as an indentured servant, though he considered me not as a servant but as a slave. He shackled me each evening so I wouldn't run off." He rolled down his pant leg and let out a harsh laugh. "And yet where would I have run to? T' whom? I spoke no English. I had no money." Her son's eyes gleamed with calculation, as he looked at her in the fading sunlight. "But I learned. To survive in this world, I learned how to make my own way. And I stopped lookin' backward. I stopped hopin' my father would come for me."

He was just a young boy when all this happened, hardly older than Felix. Just a boy. She wanted to take him in her arms and tell him that she hadn't known, hadn't known. "Your father was told you had died on the ship."

"And Jacob Bauer did not question it. He did not look for any evidence. He naïvely took the word of evildoers."

"He might have been naïve to accept their word, but he would never have left you had he thought you were still alive." She looked up at him, her eyes pleading. "You must believe that, Hans. Your father . . . he was heartbroken when he returned to Germany. He blamed himself."

"And do y' still trust his judgment? After all he's done? To you, to me. He is a man who does not listen t' others. I've sailed with many men like him. I've witnessed catastrophic results when the captain of a ship does not listen to reason." He stooped down to yank his boot on. "He was wrong then. He *is* wrong still. These plans of his—he encourages them at great risk. Why do y' still think he should be trusted with the lives of others?"

She noticed a change in his voice as his boot went on. It went flat and cold, as if the boot covered up the hurt boy who lived somewhere deep within him.

"Do you think it wise to go north toward the frontier where there is no protection for those who are vulnerable?"

No protection from the Indians, he meant. "Of course I trust your father's judgment." But she had lost some of her assuredness and her trembling voice revealed it. "He has only our best interest at heart."

Her son was not looking at her. In desperation she reached

out and caught his hand, then held it tenderly against her. "Forgive him, Hans. He is just a man."

"Bairn. Call me Bairn." His eyes flicked toward her, then settled on the ground. "Aye, he is just a man. But a man whose choices affect so many others."

She had no more answers and no more excuses.

His lips curved in a polite smile that did not reach his eyes. "Let's hope yer right."

Dorothea watched her son walk away with that hard, confident way of his. It had never struck her before this moment how much he had grown up to be the image of his father. The sun-tipped hair, the startling gray eyes. Tall and lean. Always so sure of himself. Always so tough.

No one ever contradicted Jacob Bauer . . . except for Hans. Even as a small boy, he had challenged his father, questioned him, corrected him. So unlike her. She had always felt powerless before her husband.

She didn't know where Hans got his courage to stand up to his father. Nor did she know how he had the courage to survive the difficult years after he'd been isolated—*no, speak the truth, Dorothea*—he'd been cruelly abandoned. She had never really understood her firstborn, the way his mind worked, in the way she understood Johann's or Felix's. Despite all those years as his mother, she'd never really known her son. But how she had admired him! And depended on him.

Because the main reason she had relented to Jacob's decision to take their son to the New World was that she had more confidence in the judgment and wisdom of her eleven-year-old boy than in her husband. She thought that if Hans went along, Jacob would be safe.

She was the one who had it wrong.

❧

Philadelphia
October 17, 1737

One look at Bairn's face convinced Anna that something had gone very wrong. The men had just returned from spending the day in queue in the portico of the Court House, as they had been each day since they had arrived in Port Philadelphia, excepting Sunday.

"Where is Jacob?" Christian Müller asked.

"He's gone to Germantown to purchase tools," Anna said. "He left after you went to the Court House this morning. He said to go ahead and have supper without him."

As Christian and the other men went up the gangplank to the ship, Bairn remained on the dock.

"What's happened?" Anna asked.

"I dinnae know how your people can be so naïve." Bairn's grip tightened on his hat, fingers crushing the brim, but he worked to keep his face impassive as his frustration over this immigration situation grew.

My people. The use of that pronoun rankled her. When would he acknowledge them as his people too?

"There's dozens and dozens of immigrants comin' in from the ships. They're all eager to naturalize and settle on their land before winter rolls in."

She had seen the small boats rowing to the docks, filled with German men, had seen them escorted up Second Street to the Court House. She expected the immigration process would be a slow one.

"Finally, Christian, Isaac and Peter, Simon, Josef—finally, their patience was rewarded and their turn had come up."

He leaned against the rock wall. "The way it works is that a clerk reads the Oath of Allegiance to the new immigrants in English, section by section, and the immigrants repeat it in their garbled way. Most don't understand it, anyway. Just sayin' it aloud satisfies the clerk. The clerks consider Germans to be ignorant men." He crossed one ankle over the other and studied the top of his boot. "Each man signs his name, or puts an X beside his name if he's illiterate, as most are. And that is that. Immigrants no longer, they're free to live in the New World with their families, free t' worship or not worship in the way they see fit."

Yes, Anna knew all that from Jacob's description of his own immigration process, over a year ago. "Has it changed?"

"Today, young Felix came along, sent by his father so that he would not wander the streets of Philadelphia. The laddie understood English well enough that he was able to translate the oath t' Christian Müller and the others. When the men realized that they were declarin' allegiance to the King of England, they stopped in their tracks. They asked Felix to repeat the oath, which he did. Then the men huddled together for a conference the way they do, and when it was over, they said they could not, in good conscience, declare such an oath. They gave up their spot in line—which had taken days to get—and made their way back here."

Anna closed her eyes. "I fear the men will not bend," she said softly.

"Aye." Bairn let out a deep sigh of exasperation. "Nor will the Court House. So what if they have to say a few words of allegiance t' the King? 'Tis small inconvenience for what they gain."

"A small inconvenience?" Anna said. "Bairn, it is no small thing. An oath—it is a vow. A promise made before God.

"We had few rights in Germany," she tried to explain. "We could not own land, we could not build houses. Our worship was not allowed in public places. Because the men refused to join the military, they had to pay a special tax. Any marriage was not recognized by the state church. Why, we couldn't even hold funeral services for our loved ones. Your own brother Johann was given a hasty burial, hidden from the authorities. Despite all that our people endured, we did not give up. God has blessed us and provided for us. How can we go against Him now?"

"If these stubborn men of Ixheim dinnae budge, they cannae be allowed to leave Port Philadelphia. They'll be sent back to Germany."

Late that evening, Jacob returned from Germantown. The men, as well as Maria and Anna, gathered outside to talk by a central fire because the children had gone to sleep. When Jacob heard they had returned from the Court House without success, he was astounded. "This should have taken one afternoon, not five days. Now, six! Last year, I walked into the Court House, signed my name, and was free to go."

"Did you say anything?" Christian said. "Did you lift your hand in response to the clerk?"

"Jacob," Isaac said, "did you not realize what you were doing?"

"I . . . did not speak the language. I did not know." At that point, Jacob went silent.

"Jacob, had we known this," Christian said, "if we had been made aware that is what we would have to encounter, we would not have come." In as kind a way as he could, for he was a gentle man, Christian alluded to Jacob that he had misled them by his impulsiveness, by his ignorance. It was a humiliating moment for the proud bishop.

Bairn tried to reason with his father, with Christian, Josef, with Isaac. He tried to point out that the oath was merely a way for the Provincial Council to assure itself that foreigners would agree to abide by the rules and regulations of the English government. That they truly were free to worship as they wanted.

The Amish men did not see an oath to be as simple as that. To them, it was as if they had taken God off His throne and put the King of England in His place. To them, an oath was sacrilege. Christian shook his head sadly. "No, we cannot. To swear an oath would be blasphemy against the Lord. If He wants us to be here in this New World, He will find a way."

But these delays were costing valuable time. Anna could see the lines of anxiety deepen in Jacob's face. And then he made an announcement. "The Bauer family is going on ahead to the land. Tomorrow morning."

"What about us?" Christian asked.

"The rest of you will no doubt find a way to solve this problem, then you can join us."

Bairn rose to his full height, six feet six inches, towering over the others, taller than his own father. "I will stay behind with the rest." He said he would see to it that they found a solution to the naturalization process. Once that was done, he would purchase horses and wagons to carry their trunks and barrels. And then they would journey up the Schuylkill River to arrive at the settlement.

Felix asked if he could remain behind with Bairn, to keep

practicing his English. To everyone's surprise, Jacob Bauer made no objection.

❧

That night as the baby slept in Dorothea's arms, Jacob slipped onto the pallet to lie beside her. She shifted the baby and settled him between them. Jacob lay flat on his back, one arm bent under his head.

"We are going to leave tomorrow at sunup," he said, his voice oddly gentle.

Dorothea blinked at this, for as she looked around the room, no one was making any motion to pack. "Have you told Christian? Maria will want to start packing."

"They're not ready to start out. Just you and I will head out tomorrow. I didn't anticipate the immigration process to take so long. I need to return to the land and finish the hay mowing while the weather holds."

Her senses reeled at this announcement. "You're leaving them?" She knew he was growing frustrated over the delays, but leaving them here? It didn't seem right. Her shock gave way to indignation. "We should wait so that we all leave together."

A warning look flittered over Jacob's face. "We'll only be separated for a short time. A few days. A week at the most. Hans has assured me he will see it through. Then, they'll join us."

She closed her eyes in frustration. Why must Jacob always forge ahead of the others, neglecting common sense? Hadn't he ever learned his lessons? Other than Anna and Hans, no one spoke English. They couldn't make their way without help. Besides, she couldn't bear the thought of being separated from her Hans, her son.

She opened her eyes. "Then you go. I will stay behind and come with the others."

Jacob turned to face her, surprise etched into his face. "Are you angry?"

"Yes!"

He gave her a look heavy with meaning. "I promised you that I would not leave you again."

Seething with frustration, she clenched her fist. She wanted to lash out and pound his chest, but she could do nothing with the men and women and children that shared these confined surroundings with them. She struggled to keep her voice low. "You are determined?"

"We'll leave at sunup."

She stiffened at something she heard in her husband's voice—sharp conviction, pointed and relentless.

Jacob gave her a brief, distracted glance, and attempted to smile. "It's only for a few days, Dorothea. Then we have a lifetime ahead of us." Jacob rubbed the back of his neck. "God reunited us with our son. He has not failed us. Why should He fail us on the morrow?"

Her husband's face filled with resolute calmness and she knew there would be no more debate. She was long resigned to her husband's strong will. "I'll find Felix. We'll get packing."

A guilty look flashed through Jacob's eyes before he dropped his gaze and she braced herself. "Our Felix wants to remain behind. To stay with the others, with our Hans. To practice his English. I gave him my consent."

At that moment, something within Dorothea weakened.

4

Philadelphia
October 18, 1737

As soon as the sun rose that morning, Jacob and Dorothea started the journey up the Schuylkill. In Dorothea's arms was the wee babe, a scrawny little boy child, whom she seemed devoted to. The boy's father, sixteen-year-old Peter Mast, was as equally undevoted to him. Had Anna not told him that Peter was the babe's father, Bairn would not have discerned it. It filled him with disgust. How could men turn away from their sons so easily?

Bairn watched his parents leave with a lump in his throat. For all Jacob Bauer's stern and serious ways, he did take the red Mutza with him. It was Bairn's treasured possession, the only memento he had to link to his family after he was separated from them. When the time came to say goodbye, Jacob held up the red Mutza. The coat would be their beacon, a symbol to bring them together again. He raised his eyebrows at Bairn, but said nothing. His expression wore only its perpetually tired look, deep creases lining it like the rings of a tree. They shook hands, parting, he supposed, in a type of peace.

Bairn waved to them, to his imposing father and his timid mother, telling himself everything would be fine when he felt anything but. He stared up the road until there was nothing left to see.

"So that's that, then," Anna said.

She looked at him, waiting for him to speak. But he couldn't seem to get his tongue to work, even to get enough air into his lungs to breathe.

That's that, then. His parents had actually left.

Anna gave him an intense look, as if she had much to say but knew to tread carefully. "Bairn, is everything all right? I mean, the quarrel with your father . . ."

He smiled reassuringly. "All mended." But it wasn't. Politeness soaked his voice, but he knew that Anna could hear the undertone of doubt.

Leaving ahead of the group was naught but selfish of his father. Christian and the others could not speak English; they had no idea of how to navigate through the complicated process of immigration. They would struggle to negotiate fair prices for horses and wagons. Jacob Bauer did not waste time on such worries. He was content to leave those details to someone else.

The truth was, Bairn was grateful to have time away from his father. To think, to adjust, to sift through these monumental changes he was facing. He felt such turmoil within and had no idea how to manage such conflicting emotions. It wasn't that turmoil was new to Bairn, but on a ship, there was little time to dwell on restless inner thoughts.

He lifted his hat from where it sat on the rock wall, paused with it in his hands, turning it around and around by the brim. "I'm headed to the Court House to see if I can find an understanding clerk and get this matter straightened out."

"Bairn, when exactly did you become a citizen? You've never told me."

"Long ago, when I was made cabin boy to Captain John Stedman. Anyone working on an English ship had to swear loyalty to the king. The captain held up a Bible, I put my hand on it, he asked if I was loyal to the crown, I said I was, and that was that."

That was that. As if it was nothing. To Bairn, a young cabin boy on a ship, separated from his family and assuming he'd never see them again, it *was* nothing, just a formality. Yet it was the very thing that kept stalling the immigrants. They couldn't go forward, they couldn't go back, not until this issue was resolved.

She nodded. "Are you taking Felix with you?"

"Nae," Bairn said. "Nae, I dinnae want to worry about losin' him." His brother was famous for disappearing. A few days ago, he spent the better part of the afternoon looking for him down by the ships, only to find him strolling behind a funeral procession that was emerging out of Christ Church. That brother of his, bright and curious and lacking in common sense, he troubled Bairn. Aye, and he also impressed him. The laddie was entirely uncomplicated.

Was he ever like Felix? He could not remember a time when he did not feel a burden for his fragile mother, his restless father.

A shudder rippled through Bairn. He did not like to revisit his childhood. Those memories quickly sent him down a spiral of despair and doubts. Suddenly he needed to go. Needed to get away from Anna, away from those heavy memories. He tipped his hat to her and strode down the gangplank of the *Charming Nancy*, picking up his pace with every step.

Northwest of Philadelphia
October 18, 1737

They had taken their leave in the morning, by sunup, just as Jacob intended. Dorothea had settled the baby into the pouch in front of her and gathered the reins of the mule, keeping her eyes fixed on its long brown ears.

She had said goodbye to her two sons, giving Felix multiple warnings to behave. Hans had not looked her in the eyes as she said goodbye. A public display of affection was unlikely from him, but could a son not show that he loved his mother? She was about to kick the mule to begin their journey but stopped when she felt a gentle pressure on her foot. She turned to her left and saw her firstborn son, now a man she hardly knew, standing by her side. "Take care, then."

For a moment Dorothea was too startled to react. She tried to speak when he looked up, but her voice clogged with emotions. She knew he was suffering, knew he was torn between two worlds. Yet how does a mother pave the road of life for her son? Life, she knew, was a young man's best teacher. But it was a harsh master.

Her boy had been changed by what had happened to him, scarred, altered deep, in ways that Dorothea didn't understand. It frightened her, for her son seemed more lost than ever, lost to God and the church. Lost to her.

If she forced things, tried to make amends between son and father, to attempt to have the two better understand each other, her son might resent her intrusion. Her husband certainly would. Yet if she did nothing, she left her son to suffer alone.

There was so much she wanted to say to her son. And yet she could say nothing, for fear of saying too much.

And then it was too late. Jacob tugged on the mule's reins and they were on their way north.

Philadelphia

When Bairn reached the steps of the Court House, he took them two at a time, eager to weave his way through to the front. This was a moment when his height was a great blessing, as the crowd of immigrants parted way for him. Soon, he caught the eye of the clerk and asked his advice. The clerk told him to go talk to a man named Christoph Saur in Germantown about a petition.

"Christoph Saur?"

Bairn wheeled around to face a well-dressed man. "Be y' him?"

"Not in any way, shape, or form," the man said, as if Bairn had insulted him. "But I have had dealings with him. What do you want of Mr. Saur? If it's printing you need, I can save you the trip to Germantown. I have a print shop just a few blocks away."

"Nae, 'tis not a print job I need. My business with Christoph Saur has to do with German immigrants. I was told he had filed a petition to allow the German Mennonites to naturalize without havin' to swear allegiance t' the king."

The printer nodded. "Yes. I'm aware of that petition." He peered up at the sky, eyes squinting behind his spectacles, as if he was sorting through files to find information. "February 1728. I wrote a story about it in the *Pennsylvania Gazette*. A group of Mennonites petitioned the Chester County Court—now Lancaster County—to change some wording and allow them to naturalize while meeting the dictates of their conscience. As I recall, two court officials rode forty miles on horseback to meet with the Mennonites and they came up with a solution for all." The printer pulled out his watch piece from his pocket. "You don't need to go all the way to Germantown to find out about it. I have some business to finish at the Court House, but I should be done by half past eleven. If you'll meet me at my print shop, over on Market Street, between Third and Fourth Street, I believe I can locate that article for you."

"I'll be there. Half past eleven. I thank you." Pleased, Bairn wove his way out of the jammed Court House and down the steps. He had a wee bit of time to himself before meeting the printer at his shop, so he veered down to Front Street to walk along the river's edge, to breathe in the brackish air, to look downriver toward the ocean.

This was the only place he felt he wasn't wearing a collar that was two sizes too small, just tight enough to slowly choke him. Near the water.

Far from the wilderness.

The thought of spending his life hacking and hewing his way into clearing land, backbreaking, exhausting hours spent carving farms out of forest with ax and oxcart, digging stones, hoeing weeds, felling trees—the same dull round of chores, labor and hoe. He felt a great dread.

What would Anna say if he confessed he wasn't sure he could be the man she wanted him to be? He was accustomed to the solitary life. The only ones he answered to were the captain and the first mate. His one ambition in life was to be the captain—to not have to answer to anyone. Anna wanted a partner. A farmer. An Amish farmer. Which meant that he would be responsible to an entire community of naïve, narrow-minded farmers.

She wanted him to believe the way she believed, to accept what he could not understand without doubts. She was so pious, a woman without a single doubt. He was riddled with doubts.

What if he were to lose her? That was something he could not bear. Even more than his family, he could not lose Anna. She was like the keel to his sails, keeping him balanced and setting his course in the right direction.

Everything would be all right, he told himself. He would adjust to a plowman's life. He would be the son his father expected, the son his mother wanted, the brother Felix needed, the husband Anna hoped for. He could do this. He would stifle his doubts. He must.

He heard church bells ring the quarter hour and turned around to walk toward Market Street, past the hustle and bustle of the warehouses, and search out the storefront to the printer's shop. He heard someone call his name and looked across the street to see Captain Stedman, the captain of the *Charming Nancy*, wave frantically to him. Beside him was a thin man with a dour-looking face, intense eyes, and hair graying at his temples. The man stopped to sneeze violently into his handkerchief.

Captain Stedman crossed the street, hurrying toward him. "Bairn! Bairn! I've been looking all over for you."

Felix was in no hurry to leave Philadelphia. He had developed an ideal routine for his morning: to the bake shop on

Second Street just as the baker brought cookies out of the oven and offered him one, to the print shop on Market Street as the printer's wife stopped for morning tea and offered him biscuits, to the farmer's cart on the corner of Fourth and Market as the farmer prepared to head home and gave Felix the bruised apples that he couldn't sell.

Felix had just finished his cookie, wiped buttery fingers on his pants, and brushed crumbs off his face as he reached the print shop. He stopped at the doorjamb and waited until the printer noticed him.

"Well, hello, my boy! Come in, come in. I've received another letter from that sour Christoph Saur. Here, can you interpret it for me?" He handed the letter to Felix.

It warmed Felix's heart to be considered important. He felt as if he grew a foot in the presence of Benjamin Franklin. He read through the letter once, twice. "He wants to buy paper."

"Yes, but why?"

Felix reread it. "He wants to make a German paper, to use German font. He does not like your Roman font, he says."

"Ah, I see." He took a deep breath. "At least I'll get a new customer out of this."

The printer took a coin out of his pants pocket and tossed it at Felix. "Thank you, son." He reached toward a stack of paperback books, bound in the center with two large stitches, and handed one off the top to Felix. "Keep working on your English. I could have used your help when I printed the *Prelude to the New World* for Conrad Biessel."

"Who is that?"

"Who's that? Why, he's the leader of the Ephrata Cloister. A weird or wonderful place to be, depending on your point of view. Any chance you're heading up that way?"

Felix shook his head. "No. We are going far, far away. Soon, I think."

"To Germantown?"

"No, but we are supposed to get wagon and horses in Germantown." His father had said not to trust anyone unless they lived in Germantown, and even then, only trust them partially, because they weren't Amish. He overheard his father tell Christian and Isaac about how good the food was in Germantown—that a man could close his eyes and breathe in deeply and he would be transported back to the homeland. Felix thought they should just settle in Germantown, if the food was that good.

The printer was called away by his wife to examine a board filled with tiny metal letters. "Come back before you leave for the faraway place, my boy. I'm sure I'll be getting another letter from sour Mr. Saur. Perhaps when you're a bit older, I'll make you my printing apprentice. I apprenticed for my brother, until, ahem"—he winked at Felix—"he lost patience with my charming persona."

Felix walked slowly out of the store, reluctant to leave the smell of ink and industry. He loved this city. Loved, loved, loved it.

Across the street, he caught sight of his tall brother striding down the sidewalk. Felix darted back behind the doorjamb of the Printing Office. He had to be mindful not to let Bairn see him. Two days ago, his brother found him trailing a funeral procession out of Christ Church and gave him a scolding not to cause undue worry for their mother.

But Mem was *always* worried.

Sometimes Felix wondered what Mem might have been like as a young woman, before tragedy swept into her life and swept away her happiness. Papa said she was always laughing. He could not imagine his mem laughing. Even when she learned that Bairn was not just the ship's carpenter, but he was Hans Bauer, their long-lost son—even then, Mem wept. So did Papa. Anna said they were tears of joy, but to Felix, tears were tears. If you were happy, you smiled and laughed. If you were sad, you cried. It was as simple as that. When he had found out he had a brother in Bairn, he laughed. He danced! He did a jig on the docks, a little jig that a sailor had taught him. Even his papa had laughed at his little jig.

That's how a man showed his happiness. Not with crying!

He saw Bairn stop and spin around, as if somehow he knew Felix was nearby, so he darted out of the doorway and behind a wagon. But it wasn't Felix whom Bairn was after, it was the short, round Captain Stedman from the *Charming Nancy*. He had been walking up Market Street and called Bairn's name. Felix crept under the wagon wheel to remain unnoticed.

In the gabble of greetings, Bairn and the captain stopped to speak right at the wagon—Felix could have reached out through the wheel spokes to polish their boot tops. Circumstances couldn't be more ideal to eavesdrop on their conversation, to sift through fragments of English words and phrases he could recognize and knit them together. Wasn't his father always telling him to learn as much English as he could while he was in Philadelphia? They would need his English-speaking skills on the frontier, his father said, and it made Felix feel rather important. His father should try to learn English; it wasn't very hard. Many words in their dialect sounded like English. Butter, Budder. Vater, Mater. Night, Nacht. It wasn't so hard.

And then Felix's happiness popped like a bubble of soap. He heard the words "ship . . . need a first mate . . . opportunity . . . and . . . money."

Felix connected the dots. Bairn was going to go on a ship. His brother was leaving. A week ago, he didn't even know he had a brother. And now he was leaving again. How could he do such a thing? To his parents. To Anna. To *him*!

But then Felix felt a wrench of excitement. He had an idea.

5

Philadelphia
October 18, 1737

Anna hurried down the gangplank of the *Charming Nancy* to meet Bairn as he walked toward the ship. By his determined stride, she could see he had news to tell. "Did you find a way around the oath?"

"Aye." Bairn took off his hat and raked a hand through his hair. "The credit does not belong to me but to the combination of a kind clerk at the Court House who told me of a petition that had been filed for the Mennonites. And then I happened upon a printer on Market Street who had a copy of the petition. I think the men will be satisfied with this petition . . . and the clerks at the Court House will be satisfied. It doesn't involve swearing an oath of allegiance to the king, but it does affirm loyalty to England."

"Bairn, that's wonderful news. Your father was right. God's provisions never fail."

He lifted a shoulder in a half shrug. "Well, yes, I suppose so. With a little legal advice from the printer."

"How soon will the men be able to sign the petition?"

"They'll have to get back in line at the Court House. But within a day or two, this business should be settled."

"And soon we will be able to go? To leave Philadelphia and meet Jacob and Dorothea?"

"Aye, soon." He glanced downriver and gave a slow nod. "Which means there's much to prepare for. I know of a wagon maker in Germantown who is willing to loan two wagons and two horses, for as long as they are needed." He kept his coat and hat on.

"Are you heading out?"

"Aye. I ought not be long. I heard the bells toll. A ship from Rotterdam has come into port."

"So late in the year?"

"Aye. They'd feared 'twas missin'. But in it came, with a high death toll, I heard. Mennonites, mostly, but Dr. Bond told me one of the passengers he approved fer disembarkment was alone, looking for a group that lived a straight and narrow path, he said. The doctor thought he might be Amish."

Dr. Thomas Bond was the physician who boarded the ships and examined the passengers; no one left the ship without his approval. It would be a good thing if Bairn could find this man, better still if he could persuade him to join their church.

He rubbed a hand over his face, gave her a brief, distracted glance, and attempted to smile. "Anna, darlin'. I have somethin' to tell y'."

Whatever it was, she knew she wouldn't like it.

"Let's go somewhere we can speak more privately."

She followed behind him, walking downriver.

"The weather, 'tis fine today, is it not?"

"Yes, it is a beautiful day." And it was. A golden sun shone down on the water. "But I doubt that's what's on your mind." She drew her shawl more closely about her shoulders.

"Actually, it is. We're having an unseasonably warm fall. It bespeaks a warm winter."

"That's good, isn't it? That's very good." It would be a great relief to weather a warm winter, allowing them to hasten home building. She had a dread that Jacob's cabin would be just like the lower deck of the *Charming Nancy*—crowded, with horrific smells of humanity and animals, mixed. She shuddered at the very thought.

"Anna, Captain Stedman sought me out this morning. He has a cousin, a ship captain, who wants t' make another crossing while the weather holds."

She stopped. "I thought ships didn't cross the ocean in the winter months."

"Aye, most don't, but this captain needs to make a haul."

"A haul? As in passengers?"

"Nay. Goods. Tobacco, for one. He will be traveling up the coastline of America, picking up goods to sell in England." He took a deep breath. "His first mate has been thrown into jail for brawlin' and is unable t' go. So Captain Stedman recommended me to his cousin. He said that his cousin—Captain Angus Berwick—needed an accomplished tinkerer. Since I have skills as a carpenter, he thought o' me."

Despite her intention to listen calmly, she gasped. She stared at him, momentarily tongue-tied. "And you said no, of course."

Bairn hesitated.

Prickles of cold dread crawled along her spine as Bairn's voice held a slight tremble. "Captain Berwick is offerin' a sizable salary, more than I've ever heard of fer first mate. *First mate*, Anna."

She shook her head. "There are other men to choose. There's always plenty of sailors looking for work. Men without families. Without people who are depending on them."

"Anna, 'tis one short journey. My last one. Just a few months. And then I'll be back with enough money to purchase land. Jacob and Christian and the others, they can only have land warrants, but I'm a citizen of the crown. If I can earn a fair purse on this voyage, we'll be able to own plenty of land. As far as the eye can see."

As if that would matter to her! "You've just been reunited with your family in the most miraculous way. But you would leave them? Just like that?"

"I'm crossing the sea and returning again, that's all. It happens all the time. Six months, maybe seven. And then I'll return in the spring."

Tears welled in her eyes and spilled over onto her cheeks.

He reached for her and drew her to him. "Anna," he murmured, kissing her forehead, holding her close. "Anna, think about the benefits to this plan. You told me that other Amish churches are coming next year. I can help them. As ship's first mate, I can influence Captain Berwick. I won't let him overcrowd the ship. I can do good for your church."

She had no doubt that Bairn was sincere in his assumptions—he would certainly be able to influence the captain. It was his interest in doing good for the church that she wasn't confident in. Bairn had faith in God, but his heart was not in the Amish church. She had hoped that this part of him would find repair once they reached the new land. She pulled away from him. "Tell me the truth. What's the real reason you want to go?"

"To earn enough money to buy land. To help these church people."

"They're your people too, Bairn."

"Aye, and that's even more of a reason to help them. Anna, they don't realize what they're gettin' themselves into. They speak no English and refuse to learn. They'll be taken advantage of at every turn. I've thought this through. After this sea journey, I'll have enough money t' give my father what he needs to buy the land for the church. To settle the debt between us."

"What debt? You owe your father no debt."

"I need to make sure he will be all right."

"All that he needs is for you to be by his side. He expects you to arrive at the land soon, with the rest of us."

Bairn's eyes were on the tips of his boots. He brought his gaze back to Anna, and all the distress and turmoil of the last week was betrayed by his face—he could hide it no longer. "Anna . . . I dinnae ken if I belong there."

Belonging. It was what it meant to her to be Plain, this certainty of always belonging. The church was a part of her, as much a part of her as her bones, her heart, her mind, as her soul. They would always be a part of her in ways he could not understand.

"The ship is pullin' up anchor in two days."

Her senses reeled at this announcement. "Two days?" Her shock gave way to indignation. "In two days? You're leaving in two days?"

"The sooner I go, the sooner I return."

She stared at him as if he were a stranger, and maybe, despite everything, he was. Although they had known each other as children in Ixheim, had the same childhood rearing,

Bairn had spent long, significant years separated from them, alone, first as a ship's cabin boy, then a sailor, then a ship's carpenter. The sea was part of him now, always calling to him. She'd seen him walk along the Delaware River, looking downriver as if searching for something.

"Y'll wait for me though, won't you? The rose. It's a sign. We've always been meant t' be together, you and I."

Her eyes shifted to the *Charming Nancy*, where her rose sat on deck getting sun, tucked in the basket that brought it all the way from Ixheim, Germany. That rose—it had seemed like such a miracle. But as her grandfather often said, "Ken Rose ohne Dornen." *There is no rose without a thorn.*

Right now, she could see no rose, only the thorn.

The silence stretched out between them. She drew a deep breath to still her storming heart. She was angry now, so angry the very air seemed to crackle around them. She wanted to lash out and pound his chest with her fists.

He can never change, she thought. *Never.*

She pressed on, finding courage in her anger. "If you leave, I won't promise you anything. I won't promise you that I'll wait for you."

"Anna, listen to me, lass. Listen here. I will bring back yer grandparents."

Anna stilled, considering his remark. They stood facing each other for a long moment, the only sounds coming from the water below, sails snapping, waves hitting the sides of ships.

He had found her weakness, her Achilles' heel. "If you return with my grandparents, then yes, I will wait for you." She stared up into his face, etching it into a memory that she would be able to take out and look at again and again.

"That's a promise, then." He turned to meet her gaze and the edginess that had been coiling between them began to loosen a little. He took her hand, his voice gentle. "Anna, darlin', what's a few months in a lifetime?"

But she was envisioning a lifetime in the next few months.

Northwest of Philadelphia
October 18, 1737

Hours later, still marveling over the lunacy of her husband's plan, Dorothea shifted her weight on the uncomfortable mule, the baby in her arms, with Jacob holding the reins and walking beside them. He remained silent, her husband, though she had nothing much to say to him after bidding everyone goodbye back in Philadelphia.

As she slid off her mule, bone sore and weary, Jacob led the mule to a creek for water. She took a small cup out of their bundles and filled the cup with some goat's milk to feed the baby. He was so easy, this baby. So patient. Nothing like her own three sons, who would cry and demand something the moment their eyes opened for the day. She sat down with her back against a log and gave the babe sips from the cup. Sometimes, it seemed as if this baby knew he was lucky to live and dared not create a fuss. She had said such a thing to Jacob and received a firm lecture that there was no such thing as luck.

She stretched her legs out in front of her, as long as they could go after being bent on the mule for the better part of the day. Soon enough, she would lie down and the day would end. A cloud passed over the sun and she gripped her shawl closer to her breast and shuddered. She couldn't stop the fear that was pinching her chest, fear of the night. She had always suffered a terrible dread of darkness. Especially here.

There had never been dense forest like Penn's Woods back in Germany. She hated this New World. Hated it all, the deep, dark woods and everything else about this British colony. Hated it, hated it, hated it. She didn't want to believe her hate was a sin, though she knew it wasn't the Plain way to allow hate in one's heart. She also knew not to share her sentiments with anyone, especially her husband. Always the bishop, her Jacob.

When Jacob returned from the creek, he handed her a hooped pot filled with fresh, cold water, and she drank her fill. He gathered wood to start a fire; Dorothea warmed beans from last night's supper and toasted a few slices of day-old bread. She kept silent throughout the simple meal. Jacob, too, seemed empty of words.

But then his deep voice broke into her thoughts. "There's something you want to say."

She glanced at him, taking a moment to carefully craft her words. "I've been thinking about what Hans said. That going north might leave us in a vulnerable position."

"You worry too much, Dorothea." Jacob crossed his arms as the beginning of a smile tipped the corners of his mouth. "God is working with us. Do not borrow trouble, for it is certain we shall have plenty of it before we leave this place." He reached a hand out to her. "I have no doubt it is the right place for our people."

Dorothea clasped her hand over his, but his words only intensified the storm of unrest in her soul. "But is it? Truly?"

The sharp question slipped from her lips before she could stop it, and in her husband's eyes she read the answer—Jacob *wasn't* certain . . . not at all.

"Put this fear far from your heart. The matter may seem less troublesome in the morning." He coughed once, then again. Sweat beaded his forehead.

She read exhaustion in his ashen face. "Are you feeling well, Jacob?"

"Of course, of course," he said, eyes fixed on the fire.

But she knew that also wasn't true.

Jacob Bauer had always been a strong man, hale and hearty. No longer. He had tried to hide his condition from their sons, from Christian Müller and Isaac Mast and the others, but she saw the changes in him the moment they were reunited on the docks of Port Philadelphia. He was thin. So thin! He wore two sweaters and a coat to cover up, but he couldn't hide his weight loss from his wife. He didn't eat much, couldn't rest at night because the coughing would start. She realized that he probably hadn't been well for a long time. He was insistent on leaving the others in Port Philadelphia, not because he was anxious to return to the settlement, but because he couldn't manage any longer.

The poor man.

He had worked so hard to build a new life for his family, for the church he led. He put himself in difficult circumstances, sacrificing himself for the good of others. Always alone.

No, that wasn't right. Dorothea had to continually remind herself of that truth. God was always with him. With all of them.

Philadelphia
October 19, 1737

Bairn waited on the docks as passengers were brought in from the ship on rowboats. Mennonite families were clumped together, and while there were many young men, he did not see one who stood out as Amish. Dr. Thomas Bond had said Bairn would know him by a distinguishing patch of white hair on his head. "Very peculiar," Dr. Bond had said, and Bairn had thought to himself, *Peculiar among Peculiars*.

He stopped himself. It was a bad habit to call them Peculiars and he thought he had broken it, but here it was, back again.

As a rowboat neared the dock, he saw a toddler drop his toy over the side of the boat and reach over to get it. The laddie teetered a moment, then tumbled headfirst into the dark water as the child's mother screamed. Bairn didn't even hear the splash. He was already off, pushing through the crowd to run to the end of the dock. Before he reached it, he saw a man rise up in the boat and dive in. He disappeared under the water, then emerged with the child, sputtering and crying. "Es waar alles in Addning!" he shouted to the mother. *All is well!*

The rescuer swam to the boat and handed the child up to his parents' waiting, grateful arms. As the longboat reached the dock, Bairn helped tie ropes to the cleats and watched the rescuer who, though he was dripping wet, took care to help each person disembark. Despite being soaked, he seemed full of good cheer as he shook the water out of his hair.

His hair. There it was. A shock of white.

It was apparent the man was well thought of, as the Mennonites kept clapping him on the back and shaking his hand. Even the sailors seemed fond of him.

When the man stretched a leg onto the dock, then another, he stopped and lifted his hands to the sky, repeating the words, "Denke, mein Herr. Denke." *Thank you, my God. Thank you.*

Bairn waited, watching, until he had finished his spontaneous worshiping. The man was in his midtwenties, with a lean, handsome German face, and a head of near-black hair curled into corkscrews, all but that shock of white, now entirely plastered down wet over his skull.

"Kannscht du Englisch schwetze?" *Can you speak English?*

The man stopped abruptly and looked at Bairn, startled by the question. "Nee." *No.*

Blast. Bairn would have to use his choppy dialect. It embarrassed him to speak it around people he wasn't comfortable with, and he winced as he spoke, as if ashamed. He knew he sounded stilted, using simple words, enunciating with care, and his Scottish accent colored his words. "Yer looking for a group that follows the straight and narrow path?"

"Indeed."

"Well, then," Bairn said, "follow me and I'll take you to them."

The man thrust his hand forward to firmly grasp Bairn's. Gripped his elbow. Fixed him with a sincere gaze. "I am Henrik Newman."

The man gave Bairn a palm-crushing handshake that jimmied his teeth. "Call me Bairn." He looked Henrik Newman up and down, noticing the puddle of water from his wet clothes. He took off his jacket and passed it to him. "Y' must be cold after that heroic act."

The newcomer wrapped Bairn's jacket around himself, a grateful look on his face. "A pity I do not know how to swim."

Bairn stared.

"Lach!" Henrik Newman said, with a remarkably sweet and open smile. *A jest.* "I can swim. But I'm no hero. Just a servant of God, looking for every opportunity to be a blessing."

Well, well, Bairn mused, as he started down the dock. This newcomer would be a welcome addition. Clearly, he was strong and hale, and had no fear of danger. What he did, jumping in after the child, it was a brave act. "The ship is just docked down a short ways."

"Ship? Another ship?" The newcomer's voice rose an octave.

"The church is still sequestered on the ship."

The newcomer's face fell, so Bairn quickly said, "But not for long." He couldn't blame the man—he'd just set foot on dry land after months at sea.

As they approached the *Charming Nancy*, figures appeared on the stoop, silhouetted against the light from the open door. Felix's barking dog bounded onto them. Bairn explained, in his halting speech, that the newcomer wanted to join the church of Ixheim.

There was a considerable shaking of hands with the newcomer as the dog ganged a-glee about their feet. When the newcomer explained why his clothes were wet, the women went into action, bringing him warm clothes to change into, a towel to dry his hair, and offers of food and drink. The newcomer smiled and chuckled at the fuss made over him. "Praise be to God. Delivered straight into a muddle of good cheer and warm welcome."

Maria approached him. "What may I get you? A cup of tea? A bucket of hot water to wash up?"

"If it's not too much trouble . . . both would be heaven

sent." The newcomer gave her a warm smile. Maria grinned in return, a sudden and remarkable sight, and hurried away.

"You must have a persuasive way with people," Bairn noted. "She is a woman spare with smiles."

"Who is she?"

Bairn lifted his head to see Maria pour water into a bucket. "She's the minister's wife, Maria Müller. A woman brimful of energy."

"Not that one." He pointed across the room. "Her. Over there. She's striking-looking."

Bairn looked up to find that the newcomer's eyes were riveted on Anna. She and a handful of other women were passing out slices of bread to the men, filling tin mugs from a hot kettle. A stray lock of her blonde hair had slipped and lay across her cheek. Absently she coiled it and tucked it inside her prayer cap.

"Her name is Anna König. She is the only English speaker in the church, other than young Felix. Don't let him fool you, he has much to learn though he considers himself fluent. Anna could probably teach you, if y've a mind to learn."

"Oh, I won't need English where I'm going."

Bairn rolled his eyes. He was tired of this we-think-we-still-live-in-Germany business, and nearly said so, but then something blurted out of the newcomer's mouth that stopped him cold.

"Is she unmarried?"

Bairn stiffened. "She's spoken for."

"So, then, she's not married." The newcomer's smile was easy, but a light flared behind his eyes. Bairn's eyebrows lifted and he started to say something, but Maria interrupted, holding out to the newcomer a tin cup filled with hot tea. He moved forward to take it from her, thanking her heartily as if he'd never received such a welcome gift, and once again, Maria offered him a warm smile in return.

The newcomer looked across the room to give Anna a quick, gleaming look before dropping his gaze to his tin cup, as if he sensed he was being watched.

Bairn noticed.

6

Up the Schuylkill River
October 21, 1737

Excitement was in the air, though Anna's heart wasn't engaged in the idle chatter. It was already missing Bairn.

With permission granted from the clerk at the Court House, the immigrants had declared their loyalty to the Crown of England, though not their allegiance, and were cleared to leave Philadelphia. So after a few days of gathering supplies, observing Sunday as a day of rest, the little church of Ixheim was on its way to the frontier come the dawn of Monday.

For the first few miles, the road leading out of Philadelphia was swift and smooth, but the farther northwest the convoy traveled, the more narrow the road became. Bairn had warned them it would eventually shrink into an uncharted Indian trail. Be prepared for long, hard miles over a muddy, primitive road, for the lurching and bucking of wagons over ruts.

Bairn had insisted on buying new axes for the journey. Already, they had proven indispensable along the way for clearing the trail of a fallen tree or fashioning a temporary bridge to cross a stream. The caravan stopped often in order to move or cut branches out of the way. Twice, they watered the horses and let them rest.

Christian, the leader of the church in Jacob's absence, had warned they would not stop for a meal until the day's end, hoping to make as much progress as they could. Such slow, plodding progress! They planned to arrive in a few days' time, but Bairn had warned Anna it would take longer to reach their destination far up the Schuylkill River.

Anna's thoughts wandered often to Bairn, sailing away on the *Lady Luck* today. On a windy day, a ship in full sail could slice through the water and cover one hundred miles, maybe more. For the group on their way to the frontier, they would be lucky to make a fraction of that by day's end. The women and children walked alongside the wagons to keep the load as light as possible for the horses. Wheels would get stuck in mud; the horses were new to them and poorly trained; the wagons were heavy, filled up with heavy iron tools, borrowed and purchased; bushels of apples and potatoes crowded around the large wooden chests brought over on the *Charming Nancy*.

Little by little, the group was moving forward toward a new life, unlike Bairn who, it seemed to Anna, had moved backward. Back to his worldly life.

His last words to her were, "Look for me come spring," and she had tried to give him a brave smile in return. *Please don't die*, she thought, but she lifted her voice to call, "Gott segen eich!" *God bless you*. She wondered if she would ever see him again.

As Anna trudged along beside Maria and her daughter, Catrina, she silently scolded herself. She would not let herself go down that path of vague fears. She wouldn't. Bairn had told her he would be back, that he just wanted to make one more journey, and he had yet to break a promise to her. She trusted him. She loved him. And she believed he loved her.

She thought she would never fully understand the man, but she did understand this much at least: he loved the sea. She was a jealous lover, that sea. She would not give a man up easily.

What would it take, Anna wondered, for Bairn to love farming the way he loved the sea? She mused over the similarities as she walked: The field is like an open sea, the port to aim toward is the harvest. The keel is like the plow, carving through the dark soil. And then there is the weather! Both sailor and farmer must continually adjust. They both know that nature is in control, not them. Anna spent a long part of the day pondering these points, wishing she had thought of them in time to convince Bairn to stay.

As they passed a meadow, Christian halted the lead horse. The sun dipped low on the horizon and they were all relieved to stop and make camp, tired and hungry. Anna gazed over the meadow, watching the wind play with the tops of the grass. The woods that rimmed the meadow were dense and dark, but dotted with the blazing red leaves of sugar trees.

"Peter and I will go look for water for the horses," Isaac Mast said. He and his son cut a path through the meadow toward the trees.

A light, celebratory air animated the group as they made camp. Peter and Isaac returned after finding a creek. The men took care of the horses first, leading them down to the creek to water them. Barbara, Josef Gerber's wife, and Maria started preparations for a meal. Anna found Catrina playing behind the wagon with a small kitten she had brought along. "Come help me sort the beans and put them on to cook."

Catrina stuck out her lower lip. "I'm so tired of beans. It makes my stomach hurt to think of eating beans again."

Anna was too tired to listen to Catrina's complaints. "Then why don't you find Felix and go collect dry twigs and branches for a fire?" As Catrina started toward the woods, Anna added, "Stay where we can see you."

"Because of . . . Indians?" Always anxious, Catrina looked frightened.

"Because . . . it's getting dark."

But Catrina had read Anna right. She was still uneasy about Bairn's warning that they were heading into Indian hunting grounds. Just yesterday, Anna and Felix had gone to the market to buy food for the journey and overheard talk about an Indian attack that had recently occurred in the north. She asked a farmer what had caused the skirmish. "For the most part," the farmer said as he lifted a bushel of pears off his wagon, "the causes are internal war between tribes." He set the pear bushel on the ground and looked up at her. "You're heading north?"

She nodded.

"How far north?"

"Near the top of the Schuylkill River."

His eyebrows shot up. "If you do happen upon the Indians—and you will—always have gifts ready to offer to them."

"What kind of gifts?"

"Trinkets. Pots and pans. Things that are uncommon to them." He turned away, then spun around and pointed a finger at her. "And always, always offer food. You don't need to invite trouble on yourselves by being stingy."

On the way back to the ship, Felix had asked her about the conversation with the farmer. "Anna, do you think the Indians will be friendly to us?" His face looked more excited than afraid.

"I think so," she had told him, thinking, *I pray so*. "Always remember that we trust in God. The farmer suggested that if you ever see an Indian, to offer him food. That, we do best."

Felix. Where was he, anyway? Anna gazed around the group and didn't catch sight of him. She was about to go looking for him when Maria asked her for the beans. She was cutting vegetables for a soup broth that would be cooked in a kettle over an open fire. Anna pulled a tarp off the back of the wagon and opened a sack of beans.

"And I need someone to start the fire," Maria said.

Anna sighed and looked toward the trees for signs of Felix and Catrina. That boy! Whenever work was to be done, he was far from sight.

Henrik, the newcomer, walked toward her from the creek with an armful of dry wood and kindling. "I thought you might need wood." He set the wood in an open dirt area and knelt down.

Within minutes, the fire was blazing and Maria couldn't have been more pleased.

"That's the one you should set your sights on," Maria whispered to her after Henrik walked away. She nudged Anna's elbow. "The Lord taketh and the Lord giveth. A sign from above."

"I'll hear no more of that nonsense." Anna spoke sharply, but she had learned that was the way to handle Maria's meddling. She took her turn at stoking the fire, watching the flames dance in the gathering darkness. Peter Mast had caught two rabbits, skinned them, and speared them onto a long stick to roast over the open fire. They were fortunate for this meal tonight. God's blessing on their first night.

Anna lifted the stick with the roasting rabbits to turn it once, when again she wondered where Catrina had gone to. She left Maria to mind the rabbits and walked toward the sugar trees, in the direction where the men had gone to water the horses. She'd seen Catrina run into the woods behind them, but the men had already returned and there was no sign of her. Anna was nearly to the trees when Catrina burst out of the woods and ran into her arms, trembling with fear.

Then Anna heard it. A snarl. A gray wolf appeared in the shadows, its blue eyes pinned on Anna and Catrina. The unexpected sight rooted Anna to the ground, but Catrina's frightened whimpers spurred her to take action. Moving slowly, she placed her hands on Catrina's shoulders, never taking her eyes from the wolf.

"When I say 'go,'" Anna whispered, "run like the wind to the fire. Stay in front of me. Don't look back, whatever you do." Too frightened to speak, Catrina nodded, the back of her head shivering against Anna's belly. The wolf started toward them, slowly, cautiously. "Run, Catrina."

Catrina took off toward the fire. Anna followed. Ahead of her, she saw the newcomer stand at a distance, watching.

Anna turned her head to see the wolf break into a lope behind her. She ran for her life toward the fire, as fast as she could run. She glanced back one time to see the wolf gaining ground on her. Soon, it would be at her heels. A thunderclap blasted the air, exploding against her eardrums, and suddenly the wolf stumbled. Anna slowed, then stopped when she realized it wasn't getting up. She saw the wolf's body quiver, heard it whimper in muted fury. And then it stilled.

Anna turned around and saw the newcomer standing alone, his arms still flexed, aiming a rifle, his eyes narrowed in concentration. Isaac Mast's rifle. Anna walked up to him, breathing hard, shaking with relief. "Thank you."

"Most likely," he said, smiling gently, "the wolf was lured to the camp by the scent of roasting rabbits. You and the girl stood between the wolf and his dinner."

The sound of the gunshot brought everyone running to them.

Christian reached them first and quickly surmised what had just occurred. He clapped his hand upon the newcomer's back. "You saved my Catrina, my little girl," he said, his voice choked with gratitude.

Maria and Barbara buzzed about the event as Isaac and Peter skinned the wolf for its fur coat. A light, jovial mood returned again. Maria proclaimed Henrik to be shrewd enough to grab the rifle and bring the animal down. "With one shot! Like David and Goliath."

Anna said nothing, but wanted to point out that it was a wolf, not a giant, that the newcomer slayed. Maria smoothed Catrina's wispy hair back from her cheeks, then smothered her daughter in a tight embrace and said, "I think he's a very pretty man. Don't you think so, Anna?"

Anna did not care if Henrik Newman was pretty or ugly or something in between. She was just grateful he had seen the wolf come after them and stopped it. But to object would only feed Maria's needling. "Come, let's get back to preparing supper. It will be dark soon."

As they gathered around the fire pit to stay warm, Christian asked the newcomer about his background. When Henrik told him that his grandfather had been a disciple of Jakob Ammann, the founder of the Amish church, Christian's eyes behind his shiny spectacles went glassy. "Praise be to God," he whispered.

"Now we see the purpose God had in keeping us detained in Philadelphia. To allow time for Henrik to join our church."

The newcomer looked around to see who had spoken, and his eyes settled on the minister's wife. "The Lord certainly brought our paths together." His gaze swept around the blazing fire, and his eyes stopped when he caught Anna's. He stared at her a moment, but then she dropped her eyes and felt her cheeks grow warm. "It's a miracle that I made it to the New World," the newcomer said. "And another miracle to be gathered together with like-minded believers. This entire endeavor is a return to Paradise. A return to the Garden of Eden."

Catrina sidled up to Anna. "Isn't he comely? He's the comeliest man I've ever seen."

Anna watched Henrik from across the flickering flames. Yes, his looks were striking, but she was more captivated by how Henrik's optimism lifted the spirits of those around him. When Bairn first brought him to the ship in Port Philadelphia, the entire group had been quiet and sullen, worn out by delays. It wasn't long before Henrik had everyone relaxed and laughing over an amusing story, practically lighting the room with the warmth of his personality.

He would be a welcome addition, Anna decided. They needed a young man with a strong back. They needed someone who helped them remember to face the future with a smile.

She turned her attention to stoking the fire, then wiggled the leg of a rabbit to check it for doneness. Satisfied, she lifted the rabbits off the fire and gave them to Maria to slice on a platter. Supper would be a banquet tonight: fire-roasted rabbit, some late autumn blackberries found by the creek, a rich bean broth, all seasoned with gratitude.

As twilight fell, everyone moved closer to the roaring fire to warm themselves. Joined in a circle, heads bowed, Christian gave thanks for a safe journey, for their health and the abundant food of this new land.

Anna's heart, which had just settled down to a regular beat after fleeing the wolf, started to pound again. She lifted her head and peered at the dark forest that edged their camp. Her eyes searched for every sign of movement. She saw an owl silently sail overhead and dip into the forest. She saw a beaver sit on top of a fallen log, combing its fur with its toenails. She saw a raccoon scurry through the grass. But no boy.

Her shoulders shuddered. Not waiting until Christian said the word "amen," she blurted out, "Where is Felix?"

7

Philadelphia
October 21, 1737

Felix was back on a ship, back where he belonged, where he was happiest. He was eager to explore this ship, a barque, different from the leaky *Charming Nancy* that had brought his church over the Atlantic from Rotterdam. He had learned every nook and cranny of the *Charming Nancy*; she was like an old friend to him. This new ship would take getting used to. Staying hidden did require a great deal of effort, at least until the ship was in open sea and he knew the captain would not be tempted to turn around to deposit him back on the docks of Port Philadelphia.

He grinned, brimming over with satisfaction.

Earlier today, he had carefully planned his getaway. He had stuffed his leather knapsack full of apples from a bushel in the back of one wagon, as he had no idea where his next meal would be coming from. In his pocket, he had nothing more than a Dutch dollar he'd found on the docks and about a shilling in copper. Felix wasn't worried, though.

He had taken great care to make certain that Anna, Maria,

and walleyed Catrina had seen him frequently during the early morning so as to not arouse any suspicion. He had to be especially mindful about Maria and Catrina. They kept their beady eyes on him all the time. And Catrina was everywhere he turned.

Felix even made a big show of crocodile tears as he said goodbye to his brother Bairn. Very convincing, he was, and proud of his theatrics. As the wagon caravan began to roll forward, Felix walked beside it for a number of city blocks, chattering happily to Anna. He even carried the awful dog in his arms, just to throw her off. But then Maria and Catrina came alongside and distracted Anna with the day's complaints—Maria was always complaining about something!—and as Catrina patted the awful dog, Felix saw his chance. He let Catrina hold the awful dog, which kept her occupied and would restrain the awful dog from following him. Two birds, one stone. Little by little, Felix dropped back behind them, still adding something to the conversation until Maria scowled at him and said that children should be seen and not heard.

And there was his moment. He slipped farther and farther behind them, scooted around one wagon to get to the other side of the road, then kept walking more and more slowly until he was at the back of the caravan. He reached his hand into the apple and potato wagon, felt around for the leather satchel he had hidden, grabbed it, then ducked behind a tree. The caravan moved along on its lumbering journey.

Felix stayed behind the tree until the caravan was out of sight and out of earshot, then he did a little jig step before he set off briskly, moving toward Philadelphia with bold, broad strides.

When he reached the city, he made a quick detour to Market Street to say goodbye to the printer, Benjamin Franklin, who had been kind to him, then made a beeline toward the waterfront. The barque had been brought to the docks to load cargo into its hold. This was a welcome change from last evening, when he had seen the barque still anchored midriver. He kept out of sight, crouched behind barrels on the docks, seeking a glimpse of Bairn. He heard him before he saw him, giving orders to the stevedores on which barrels to load first.

This had not been good news. Trying to get around Bairn was like trying to get around Anna—they both had eyes in the back of their heads. But here was where Felix's English came in handy. He saw one of the dock workers lift a barrel lid and peer inside. "Why are these ones empty?" The dock worker sounded puzzled.

"They're heading north to fill them," another dock worker answered back, lifting his hand to his mouth as if he were drinking from a bottle.

Then Felix had a brilliant idea.

He waited until a load of barrels was getting uploaded by the capstan, cautiously crawled around the barrels still to be loaded, lifted the lid partially off the barrel that the dock worker had indicated was empty, and dove into the barrel, then closed the lid. It was a bit topsy-turvy when the barrel was loaded, and his head, elbows, and knees got bumped more than a few times, but with all the noise of the docks, his hiding place went unnoticed. As soon as he heard the footsteps of the deckhands climb up the ladder to the top deck, and he didn't hear any other sounds, he lifted the lid of the barrel and peered around. Satisfied he was alone, he jumped out of the barrel, only to be nearly discovered by a sailor, an older fellow as wrinkled as a dried apple, who was coming out of the fo'c'sle. Fortunately, the lighting was so dim that the old sailor probably thought it was a rat he'd heard. He walked around the lower deck, muttering to himself about needing to put more arsenic down.

Felix was as nervous as a cat. He held his breath until the old sailor climbed the companionway ladder to the upper deck, then he let out a huge sigh of relief. He had to be careful and not be found. Not yet.

He heard the familiar rhythmic cadence of his brother's boot steps up above, striding up and down the deck in that long stride of his. Felix would know his brother anywhere. His heard Bairn's voice as he spoke to someone, then he heard that someone answer in response, with intermittent sneezes and coughs like he had the plague. Bairn shouted out to the deckhands to make way, and Felix realized he must have been talking to the captain.

Felix hoped Anna would get the letter he left for her, telling her not to worry, that he was with Bairn and would make sure they returned safe and sound, come late spring. With her grandparents.

Ohhhhh, wait.

He patted his pockets and heard a crunching sound. The letter! He'd forgotten to slip it into Anna's basket with her rose.

Oh well. She'd figure out where he went. Anna was smart like that. She could calm his mother down so she didn't dip back into her sadness. He felt another sting of regret. His mother was not like other mothers, not like Maria or Barbara. His mother carried sadness around like a burden, almost like the way Anna carried her rose basket. It was never far from her.

Would his mother understand that he was with Bairn, that he couldn't bear to be parted from him? Surely, she could understand that.

And if not, spring would be here soon enough. He dismissed the ping of worry about his mother and settled down, leaning against the ship's exterior wall, waiting for the tide to come in and the ship to go out.

Felix did not dare venture from the lower deck quite yet—not until the ship was well under way, far from any chance of it turning around if he were discovered, and not until he had a sense of the ship's rhythm. He had much to learn—to listen for the watch bells, to instantly recognize this new captain's voice, to count the deckhands and know where they were at all times.

To Felix's reckoning, he should stay below deck for at least two days, longer if he could stand it. But oh, he was getting so hungry! The growls of his stomach sounded like angry tigers lived inside him.

He dug into his satchel to find an apple to eat. Inside it were not the apples he had grabbed from a bushel, but a bundle of papers, a tan linen shirt, a blue woolen scarf. In Felix's haste to slip away unnoticed from the wagon caravan, he had accidentally grabbed the wrong leather satchel. Rats! He was famished.

He heard someone come down the ladder and hid behind a barrel near a cannon portal. A sailor—the cook, perhaps?—was rooting through a few barrels and filled his apron with something, then climbed back up the ladder, knees creaking with each step.

Remember that, Felix told himself. *Cook has creaky knees.*

It was surprising how much a person knew about another person, without really knowing him. Already, he was learning. Cook had cracking knees, the captain had a persistent sneeze and hacking cough, Bairn had bold, strong footsteps. All clues to their identity, when a person lived hidden in the lower deck.

Why so many cannons on this ship? The *Charming Nancy* did not have nearly as many. He was beside himself with excitement, eager to explore this ship—every inch. But first, he was desperate for something to eat.

He crawled on hands and knees over to the barrels where the cook had filled his apron with supplies. He had left a mess getting flour from one barrel. Maria would box the cook's ears if she saw such a mess, but he would leave good clues for Felix to figure out where the food barrels were. He peered into the barrels, opened one to find onions—no thank you—and then hit a gold mine. A barrel filled with apples, so freshly picked that leaves were still on the stems. This, Felix believed, was a sign from God that he would be provided for. He could live on apples for weeks. Months, if necessary.

He heard sailors shout to each other as they unfurled the sails from the masts. Sails snapped. The ship creaked and groaned, lurched, tipping one way, then another, as it started to move away from the dock. Once it went roundabout and more sails were unfurled, one by one, so that the ship gained speed and hit open water, it had a kind of music all its own. Creaks, groans, rattles, bangs, slapping sails.

He hurried over to the cannon hole to watch the ship make its way slowly down the mouth of the Delaware River. He ran to the other side of the ship to see Port Philadelphia pass by. He gave it a salute, the way he'd seen sailors do.

He took a deep breath, filling his lungs with the scent of the sea.

And now Felix was quite free to do as he pleased. No boy could ever have been as happy as he was at that very moment.

And then, out of nowhere, down the ladder came Squinty Eye's awful dog, his tongue hanging out, nails clicking along the wooden planks, his short, nearly hairless tail wagging back and forth, pleased to have found Felix.

Bairn stood at the helm of the ship, overlooking the dock, the port, the river filled with bobbing ships. A thousand times his eyes must have taken in such a scene. It was all the same, and so was he. He hadn't changed at all, not at all.

Or had he?

He threw off that jabbing thought and let the old rhythm of the sea return to him. How he'd missed this.

Sail ships had distinct personalities. No two had been built alike, no two handled alike. Bairn had learned to familiarize himself with the sounds of each sail ship he served on, grew to know them like they were people. He closed his eyes, listening carefully to adapt himself to the unique sounds of the *Lady Luck*. The noise of a ship was similar to the effect of heel taps on a boot—it let a man know he was alive, breathing, and had someplace to go.

Someplace to go. Someplace to return to.

A cold, clear reality swept over Bairn in a terrible wave, one so powerful it stole his breath. He was alone again, truly alone. This time, the fault was not his father's, or greedy redemptioners', but his own foolish judgment.

Why had he left Anna? Why had he left his mother, his father, his brother? He himself couldn't grasp what it was inside of him, where it came from, that made him walk away from what was right there, right in front of him, everything he'd ever dreamed about and longed for.

What was the matter with him?

Before he could answer, wind and tide came together and the captain gave the signal to prepare the ship to make way. Bairn set aside his turmoil and snapped into action as first mate. Exiting the port required his full attention, especially at twilight, and he was grateful. It took skill to maneuver the ship around anchored vessels and approaching ships, and this barque was new to him.

Its load was light as it left Port Philadelphia, which required an adjustment of sails to slow its movement. And then, as the river widened and they headed toward the Delaware Bay, Bairn cupped his mouth and shouted, "Hard-a-lee!" to the sailor who manned the wheel, to turn the ship's head. He hollered another command to the sailors on the masts, to unfurl the last of the sails and let them billow.

"Aye, sir!" echoed back.

He stood at the stern, taking a deep breath, and watched the receding wooded shoreline of Pennsylvania. His thoughts returned to Anna.

Anna cried when they'd said goodbye and it tore his heart in two. She was not one to cry. It touched him with a grave longing for something he couldn't name.

Was he wrong to leave her? It was for such a short time, five, maybe six months. Bairn had learned a great deal about time in his life on the sea. Time wasn't meant to be hoarded but to be mastered. Use it well, or lose it poorly. He told as much to Anna and she strongly disagreed. She said time was to be measured. Exchanged like a value. She made it sound like gold.

He'd done everything he could to leave things right between them: He worked out the compromise to have the men affirm submission to the British Crown rather than swear an oath. He helped the church gather supplies and tools, horses and wagons. He explained to the minister that he was not accompanying them. Christian said he was disappointed but not surprised, and he wished him well. And then Bairn bid them goodbye as the wagon caravan got on its way.

It wasn't fair to promise Anna that he would return with her grandparents. He didn't say it aloud to her, but he wondered if they might have already passed to their glory. He remembered them as quite elderly. Or what if they refused to come, like they had done on this past year's journey?

Her grandparents had made the right decision. The journey was a brutal one, made increasingly difficult by things that were out of anyone's control. He'd heard of one ship, bringing German Moravians, whose whereabouts were still unknown.

Surely, this last year was atypical. The captains were more experienced now, toting passengers in the lower decks and not just cotton and woolens. Surely, next year's crossing would be much easier.

And then what? Would he be ready to return to Anna, to his family? To take his spot beside his father and become one of the farmers who tamed the wilderness?

Or would he be wrestling with the same doubts? The same

despair? Anna thought so. She said it wasn't a problem of his vocation. It was a problem with his heart.

A gust of wind billowed the mighty sails, so strong it lifted his hat. He grabbed the brim with both hands, firmly settled it on his brow, and tried to dismiss the distressing emotions that followed him like shadows. It was the old melancholy that was returning to him—confusion and heaviness. Loneliness.

He walked around the upper deck, checking spars and halyards, looking for any loose ropes. As he jumped down from the fo'c'sle deck, he stopped and turned in a full circle.

He was not a man prone to superstition or funny feelings, not like most sailors and deckhands. They drew meaning from every jot and tittle, in every dream, every cloud that floated by. No, he'd never paid any mind to that nonsense about premonitions.

But there was an odd feeling he couldn't shake. All day long, he had the strangest feeling that he was being watched.

And then he heard a familiar bark.

8

***Lady Luck*, Atlantic Ocean**
October 21, 1737

Everything had been going so well, just as Felix had planned.

The ship's bow sliced through dark water as sails billowed. *Lady Luck* was on her way down the Delaware River to meet the Atlantic Ocean.

From the top of the companionway ladder, Felix had peered through the hatch to watch his brother walk along the upper deck and climb onto the ship's bowsprit. Bairn had simply stood there, with his arms straight at his sides and his head slightly lifted, and though Felix couldn't see his face, his brother's very presence seemed to alter from the inside out. Suddenly it was all there, in the set of his shoulders, in the way he braced his legs on the deck. His brother looked every bit the sea captain.

Felix's heart swelled with pride. No wonder Bairn had to go back to sea! This, *this* was where he belonged. A leader among men who tamed the mighty ocean. Not stuck in the wilderness, pushing a plow or yielding an ax.

It was all going so well, just as Felix had planned.

And then the dog let out a bark.

That dog! That awful dog. It always, always found Felix and gave him away. His brother must have heard its bark because he bolted toward the companionway, down the ladder to the lower deck, and let out a whistle, a signal to the awful dog to come. The dog barked, ran to Bairn, and ran back to Felix with its dumb tail wagging in a circle. Ducking his head so he wouldn't hit the beams, Bairn marched right over to Felix's hiding place by the cannon. Slowly, Felix lifted his head to face his brother's glare.

Bairn stared down at him, his hands on his hips. "I should have ken! I should have ken! Y' jumped the wagons and ran t' the docks. I should have ken y'd do such a dastardly thing!"

Felix slowly rose to his feet. "Are you going to turn back the ship?"

Bairn's face went from shock to fury. "Return? Are y' daft, lad? We're too far from shore to return." His eyes narrowed. He pointed at Felix. "Which y' surely ken—why else would y' be hidin' down here?" Bairn shook his head. "Did y' have the wits about you to let anyone ken y've gone missin'?"

Felix pulled the letter from his jacket. "I wrote a letter to Anna." He opened it up. He'd been quite proud of that letter. "But then I forgot to leave it in her rose basket."

Bairn leaned against a barrel. "So now y've caused them undue worry and delay. You ken Anna will return t' look for y'. She thinks of y' as her burden." He covered his face with his hands. "Felix, dinnae y' think of what this would do t' yer poor mother? The sea devils will return to her."

Sea devils were the sailors' way to speak of sadness. "I guess I didn't think much about sea devils." Though he did like the way it rolled off his tongue. Sea devils. He would be completely fluent in English by the time he came back to Port Philadelphia, and wouldn't his father be proud of him then? Wouldn't Anna? Yes. He could just see the delight in their faces as he negotiated trades for them. Then they would see that he had made a wonderful decision. Even his mother wouldn't be so terribly bothered.

"Why did y' do such a thing?"

"I heard you and Captain Stedman talk."

"What? When?"

"I was hiding under a wagon wheel. Right by your boots."

"So y' decided then and there to run away?"

"I'm not running away! How can I be running away when I'm with my brother?"

"Y' have a wee brother now."

"That's just it. Mama is happy as long as she has a baby to fuss over. She has Papa and the new baby. And Anna too. They all have each other. But you, Bairn, you don't have anyone. You need someone with you. You needed me."

For a long time, Bairn stood silently, watching Felix.

Felix lifted a finger in the air the way Captain Stedman did when he tried to drive home a point. "And soon enough, you and I will be back in Port Philadelphia. You said so yourself. We'll go straight to the new settlement and help Papa chop down trees." He brought his hand down in a chopping motion. "You'll see, Bairn. They'll hardly know we've been gone. They might not even miss us."

Bairn gave him a look as if he might be sun touched, but Felix had the utmost confidence in his logic. "So, what's the plan?" he asked Bairn, who always had one.

"I'll not be hiding y'."

"Understood."

"We're goin' to find the captain to explain yer sudden appearance." Bairn gave him a little push in the direction of the stairs. "Go, then. Go on."

"What will he do?"

"My guess is he'll put y' on the next passin' ship to return y' to Port Philadelphia. From there, you'll be on yer own to find yer way t' the settlement."

Oh no. The wheels in Felix's mind started to spin. "Here's a better idea. I could be cabin boy. The captain will listen to you, Bairn. And there's no cabin boy on this ship." He didn't think there was, anyway.

Bairn frowned, but he turned and headed to the upper deck to find the captain. At the top of the ladder, he turned and shouted, "Are y' coming or not?"

Felix ran to the ladder to catch up with Bairn. The awful dog trotted behind him.

Up the Schuylkill River

Anna gazed at the flickering flames of the fire, wanting to sleep but her mind was spinning. Beyond, in the dark infinity of the deep woods, a wolf howled at the moon. She wondered if it might be the mate of the wolf Henrik had killed. Was that poor she wolf waiting for her mate to return, wondering what had happened to him?

The she wolf would have a long wait.

She ducked her head to hide a tear that slipped down her cheek. How ridiculous. To cry over a wolf. But that wasn't what was upsetting her. She was thinking of Bairn. Of Felix.

As soon as dawn broke, Anna was heading to Philadelphia

to look for the boy. It had taken some finagling for Christian to acquiesce. When she first told him she wanted to return, he refused. "Absolutely not," Christian had said. "The men will go. Josef and Isaac."

"I'm the only one who can speak English," Anna said. "And I think I might know where Felix might be." Near the docks would be her first guess. "I can find him in half the time."

"Not alone," Christian said. "Far too dangerous."

It would be dangerous to be alone, she knew that. But she was worried Christian would consider letting Felix fend for himself. He was *that* exasperating a boy. And yet he was one of theirs, and she loved him dearly. As soon as she found him, she would hug him, then scold him furiously. Then hug him again.

"Jacob is expecting all of you, as soon as possible. If the weather stays mild, think of the work that can be done before winter arrives. I'm the logical choice." They were all anxious to reach the land. The newcomer had likened their situation to the last journey of the Israelites as they faced the land of milk and honey, perched on the border of the Promised Land, eager to go in.

But Anna couldn't go to the Promised Land with Felix gone missing. She had to go find him.

But Christian would not hear of it. Naturally, the dilemma of missing Felix went to committee. Christian, Isaac, Josef, and Simon gathered by the fire, debating different ideas. One of them could take a horse and ride back to Philadelphia—there and back in one day's time, rather than two or three days for a return trip on foot. But if a horse were to be used, it meant a wagon would have to be abandoned, stolen perhaps by wanderers or Indians.

Another consideration was to make camp for a few days, while the men went to the city and returned. Even Christian, a slow-moving man on his best day, was reluctant to go along with that decision. He tapped his fingertips together in a meditative rhythm over his round belly.

Too much time would be lost, they decided in the end. Then the newcomer stepped toward the circle. "I've got an idea," he said. "I'll accompany Anna to Philadelphia. We'll find the boy and bring him back."

Maria's eyebrows shot to the top of her head. "Not the two of you together. Not alone! I promised Anna's grandparents that I would not let anyone damage her honor."

Anna turned to her, astounded. This was the first she'd heard of such a promise. More to the point, hurrying to Philadelphia, on foot and back again, on a mission to find Felix, would hardly provide any opportunity for her honor to be damaged.

"Then I'll go along with them," Peter Mast volunteered. "The three of us will go." Peter was closer to a boy than a man.

"He is like a brother to me," Anna said, which made Peter frown.

Maria's eyes widened for a moment, then her narrow lips curved in a smile. "That would be a satisfactory arrangement."

Christian and Josef and Isaac leaned together for another conference. Then their heads popped up and Christian said, "Go to Philadelphia. Find the boy. Then return to us. We will keep going."

"But how will they find us?" Maria said. "How will they know where we are?"

"Flour," Anna said. "When you come to a fork in the road, leave a trail of flour. We'll find it."

"What if it rains?" Maria was always one to find what was wrong with a plan.

"Then leave some cloth around a tree. We will find you. We'll be looking for tracks, for signs that we're following you."

The newcomer looked around the circle to catch the eyes of the decision makers, nodding at each one. "There's a solid plan. We'll go, we'll find him, and we'll catch up with you. You'll hardly know we've been gone." He snapped his fingers. "There and then back. Back with the boy."

Anna appreciated the newcomer's confidence, his kindness, but she wasn't quite as convinced that the plan would be swift and successful. He did not know Felix like she knew him.

Lady Luck, Atlantic Ocean
October 21, 1737

Bairn went to the bunk and pulled the covers around Felix's shoulders, and stood looking at him, bemused. He wanted to shake sense into him . . . yet he also had a profound admiration for the little bugger. How in the world did Felix have the kind of gumption that he did? What boldness was set in that child's soul? Where did it come from? Bairn had seen all kinds of men in the last ten years—good ones, bad ones, sour ones, corrupt ones. But the fearlessness in Felix—that he had rarely seen in any man. Most every man he knew was motivated by greed. Felix was motivated by love.

Along with, to be fair, an overly developed streak of curiosity.

The look of alarm in Captain Berwick's eyes was hard to miss. He was a hard man, that captain, not like his kind-hearted cousins. But the captain was willing to permit Felix to remain as cabin boy so long as he obeyed orders, and he acquiesced readily as soon as Bairn said no wages would be required.

Bairn felt a great responsibility to care for the boy—to return him to his mother and father, to Anna.

Anna.

Was she still searching for Felix in Port Philadelphia? He hoped someone had seen the boy get on the ship, just to put her mind at ease. Surely, she would know that Bairn would mind him for her.

Felix turned to his side, flopping an arm outside of the covers. The air was brisk and Bairn worried he might get a chill. He took the blanket off his own bunk and covered him with it. A memory flashed through his mind: of his own father covering him with his red Mutza the way he was covering Felix.

He wondered what he would be like if he hadn't gotten separated from his father on the ship, all those years ago. Would he be like Felix? Content, untroubled. Maybe he would have always been more like his mother—a worrier, a churner.

Strange. It was new for him to allow himself to let those thoughts carry forward, rather than cutting them off the second they filled his mind. He took a deep breath and felt a dozen different emotions collide. As much as he loved Felix, he envied him too. The lad had been given a true childhood.

Felix was doted on by his mother and father. As firstborn,

Bairn could not remember receiving such adoring love. His parents had always given him more responsibility than affection. He recalled mastering an impressive array of tasks, taking on more work and responsibility every year. Starting at age six, considered tall for his age, he rode the horse to steady it while his father followed behind with the plow. He would plant the wheat seeds as his father covered them, working from sunup to sundown, coming in from the field at night covered with insect bites and scratches from the prickly burrs. During the wheat harvest, he would bind the handfuls of cut wheat that his father had sickled and carry the sheaves to the hay barn. In winter, he hauled wood and chopped it four or five feet long for the fireplace and carried rails to the fields. As he became stronger and more skillful, he took on more adult tasks, even splitting rails and building fences. By the age of eight, he was holding the plow and guiding the horse himself. By the age of ten, he was given care of the stock. During summer nights, he would stay out in the fields all night long, alone, to guard the sheep and goats. His father gave him his old gun to scare away the pests and predators.

His mother treated him more as a man she relied on than as a child. When he accompanied his father on the journey to the New World, the last words his mother had told him were to be sure to bring back his father, as if that were his responsibility. She did not give a similar warning to his father. She did not feel worried about Bairn, only Jacob.

And why didn't Jacob make sure his son was truly gone off that ship? It needled Bairn, all through those years. Why had his father accepted the word of the ship's captain that his son had died?

Suppose his mother was right, that his father could not

be held responsible for that—he had taken ill too, after all. And the ship was a chaotic place.

Even still, why couldn't his father just say he was sorry for those lost years? He could not forgive him for that.

Getting humility out of Jacob Bauer was like squeezing water from a stone.

He went to the upper deck, to the bowsprit, and looked out to a shroud of fog. There was a stinging chill in the air. He fastened the top button of his coat collar around his neck. *Slainte*, a Gaelic word meaning "health," sounded from the crew's quarters more than a few times tonight. The crew was celebrating, and they had every right to—the first night that the ship sliced her way onto her journey.

Like a cat scenting the breeze, Bairn lifted his head and narrowed his eyes. He thought he smelled coffee wafting from the galley, and it took him right back to a moment, not long ago, on the *Charming Nancy*, when Anna handed him a warmed mug of the stuff.

Not that long ago.

The wind felt cold and he rubbed his arms, shivering a little. He should go inside and get some sleep before his turn at watch, but he knew he wouldn't sleep, he would only lie there and stare at the top of his bunk, his thoughts churning. Something of the old melancholy was settling upon him again.

Maybe he was just designed for a life at sea. Like most sailors, he would always be on the move, never have a home. Maybe he was more like his father than he wanted to think—always restless, always looking for greener pastures. Never content, never at peace.

But Jacob Bauer, right or wrong, never had a single doubt. Bairn, on the other hand, was a man full of doubts.

Outside Philadelphia
October 22, 1737

The newcomer moved at a fast pace. By the time the sun was climbing in the sky, Henrik, Peter, and Anna happened upon a farmer who was driving bushels of apples to the market in Philadelphia. He offered them a ride and they gratefully accepted, climbing onto the back of the cart. Peter made a pillow of his jacket and curled up against the side of the cart, falling asleep within minutes. He looked so young and awkward as he slept, with his long, sleek hair covering his sharp, bony face.

Anna wrapped her arms around her bent legs, her head tilted back. The sun was a bright glow behind her closed eyelids. The day was warming up and the wind had a hint of autumn in its scent. She stretched her arms, and opened her eyes to look at the newcomer. He sat with his long legs sprawled out, one ankle over the other. His hat brim covered his face. She could barely see his chin resting on his chest.

Catrina's comment floated through her mind: *He's so pretty, don't you think?* The newcomer was a particularly comely man, with dark hair and blue eyes that twinkled and snapped. She wondered how old he was. As she observed how he interacted with Christian and Isaac, she noticed an intensity to him, a boldness, an ability to absorb the circumstances that surrounded him and sort through them at lightning speed. The way he managed Christian, even Maria—those skills could only be developed by someone with significant life experience. Or someone with an unusual gift with people.

She leaned a little closer to him to see if she could decide how old he was, when he shifted and lifted his head. She jerked back, her startled gaze sweeping over his face. But his eyes were focused not on her but on something beyond. Or perhaps something deep within.

They didn't speak for a long while, which didn't bother her. She was accustomed to quiet, because she was raised believing that an excess of words was not pleasing to God. The newcomer seemed to hold the same view, because he didn't say much along the way. When he did talk, it was with concern for Peter and Anna, making sure he hadn't been walking too fast, wondering if they needed rest or food. Now, seated opposite her on the cart, he lifted his head to ask her a question. "Anna, how did you learn English?"

Anna drew her knees back up and circled them with her arms. "My grandfather. He knew many languages and taught them to me. Languages come easily to me, but there are times it's been more of a burden than a blessing." She glanced at Henrik. "You can join the English lessons I give to the others." To Felix and Catrina. She tried not to let her mind worry over Felix; if she even started to think of him, she felt a swirl of anxiety.

"I won't be needing English, not where we're going."

She lifted an eyebrow. "You're not in Germany any longer."

"I am in a world where I can keep my German language, beliefs, traditions. My religion. That's what I've come for. That's more than enough for me."

"So you think this settlement will be so isolated that you don't have to interact with anyone who's not German?"

"I don't expect to have to interact with those who are tainted by the world. It's Paradise we're heading to." He gave her a grin, and it was dazzling, full of confidence. "We've been given another chance at the Garden of Eden."

She'd heard him say this before, but she thought he was jesting. Could he be serious? Her face must have revealed her skepticism because his mouth curved with amusement.

"I see you have doubts, Anna. Doubts don't belong on this wondrous and mysterious path that the Lord has set before us. A holy experiment waits for us." He leaned forward. "And we will not disappoint Him."

Words failed Anna. Instead she gripped her knees tighter and held her breath. Never once had it occurred to her to think about the New World in such a way. To her, it was a reluctant undertaking, perhaps even a foolish one. And the way the newcomer was staring at her now made her wonder if he knew how small her thoughts were, how unworthy she was. She rounded her shoulders, pressing her mouth to her knees, feeling suddenly shy and oddly exposed. She looked over at the newcomer, whose gaze was fixed ahead on the road toward Port Philadelphia, looking as pleased as a man could look, as if he had found a wonderful secret to life and it lit him from the inside out.

She wondered what Bairn would think about the newcomer's bold expectations. Laugh at him, most likely. Consider him naïve.

And yet it was refreshing to be around someone who had such confidence, such assurance, that their journey was God-inspired. Why was it so easy for some people to be happy? And others . . . not at all.

9

Philadelphia
October 22, 1737

Hours spent searching along the waterfront in Philadelphia turned up not a single clue about Felix's whereabouts. Twelve thousand people in this city—you'd think that someone, somewhere, would have caught sight of him. If not Felix, then the dog that followed him everywhere.

They had started on the docks at Penn's Landing, then made their way up to the city streets. Peter suggested they split up to cover more ground, so she found a paper on the ground and wrote questions on it for Peter and Henrik to ask. The newcomer had told her he wouldn't need English. Didn't he need it today? But she was too distracted and filled with worry to bother with his curious thinking.

She crossed the street, hurrying up the root-cracked sidewalk, the wind skirting yellow and red leaves around her feet. She went to a brickmaker, to Christ Church where Felix had confessed to her that he had wandered inside and dipped his hand in the baptismal font—because he found out it was the very same font that William Penn had been baptized in as an infant, imported all the way from England! Then she went to the City Tavern and found the servant girl who gave Felix the Sally Lunn buns. The servant girl said that just a few days ago, she had caught sight of Felix and his little dog cutting through the green of the square, moving fast and looking over his shoulder. She promised to hold on to him if she did see Felix again, and she gave Anna a Sally Lunn bun. Though hungry, Anna ate only one third of it—saving the other pieces for Peter and Henrik.

She wracked her brain to think of any passing comment Felix might have made about unique individuals—but to Felix, everyone was a unique individual. All of Philadelphia was a curiosity to him and he talked incessantly.

She met up with Peter and Henrik in front of the London Coffee House near Penn's Landing. Henrik had found a German farmer who had finished his business in the city and was returning northwest. He said he would be willing to let them ride in his empty cart. "Come, Anna, we must take this offer. We've done the best we could to find the boy." Even the newcomer, who seemed to be perpetually optimistic, was ready to give up.

Footsore and weary, she knew Henrik was right.

But where, where, *where* could Felix be? Who else might he have visited? A man walked past them with a newspaper in his hand—the *Pennsylvania Gazette*.

"The printer!" Her mind raced with fragments of Felix's endless chatter. "He had become friendly with a printer at a bindery. I can't leave until I talk to the printer."

"Anna! We must go!"

She turned to answer him, but kept walking backward. "Wait here, Henrik. I'll be right back. A few minutes more.

Please. I have to check one more place. The last possibility." It was the only way she would have peace of mind that Felix was not in Philadelphia.

Renewed by a spurt of energy, she ran down the brick sidewalk along Market Street. She hurried across the busy street, darting around a horse and wagon, and burst into the shop. A man in a leather apron looked up in surprise.

"Have you seen a boy? About this high." She lifted her hand to her shoulders. "Dark hair and eyes." She was gasping for breath. "A German boy who speaks English. And a small dog that follows him everywhere."

The man had long hair that fit like a horseshoe around the back of his head. His eyes twinkled, as if he found her amusing. "What language does the dog speak?"

At first Anna was confused, until his eyes gave away his teasing.

"Ben! Stop that." A woman stood by the large printing press. "Answer the girl. You can see she's frantic with worry."

"My apologies, madam. Yes, I think I know whom you are seeking. A young boy, around the age of eight or nine, with a very lively mind."

"You've seen them? When? Where?" She drew out the words with the slow easing of pent-up breath.

"Yesterday. Midmorning, the boy burst into my printing shop . . . much the way you just did."

"Out of breath," the woman added. "He'd been running quite a distance."

"Yes. Deborah's right. He was quite out of breath. He was on a mission, to be sure."

"What did he want?"

"He wanted me to know that he would accept my apprentice job, but he wouldn't be back until the spring. He asked me to hold the job open for him."

The spring? Anna's heart started to pound. "Do you know where he is now?"

"On a ship called the *Lady Luck*, he told us," the woman said.

Anna knew it! In her heart, she had known all along where Felix had gone: he was on Bairn's ship.

The couple was waiting for some response from her. "Thank you. You've set my mind at ease."

"If you happen to see the boy," the man said, "tell him that I'll hold the job for him. I think he would provide excellent fodder."

"Oh, you can be sure that I will be seeing him, and that I'll have plenty to tell him." She took a few steps, then turned around. "May I tell Felix who wants to hire him as an apprentice?"

"Tell him Ben Franklin wants to hire him. The printing press man. This is my wife, Deborah. She's the chief typesetter and proofreader."

"I'll do that. However, I wouldn't hold the position for him. His parents won't hear of it."

She thanked the couple again, and hurried back to meet Henrik and Peter, sending up silent thanks to God for that timely encounter. At least she knew Felix was safe. And she knew that he was with Bairn. She took off down the street at a run, her skirts tossing, but as she crossed the street, her feet slowed and her smile faded.

How in the world could she tell Dorothea and Jacob that both of their sons had left the New World?

As soon as Anna met up with Henrik and Peter, she told them the story of Felix following Bairn onto the ship.

Henrik was visibly relieved. "Good. We can be off."

"Anna."

She swiveled to face Peter. His long bony face had a pale, drawn look.

"I'm not going with you. I'm staying here, in Philadelphia."

"You're *what*?"

"I don't want to cut down trees for the rest of my life. I see how thickly wooded that wilderness is."

"It's only for a short time. Clearing the land won't last forever. You'll be able to farm the land."

"I don't want to be a farmer. I want to make my own way in the new world. I heard men in the city talk about getting rich. German men, Anna. There are other ways to live than on a farm."

"Peter, you can't possibly leave now. We need you. You need the church."

"No, I don't. Maybe if Lizzie hadn't died on the ship, maybe I would have wanted to stay in the church. But I feel like I've been given a second chance. I'm only sixteen years old. I want to have a life that counts for something more than pulling tree stumps."

"Peter, you have to think clearly."

"I am thinking clearly! I've thought of nothing else since the moment the ship docked in Philadelphia."

"What about your son? Lizzie's child?"

"I've entrusted his raising to Dorothea and Jacob. They'll do well by him. Much better than I could ever do."

"Then, think of your father. He'll be heartbroken."

Peter dropped his chin to his chest. "That's why I'm asking you to explain to him why I'm not returning. I can't face him, Anna. You know what he's like."

She looked to the newcomer for help, but he said nothing. Then the newcomer clasped the boy's shoulder, giving it a rough shake, the kind of touch men gave one another. "Take care, then, boy."

"We can't just let him stay behind! I'm responsible for him."

"Anna, he's nearly a grown man. He's lost a wife already. He can make his own choices. I did the same when I was his age."

Peter looked at the newcomer in sheer amazement. "Thank you, Henrik. You understand."

The newcomer shook his head. "To be truthful with you, I don't understand. I don't know how someone can turn away from this wonderful new adventure."

"What adventure?" Peter was wavering. "I thought we were just cutting down trees to farm land. I've already done plenty of that."

"So much more than that." The newcomer gave him a look as if it was so obvious. "Boy, we are seeking Paradise." He tugged on Anna's arm. "We must go. The farmer is waiting for us. I fear we've already taxed his patience."

"Peter, please come with us." She saw a slight hesitation written on his face. "Talk to . . ." To whom? His father, who would be as unbending as Jacob Bauer? Talk to Christian? Thinking over the leadership options of the church, she could understand why Peter wanted to avoid a face-to-face confrontation.

"The boy knows where we'll be. He knows the road home is always available." He grabbed Anna's arm and pulled her along after him. "We have a responsibility to the others."

"But . . . wait . . . Peter, have you shillings? Any food?"

"Don't worry about me, Anna. I'll fend for myself."

He thought he was a man, but he was such a boy still. "Follow the Schuylkill River, Peter. Go north. That's where you'll find us."

As the afternoon sun began its descent, Philadelphia fell behind Anna, the newcomer, and the German farmer, who, it turned out, wasn't a farmer at all.

The man drove the cart due west, toward Lancaster, a more well-traveled road than the one Christian had led the convoy on. Eventually, he said, he would take another road to go north. Anna sat in the cart, nestled against the corner. The cottony clouds scuttled away like ships in the harbor, while the setting sun filled the sky with hues of red and gold.

Hours passed as Anna tried to sleep, dropping off and waking abruptly whenever the cart hit a bump in the road. She listened drowsily to Henrik and the German man—Peter Miller was his name—carry on a long, animated conversation on the wagon seat. He was a surprisingly learned man, an ordained German Reformed pastor. "I began preaching to the German Reformed congregations on the frontier but now am a disciple at the Ephrata Community." He glanced at the newcomer. "Surely you've heard of us."

"Surely not," Henrik said affably. "I'm fresh off the ship. I joined a group of Palatinate seekers."

Seekers? Anna mused. She did not see her church as made up of seekers but of believers.

"Ephrata." The newcomer took off his hat and scratched his head. "An unusual name, Ephrata."

"It's from Scripture. It's a word that denotes suffering."

"So this community . . . is it a monastery?"

"Yes and no, and so much more. It is north of here, made up of Brethren like us. You and me . . . and your sister in the cart."

"She's not my sister."

The German smiled. "Ah, but in God's eyes, she is. That's what the men and women call each other. Sisters and brothers."

"And these men and women—they are all Brethren?"

"Anabaptists. Pietists. Mennonites, Dunkers, all devoted."

Anna's ears perked up.

"The community is only a few years old," Peter Miller continued. "It's led by Conrad Beissel, our Vorsteher." *Founder.* "He was a journeyman baker who followed God's calling."

"A calling by God," Henrik repeated softly. "Tell me more."

"Some think him radical, but his followers—and I include myself—believe he has an unusual understanding of God. He tried to live the life of a hermit but a small group of followers couldn't leave him be. They needed him as their guiding light. And that's how the community at Ephrata began—not because Conrad Beissel was looking for a church but the church was looking for him."

Henrik straightened up with a start. "So what *is* this special understanding that Conrad Beissel has?"

"Now he is known as Father Friedsam." *Father of peace.* "I am known as Brother Agrippa." He slapped the reins to get the horse trotting through a straight part of the road. "Father Friedsam stresses the need for separation from the larger world. He united his dispersed followers so that, together, we could oppose the tainted influence of the world."

"That is a virtue shared by many." Henrik nodded his head in full agreement. "So is this community self-sufficient?"

"Almost. Not completely, though, not yet. We have plans to

construct many buildings on our settlement. Before my stop in Philadelphia, I went to Germantown to order windows and raw iron for door hinges and latches. We have many plans—a paper mill is under way, a bakery. Father Friedsam has ordered a printing press from Germany. Many of the sisters practice the work of Fraktur."

"A worthy ambition, to be separate from the world in all matters. We have much in common, it seems."

"Father Friedsam is convinced that Christians who worshiped on Sunday had chosen the wrong Sabbath. So we observe Saturday for worship."

Henrik tipped his head. "What else does Father Friedsam emphasize?"

"We are waiting for Christ's Second Coming, which he believes could happen at any moment."

Henrik's entire body posture changed. Anna could see it unfold. He leaned closer to Brother Agrippa, eyes intently on him, clearly fascinated. "Do you mind if I ask what the purpose of the community is?"

"I don't mind at all. Questions begin the journey. The purpose of Ephrata Community is to share spiritual experiences and search for the desired union with God. And to wait."

"To wait?"

"For Christ's Second Coming, of course."

"Union with God? But . . . what does that entail?" Henrik's shoulders were rolled forward and his hands tucked between his knees, full of anticipation like a child. "Please, tell me more."

But before the conversation could continue, Brother Agrippa surprised them by pulling the reins of the horse to a stop at a fork in the road. "That will have to wait for another day. You are always welcome to come to the Ephrata Community. See for yourself how we live." He jumped off the cart and handed the reins to Henrik. "Father Friedsam has recently decided that it's wrong to ask a beast to take our burdens. I had intended to sell the horse and cart in Philadelphia, but after meeting you there, I sensed the Spirit's prompting to help you along on your journey. The horse and cart are yours. Do with them as you will." He also left them with his evening meal—an apple and two hard soda biscuits—and a crudely sketched map of the Schuylkill River drawn on the corner of brown paper. He bid them well and went on his way.

Anna remained in the back of the cart, astonished. She watched the man stride down the road with only the moon to light his path, as if he had not a care in the world. "Do you think he is an angel?"

"Perhaps," Henrik said, reins in hand. He swiveled on the bench to look at her. "He was certainly sent by God to provide for us, just when we needed the help." He put out his hand to help her climb over the side of the cart to sit on the bench beside him.

"If they think Christ is returning soon, why are they constructing buildings?"

Henrik shrugged. "I suppose that they need to find ways to live while they wait. Brother Agrippa told me they are working on building a printing press for German books. That's why he was in Philadelphia. To meet with a printer."

"Benjamin Franklin?"

"Yes, I believe so. You know of him?"

"In fact, I do. His print shop was where I went while you and Peter waited for me. Felix had met him and must have somehow made a positive impression on him. He told Felix he would apprentice him when he returned in the spring."

Henrik slapped the reins to get the horse moving along. "Why does this Ephrata Community interest you so?"

"Because I believe this New World is God's way of starting again. Just like after the flood. Noah was given a fresh start—the old evil ways had been done away with. The New World is our Garden of Eden."

"So that's truly why you've come? To find the Garden of Eden?"

"It's here." He looked down the road at Brother Agrippa, barely visible in the moonlit shadows as he sauntered down the road. "It's here. Somewhere in this New World." He slapped the horse's reins to get it going and winked at Anna. "And you and I are on our way to find it." He gave her a nudge with his elbow. "It's our destiny."

Anna laughed, and it felt so good. "You're a very different sort of man, Henrik Newman."

He grinned. "I've been told such a thing once or twice in my life."

Many times, no doubt.

"Will we meet up with Christian and the others soon?"

"We're heading north on a different path, but the German said we should intersect with them at some point." He flashed a grin. "I hope."

He fell silent, and they went without speaking for a long while. She stifled a yawn, wondering if he would mind if she returned to the back of the cart and slept the rest of the night. He seemed determined not to stop and he seemed equally determined that he knew where he was going.

Bairn would know where they were and where to go next. He could navigate anywhere as long as stars were visible in the sky. She tried to ignore the ache that rose in her chest whenever her thoughts wandered to Bairn.

"Henrik, I do appreciate your help in the search for Felix, for allowing me to pursue that last hunch." She couldn't imagine how she could have left Philadelphia without knowing for certain what had happened to him.

"Anna, do you think the Bauer brothers will ever return?"

"Yes. Of course." She glanced at him. "What makes you think they won't?"

"It sounds like the older brother is a man with a strong inclination for the sea."

She twisted the string ends of her prayer cap. "Just one more crossing, he said."

Henrik's brows rose. "Just one more?"

"Bairn's not like most seamen."

"Can he read? Most seamen can't."

"Yes. He reads quite a lot."

"So what are his favorite books?"

"Books about voyages . . . oh." She looked away.

"How will Felix's mother take the news that he is a stowaway on a ship?"

Anna took her time answering. "I don't know. She's not a sturdy woman." She dropped her chin to her chest. "Let's hope for the best."

The newcomer beamed. "Always."

10

Northwest of Philadelphia
October 23, 1737

At some point in the night Dorothea woke with a start. She wasn't sure what roused her, but as she sat up, the skin on her arms began to tingle. She looked over at Jacob and saw him struggle for breath. She checked his forehead for fever and found him burning up. "Can you speak?"

"Dorothea," he rasped, his voice threadbare, "I am greatly suffering." He looked at her, his face rippling with anguish. And yet she was completely unprepared for his next words. "I fear I am dying." His eyes fluttered shut, his breathing remained labored, puffing with each heartbeat.

She sank onto the ground beside him, too astounded to reply. A horror gripped her: they were in a desperate situation and she had no idea what to do next. It was the middle of the night and Jacob couldn't travel. As she added kindling to the fire to keep Jacob warm, she tried to stay calm but her hands were trembling. She lay down beside him, with the baby between them to give the child warmth, listening for Jacob's labored breathing . . . and tried not to let her thoughts run amuck.

She had always assumed she would be the first to die. Not Jacob. Never Jacob. He was so strong, so resilient, so determined.

She had thought death was certain on the *Charming Nancy*. The storms, the cracked beam in the ship, then the drought—death was always lingering. At least it would have been quick. She heard the howl of a wolf, or a coyote, or some kind of vicious predator. Why had God brought her this far, saved the life of this little babe, returned Bairn to his family, only to have them all face a horrifying end?

God is both a deliverer and a destroyer. How often had she heard Jacob say those words?

Why had God brought her from Germany? She should have stayed in Ixheim, near her parents' graves, her son Johann's grave, and one day she would have been buried on the hillside. She had no heart for conquest and no patience for new ideas. She had witnessed too many painful scenes. "God," she whispered, and the word came out like a gust of hard breath. "If You are at all merciful, help us. Help me."

A sudden spasm knit Jacob's brows. His eyes opened, and when he spoke again, his voice was whispery soft and tinged with terror. "I should have better prepared you." Jacob lifted his hand and stared at the trembling fingers as if he'd never seen them before, then closed his eyes. "I should have prepared Christian. He won't know what to do, which means he won't do anything. He doesn't know how to build. He doesn't know how to lead. Only to follow."

"Hush, Jacob. Don't talk. Save your strength."

He opened his eyes. "You must tell Christian what to do. And make sure our Hans hears this. He is a builder."

He closed his eyes again, breathed in deeply, and it sounded so difficult for him that it frightened her even more, if that was even possible. She was shaking with dread, expecting each breath to be his last.

But then he mustered his strength and opened his eyes wide. "Listen to me, wife. Listen carefully. First each man must select a tract of land for his family. Remind them to look for water sources—springs and creeks. Then everyone must assist each other in the building of cabins before the cold of winter sets in." His voice fell to a whisper.

"Please, please. Rest now. You'll feel better in the morning. See if you don't."

He shook his head. "In the morning, first light, you must go. Leave me here. Follow the trail. For our sons' sake. For the babe's sake. For your sake. By day's end, you'll reach the cabin."

"No, Jacob," she said softly. "No, I won't leave you." She raked her hand through his disheveled hair. The sweat was running cold down his forehead. "Don't quit on me now, husband." She thought she saw a smile flitting in his eyes, but it might have been her imagination.

She added wood to the fire, warmed water in the cup for Jacob to sip, fed the baby the last little bit of bread softened in water, and prayed. Oh, how she prayed!

She felt the air stir beside her. Her thoughts came to an abrupt halt. She looked up and her lips parted in a silent gasp. Standing not ten steps away was an Indian, bare-chested, with long hair the color of dirty snow. Scared speechless, she felt her heart start to stutter, beating too hard for her to hear anything but her own fear. She took a quick scan around the campsite, terrified. She scrambled for a weapon, seeking Jacob's knife, but the only item within reach was the flint she had used to strike the fire. Slowly she rose to her feet, though her legs trembled so badly she could hardly hold herself up. Even still, she steeled herself, holding the flint in front of her.

What was she doing? How could she prevail against a man? She felt a scream rise in her throat and choked it off, for screaming would not help. No one could hear her. Nor could she fight off this attacker with physical strength.

But he did not attack.

The Indian merely looked at her, at the baby, and then his eyes rested on Jacob. She glanced at her sick husband, whose eyes were open. And she saw a flicker of recognition in those bloodshot eyes.

"I should've known," Jacob said in a raspy whisper. "You've been with us the entire time. God will bless you, my friend."

In that instant, comprehension flooded Dorothea's mind. Her thoughts ran backward, clicking off the things she knew. Jacob told her of an Indian who had helped him build the cabin, working beside him for months, showing him how to choose the best timbers. He was a Delaware Indian, Jacob said, who had shown him great kindness. "You are . . . Jacob's friend?"

The Indian ignored her question and kept his eyes on Jacob.

"Please, can you help us? Is there anything you can do for my husband?"

Just as suddenly, the Indian spun on his leathered heel and disappeared into the woods. Dorothea didn't know whether she should feel relief or sorrow.

Before daylight, the Indian returned with a pallet—two wooden poles held together with sewn animal skins. He lifted Jacob onto the pallet, covered him with the red Mutza he'd been lying on, and attached the pallet to the mule's harness. Then he handed Dorothea something round, made of animal skins with sheepskin on the inside. He put the baby into the carrier and then onto Dorothea's back. He pointed to the mule and folded his hands together so Dorothea could step onto his hands. He helped hoist her onto the mule, the baby on her back, and led the mule by the reins as Jacob had done.

They rode all day, with short stops near creeks to get water, feed the baby, check on Jacob, who slipped in and out of unconsciousness. When he came to himself, he whispered to her, his voice threadbare from his struggle. "Fear not, Dorothea. God is with us."

Once the old Indian disappeared into the woods and returned with some plants to eat. She found herself wishing she had the skills of Anna's grandmother, left in Ixheim, for she had known how to find plants to provide food or medicine.

She thought the Indian was leading them to the cabin that Jacob built, but as the last light of day lit their path, they arrived at a clearing in the forest. Then she saw, across the grassy expanse, an enormous wooden building, and in the air she smelled a scent of chimney smoke. As she gazed at the building, she had the oddest sense that they had gone through the deep dark woods of the New World and come out the other side into the Old World.

She blinked a number of times, sure she was hallucinating, but the building did not evaporate into thin air. It remained solidly in front of them. Its steeply pitched roof was covered in shingles, the siding was made of clapboard, and the narrow dormer windows reminded her of German architecture. Candlelight flickered through many of the tiny windows, and she felt cheered by the sight.

The Indian helped Dorothea climb down from the mule and unlashed the pallet from its harness. He knelt by Jacob and put his hand on his heart, as if he was passing something on to him, a wordless blessing. Jacob murmured something to him, words Dorothea couldn't understand. Then he grasped the red Mutza with his hand and pressed it upon the Indian. He spoke some words to him in a language she did not know.

The Indian stood and held the red Mutza in his hands for a long while. Then he simply walked off, without a backward glance. The baby let out a cry and Dorothea looked down at his little innocent face. She looked at Jacob's fevered face, listened to his labored breathing.

But they'd gotten this far. She had to keep going. She reached out a hand and knocked on the door. Then she knocked again, louder this time.

A hooded figure opened the door and a woman's face looked at Dorothea in surprise. She saw the baby in her arms, Jacob on the pallet behind her.

"Bitte," Dorothea said, her voice breaking. *Please.* Every ounce of strength had poured from her bones. She was so cold. She had to get inside the house by a fire and get warm again. She didn't think she would ever be warm again. "Bitte."

"Brauchscht Hilf?" *Do you need help?* A woman's voice emerged out of the hood, speaking in the German dialect Dorothea had used. "Kumme." *Come in.*

Jacob's Cabin
October 25, 1737

Anna smelled it first. Chimney smoke in the air. Soon they reached a clearing that led up to a cabin. Jacob Bauer's timber-framed log cabin.

"It's larger than I expected," the newcomer said as he slapped the reins of the horse to get it trotting. "How in the world did one man build such a frame? A stone chimney? And the roof too. Think of splitting all those shingles. Didn't you say he'd only been here a year?"

"Jacob Bauer is known for his unusual strength," Anna said. "Back in Ixheim, he once carried a donkey laden with baggage across a swollen stream. Another time he broke the horns off a vicious bull."

"Is he as wise a leader as his building is sturdy?"

She hesitated a moment and the newcomer noticed. He turned to her with a question in his eyes. Sturdy, yes. A fine builder, yes. But was Jacob a wise leader? In some ways, wise—filled with vision, determination; in other ways, not at all. Impulsive, strong minded, domineering. She didn't want to share such an assessment with the newcomer, so she dodged the question. "What makes you ask?"

"I don't understand how he could have left Philadelphia ahead of everyone."

"With winter approaching, there can be no wasting of time. He wanted to finish mowing the meadow, he said. The livestock depended on that hay for winter."

"From what I understand, he left them with the issue of the oath unresolved."

"He left the matter in the hands of Bairn, who did resolve it for the men."

"Yes, and look where the sons of Jacob Bauer are now." His sparkling blue eyes fixed on her, intense and unblinking, like those of a cat about to pounce on a mouse.

Anna dropped her eyes to her lap. What could she say?

"Jakob Ammann would not have allowed his church men

to take an oath that allied them to the world. He would not have left them until everyone could leave together. Instead, he would have forsaken the world's concern to care for his church."

The newcomer's stories about Jakob Ammann were interesting, though she suspected that his reputation grew exponentially with the retelling of stories. Her grandfather had also known of Ammann, but he had a more temperate view of the man—he had known Ammann to be an angry man, demanding and harsh, combative, divisive. Despite misgivings about Ammann, Anna's grandfather had become Amish to appease her grandmother.

Anna felt the need to defend Jacob Bauer from the newcomer's criticism. "Jacob Bauer didn't anticipate that it would take a week for the men to be cleared through the Court House. He thought it would only take a day."

But that, right there, might be the reason she had doubts about the depth of wisdom in Jacob Bauer. He charged ahead, with little to no patience when things didn't go as planned.

Up ahead, Anna saw Christian and Maria, Catrina, Barbara and the twin toddlers, standing outside of the cabin, waving to them. What a glorious sight! They were home. A journey that had begun last spring—seven months ago—covering a long trip up the Rhine River, a difficult stay in Rotterdam, three arduous months on the Atlantic as they traveled thousands of ocean miles, an arrival into Port Philadelphia, only to be forced to stay on the ship until the illness of a few passengers passed one way or another, and a lengthy trek into the wilderness. At long last, they were home. God's goodness knew no bounds.

Christian ran to meet them.

"When did you arrive?" Anna asked.

"Just hours ago," Christian said, grinning. "I have not said this often as a farmer, but it was a great blessing to have no rain. Day after day! Not a drop. The travel went swiftly and smoothly."

Maria joined them. "If you overlook the fact that every bone in my body has been jarred and jangled, then yes, it was a fairly smooth journey." She looked around. "Where is Felix?"

Anna and the newcomer exchanged a look. "He's safe. We learned that much."

"But where is he?"

"He's on the ship. He went as a stowaway. He wanted to be with Bairn." She looked at Maria. "I'll tell Dorothea and Jacob. I'll make them understand that Felix is safe. Bairn will take good care of him. They'll be back, come spring."

Something passed between Christian and Maria.

"What's wrong? Is it Dorothea? Is the baby not well?"

Christian lifted his chin. "Jacob and Dorothea and the baby—they have not arrived."

"Not yet," Maria said.

Christian dropped his chin. "No. Not yet." Then a thought occurred to him and he walked to the cart, peered inside, and looked at Anna. "Where is our Peter Mast?"

Isaac Mast had come out of the cabin to join them, and others were trailing out. "Where is my son?"

Anna's shoulders lifted, then sagged. "Peter . . . he chose . . . to remain in Philadelphia." She looked at Isaac. "That was his plan all along, he said. He did help us look for Felix, but then he was determined to remain behind. We tried to change his mind, Isaac. He knows where to find us. I feel confident he will return." She prayed so, anyway.

Maria leaned against Christian and covered her face with her hands. “Everything is falling apart. We should never have left Ixheim.”

The newcomer flung his arms out in a flamboyant embrace and held them in the air a moment. “Maria, don’t despair! There is a purpose in all things. Our work is not to question. Only to obey the Lord.”

In the front of the cabin was an open fire pit, with flames licking a roast.

“Is that venison I smell?” the newcomer asked, sniffing the air appreciatively.

11

***Lady Luck*, Atlantic Ocean**
October 25, 1737

Captain Berwick hauled forth a handkerchief, gave his nose a fierce blow. "The sinuses!" he said, scowling. "Bairn, ye must better mind that laddie."

"Mind him?"

"He's a useless cabin boy. Never can be found when he's needed. He's turnin' into a menace. Sneaks around when no one is lookin'."

That, Bairn did not doubt. He had given Felix a loose leash, hoping the laddie would settle down as soon as he got the lay of the ship and before it headed out to open sea.

The captain had given Bairn orders to plot a course south, to the James River of Virginia, with plans to dock along a riverside plantation from which he had bought a large shipment of dried tobacco to trade.

There was scarcely any type of legitimate trade that sea captains did not engage in for their vessels, for they were resourceful businessmen with ship investors to please. Any seaman knew that the transport of products wanted by the rest of the world was how money was to be made. Captain Berwick was happy to take products from the New World to sell, barter, and exchange in England. And he was also happy to return to the New World with what it wanted most: Germans. They had reputations as highly skilled hard workers. Cities in the colonies exploding with growth needed such a labor force.

The trip to Virginia did not take long, a few days' journey. But then the captain told him to set a course north to Boston. Bairn felt a hitch of worry. That meant they would not be crossing the Atlantic until mid-November. While the journey east would be much shorter than the return—the prevailing global winds blew from west to east, and there was that odd stream of warm water that provided its own benefits of plentiful fish for the catching and mild temperatures—even still, he knew not to tempt Mother Nature.

"Captain Berwick," Bairn said carefully, for he didn't know this captain well, "it concerns me to delay crossing the ocean. Winter won't be staved off for long."

"Nonsense! You need to read this. We're in fine shape this winter." He thrust a copy of *Poor Richard's Almanack* in his hands. "Warmest winter in a decade." He coughed into his handkerchief. "In Boston, we'll fill *Lady Luck*'s hold and be off on our journey."

The captain walked a few paces to the water bucket, reached down for the dipper and filled it, then slurped it down.

The *Lady Luck* was an American-built barque, with three large masts and a foremast rigged square, a ship designed for cargo transport. The great object of a cargo transport was to always be full. The fact that there was such little cargo loaded in Philadelphia was curious to Bairn, though he had more sense than to rag the captain about it. He had already discovered that if you were going to get along with Captain Berwick, there were things you did well not to notice or comment on. The endless nose blowing, for one. Bairn had asked him if, mayhap, he was a user of snuff, and the captain snarled back at him to mind his own business, adding a few unrepeatable adjectives. “Sir, what would we be loadin’ in Boston Harbor to sell in England? I can help negotiate prices for you. I’ve done it many times for Captain Stedman.”

“A fresh avenue of trade.” Captain Berwick gave him a wink. “I won’t be needin’ any help with negotiatin’.” And he had no more to say to Bairn.

Tending to Felix was all consuming. Bairn already had quite a bit of responsibility on his shoulders as first mate, as the captain had only a skeleton crew on the *Lady Luck*. The captain spent much time in the Great Cabin. His frequent absences provided Felix unlimited freedom to roam the ship . . . until something happened. And it often did.

So far Felix had broken a mirror in the sextant, untied a sail on the main mast, and tipped over a molasses jug in the galley. Cook banned him from the galley, the second mate Squivvers banned him from the upper deck. Not that Felix paid bans any mind. He went where he wanted to go. Bairn tried to keep the lad out of trouble, but trouble seemed to find the lad.

Whenever Bairn threatened Felix that he would oust him at the next port, the boy would look up at him, eyes glittering with hurt, watering with worry, and he’d lose his resolve.

When the watch bell rang this morning, Bairn went to his quarters as soon as he was relieved from duty, expecting to find the boy. The room was empty. Felix had gone missing again. He lay down on his bunk and stretched, exhausted. He missed having a hammock, like those in the *Charming Nancy*. He'd been up since second watch. His hand dangled on the floor and a warm, fuzzy ball of fur brushed up against his fingers. He jerked his hand up, looked down, and saw a fat gray cat sitting inside Felix's leather satchel. He reached down and drew the cat to his lap. He noticed an envelope in the satchel, smashed by the weight of the plump cat. Bairn lifted the satchel to his bunk, pulled out the envelope, sealed by wax, though the seal had been broken. Thanks, no doubt, to Felix. Bairn opened the envelope. The pages inside were on good rag paper, a letter written in precise German script, made out to someone named Karl.

He felt a movement beside him and turned to look into Felix's face. "You found my cat!"

"Yer cat? Have y' been hiding it?"

"Not hiding it. Just trying to train it so it will catch the rats."

"Where is yer dog?"

"Locked in the lower deck. I hate that dog."

"Y've been hiding other things too." He held up the envelope. "Where did this come from? You dinnae take this from your father, did y'?"

"*Our* father. He's *our* papa. Yours and mine. And now that little baby of Mem's too."

"Don't avoid the question. Did y' take it from him?"

"No. I don't know whose it is." The cat jumped out of his hands and off the bed. "I grabbed the wrong satchel when I left the wagon caravan."

"Are y' able to read proper German? In German script?"

"What's proper German?"

"Luther's German. Before Martin Luther, there was no proper German. Only dozens of dialects."

"I can read the Bible."

"So, then, surely you must be able to read this letter."

Felix read the page silently. "It doesn't read like the Bible. I don't know these words. And it's hard to read the handwriting." He frowned. "Isn't there any German on the ship?"

"In case y' hadn't noticed, 'tis a British ship." Bairn lifted an eyebrow.

Felix turned the pages, one after another. "Maybe you should give it a try."

"My German is worse than yer English."

Felix frowned. He pointed to the heading. "Mein lieber Karl, mein Mann. My dear husband." He looked at Bairn. "It's written to a man named Karl."

"Excellent. Yer a genius. Can y' make out the rest of the letter?"

Felix scanned the pages again. "It'll take me some time. And a dictionary."

Good. Something to keep the laddie's busy mind occupied. "Where did you find this satchel?"

"From one of the wagons. Those horses and wagons we borrowed from a farmer in Germantown."

"But that farmer's name wasn't Karl. His name was Christoph Saur."

"I recognize that name! The printer in Philadelphia had letters from Christoph Saur. He's a printer too." Felix yawned. "They don't like each other."

Bairn nodded, distracted. He felt a little tug in his guts,

a hunch taking root. There was something going on here. It was too soon to tell just what yet, but there was something . . . something . . .

Felix stretched out on the bunk, one ankle over the other, reminding Bairn of himself. "So where are we going next?"

"Boston Harbor."

Felix grinned. "There's no place I'd rather be going."

"Have you any idea where 'tis?"

"None at all." He stretched his hands behind his head. "What's molasses?"

"It's a by-product of cane sugar. A little like honey. Dark and smoky."

"Bostoners love molasses."

"Aye, they do. They use it in everythin'. Baked beans and brown bread."

"I heard Bostoners like it best in Demon Rum."

Bairn whipped his head around. "Where did you hear such a thing?"

"From the sailors. They said Boston is famous for rum." Felix smiled his naughty-boy smile. "One called it Oh Be Joyful. Then the other one, the one with the weird glass eye—"

"Squivvers. Mr. Squivvers to you. He's second mate. And just look at the good eye so you don't lose track of what yer tryin' to say." Poor Squivvers had a very ill-fitting glass eye.

"Understood. So Mr. Squivvers with the weird glass eye called it Rumbullion. And still another called it Kill-Devil."

Bairn sighed. Anna would be horrified. The boy needed schooling. He needed someone to watch over him. He needed a family. The heel of his boot bumped against his trunk stored under his bunk. He bent over the bunk, pulled out the trunk, and opened it. "Felix, we're going to start your schooling. Today."

"Thank you, no. I do not care for schooling."

"I dinnae give y' a choice."

Felix sat upright. "What? You're *serious*? But I don't need any more lessons."

"Nae, y' do. Despite not being overburdened by the need for an education, y' need things to fill that busy mind of yours. Yer going t' read English books, so you keep practicin' the language. That church needs English speakers, even if they think they dinnae." He pulled out an old newspaper, the *Pennsylvania Gazette*, that could be used for scratch paper and vocabulary building. "Sums too. Addin' and subtractin'." He dug under a folded sweater and found a map of the world. "And geography."

Felix's face crumpled with frustration. "Schooling will take up my valuable time."

Bairn stifled a laugh and handed him the rolled-up map of the world. "First assignment. Find Boston Harbor. Second assignment. Decipher that German letter."

"But Anna wants me to learn English!"

"You're getting plenty of English when y' prowl around the ship and get in the sailors' way." He pointed at Felix. "And those aren't the words y' should be committing to memory." He grinned. "But I'll make you a deal. You help me with the dialect and I'll help y' with the English."

"No one understands you. You speak the dialect with a Scottish accent." Felix giggled. "Even your English is hard to understand. Remember, back in Philadelphia, when you told Catrina to tell her mother that you were going to the shops over there?" He mimicked Bairn's accent. "Am gan tae the shoaps oor air." He burst out with a laugh. "She told Maria that you headed out to shock wheat."

"Aye, I remember. When I returned, she saw the loaves of bread in me hands and asked if I'd baked them meself." Bairn chuckled. "But that's enough of yer mockin', lad. At least I am workin' on bein' understood. We both need schoolin'."

The laddie pressed his face into his hands hard, then took a deep, groaning breath and slowly raised his head. "I'm thirsty." He jumped off the bunk and went to the bucket of water. "Empty. Schooling will have to wait." The cat stretched and yawned, then curled into a ball on top of Bairn's pillow. "The cat has a shock of white on its forehead just like that fellow."

"Which fellow?"

"The newcomer. The man who joined up with the church."

Bairn stilled.

Felix set the empty bucket on the ground. "Do you remember when the *Charming Nancy* stopped in Plymouth to water the ship?"

Bairn was only half listening as he tucked the letter back into the envelope. "Aye. It's the first and most important task before the long sea journey."

"Why hasn't the captain watered the ship?"

"Probably because he wants to wait to fill up in Boston."

"Maybe . . . but the cargo hold is already full. Big heavy barrels."

"With water?"

"No. Not water. I could tell when I knocked on them."

Bairn sighed. "You should nae be down in the cargo hold at all."

But something Felix had said triggered that odd feeling

to dance again on the edge of Bairn's consciousness, a little hunch that was about to become a full-blown thought, when he heard the bells ring, sounding the watch change.

"Time for supper!" Felix jumped off the bunk and ran to the door.

And the thought was gone.

12

Jacob's Cabin
October 26, 1737

The log cabin was crude, dark and dim inside, but it was watertight, snug, and well constructed, as Anna would have expected from Jacob Bauer. It measured sixteen feet wide by twenty-four feet in length. There was one door and two small windows. A large open-hearth stone fireplace at one end of the cabin furnished heat and was the only source for cooking. The walls were fairly crammed with trunks stacked on top of each other, and barrels filled the corners. A loft above served both as sleeping quarters and a place for storage of dried hay that the men would bring in from the meadow.

It was a fine cabin for one family, but crowded and claustrophobic with five families, plus Anna. Plus the newcomer.

On this morning, Anna's first full day at the new land, she was outside by the fire pit, stoking it to get the flames going. The sun was shining and the wind was gently blowing—an ideal day to wash clothes. She probably should be inside helping the other women clean up after breakfast, but Maria was in a snit about something or other.

She had asked Anna about the newcomer. "So what's he like then, this man?"

Anna wondered herself, and had no answer to satisfy Maria's nosiness.

"But you've just spent days with him!"

Still, Anna had nothing much to say about the newcomer, nor did she want to share her thoughts with gossipy Maria. Her reluctance only convinced the minister's wife that there was something she was holding back—she wasn't!—and the morning skidded downhill from there. After months on a small ship with Maria's moodiness, Anna preferred to stay clear.

She picked up the fire iron and poked at the logs, studying the fire. Bairn's face flickered in the flames. She sucked in a breath and closed her eyes. *Bairn, Bairn, how could you do this, how could you have left us? How could you have left me?* She opened her eyes, forcing herself to shift to the matters of the day as she lifted the heavy cauldron of water onto the trammel. She looked around for something else to do while the water heated. If she could stay busy with ordinary things, maybe she would be able to convince herself that nothing was wrong. Bairn and Felix would return, Jacob and Dorothea would come up the path through the woods today, and all would be well.

Catrina was suddenly at her side, handing her a tin of hot coffee. "Mama said you seemed out of sorts today. She said it would be just the thing to help you get over Bairn's desertion. You know, since he only drinks tea."

"I don't need help to get over anything, as I haven't gotten under anything to begin with." Exasperation clipped her voice.

"Oh." Catrina spoke in a quiet, wounded tone.

Anna's sharp reply had clearly hurt her and her conscience smote her. "Catrina, I am sorry." She cradled the tin between her hands. "I didn't sleep well last night. Forgive me for being short with you."

Maybe it wasn't Maria's moodiness that was the problem, but hers. Bairn's absence in this place did make her feel brittle and blue.

The newcomer stood at the cabin door with his hands on his hips, staring at the forest as the sun limned the top of the trees. "Your bishop chose well. This is a pioneer's paradise."

Anna glanced briefly at him, then looked again, longer this time. The open narrative of his face drew her right in, his warmth and cheerfulness.

"To be among the first to settle in an untouched wilderness, especially in a setting as blessed with natural assets as this land. Surely this was how Adam and Eve must have felt at the dawn of creation. Surely God is in this place."

Christian joined the newcomer at the door's threshold. "And God will be with us today as we sickle the hay in that meadow."

The newcomer stepped outside to make way for him. "Is that the best way our time should be spent, sickling hay? It seems we should concentrate our efforts on scouting out the land, to choose building sites. To start building cabins."

"That is what Jacob Bauer talked about doing. To mow the hay, rake it, and leave it to dry."

"And then what?"

"I suppose, to build fences for the livestock." Christian seemed perplexed. "Unless Jacob has something else in mind. He should be here soon. Any day. Maybe even today."

Josef Gerber chimed into the discussion, his head appearing at the door behind both men. He was an energetic man, small and thin, like his wife, Barbara. "I think we should prepare the meadow to sow crops before winter arrives." All three men peered up at the azure sky, empty of clouds.

Christian nodded. "Yes, that should be done, as well." He sighed a tired sigh. "There's so much to be done."

"But spending all that time and energy on sowing crops doesn't seem necessary, Josef," the newcomer said. "Not this first year, anyway. There's an abundance of wild animals to hunt for food. Just look." As if on cue, a V-formation of honking geese passed overhead. "Ducks, geese, they're filling the sky as they head south for the winter. And there's plenty of fish in the creek."

Isaac appeared at the door. "So what do you propose, newcomer?" There was a tone in Isaac's voice that made Anna stop stoking the fire and turn toward the men.

"We don't have long before winter settles in, a few weeks at the most. I think that our time would be best spent felling trees to clear land and build shelters for each family, and also for the livestock. With everyone helping, we can build cabins in no time. Most of the building materials are right here—logs, stones, sand, lime, and clay. Ready for the taking, if we all worked together. If we lack for anything, nails or windows or iron hinges, I will go to Germantown."

Isaac gave him a doubtful look. "Always eager to run off to the city, aren't you?"

"Just to get supplies to help keep the work going. That's our way, is it not? Neighbor helps neighbor. There will be time enough for farming."

Isaac's eyes narrowed. "So, newcomer, you think you know more than our bishop?"

"No, not at all." Henrik looked surprised at Isaac's harsh tone, but Anna knew what lay behind it. Isaac blamed them both for Peter's unexpected departure.

"Then we will wait until Jacob arrives before we start building shelters. And in his absence, we will do what he wants us to do. *That's* our way."

Henrik acknowledged Isaac with a slight dip of his chin, nothing more, a sign of humility, Anna thought, before he went inside the cabin. She overheard Isaac grumble to Christian, "That boy doesn't know anything about sickling hay or felling trees. Have you seen his hands? They are not the hands of a farmer."

Christian looked out at the forest. "Perhaps he's right, though. We're spending precious days bringing in hay for livestock we don't have."

Isaac lifted his eyes to the sky. "Jacob always knows what is best." When he lowered his head, he caught Anna staring, but she didn't look away.

Did Jacob always know what's best? She wasn't sure. Isaac frowned at her and turned on his heel to start off to the meadow, saying over his shoulder, "There's plenty of hay that needs cutting, if that newcomer can stop talking long enough to get himself down to the meadow to work."

Henrik had returned to the cabin's door and heard Isaac's biting words. His gaze followed the man's stiff back as he stomped down the path to the meadow.

"Don't pay him any mind," Anna said, walking up to him. "He's upset about Peter."

Henrik rolled his shoulders in a half shrug. "I suppose I don't blame him."

A soft breeze plucked at her loose capstrings, making them dance. She tossed them out of the way, over her shoulders, then tucked a strand of loose hair behind her ear. He watched her, half smiling, and she wondered what sort of look she was wearing on her own face that he felt he had to smile at her in that way.

"No doubt I'd be just as tetchy if I were in his shoes," he said. "I can't imagine what it would be like to have a son depart his family, without warning or explanation. A betrayal to everything—*everything*—a father holds dear."

But were they still talking about Peter Mast?

Lady Luck, Atlantic Ocean
October 27, 1737

Bairn walked the entire deck, checking spars and halyards. He had finished making the midnight bearing with the sextants, wrote it in the logbook, while Felix was fast asleep. This was the time that Bairn felt completely at ease. The only sound to be heard was the slapping of the waves and the sharp prow of the ship cutting through the sea. Something about the inky black of the sky around him released the tangled thoughts Bairn held tight.

On duty, he held himself responsible to the captain and crew and gave the ship his whole attention. He liked keeping watch, walking the ship, knowing what was working and where trouble might be brewing. He liked to see the sun coming up. He walked around the upper deck with a lantern in his hand, stopping to breathe deeply of the salt air, to gaze out over the black surface of the water. He realized someone was at his elbow. A seaman stood beside him, waiting to be noticed.

Squivvers.

"Do y' always take the night watch?"

"No sir. Captain Berwick just puts me on it, sir." Squivvers remained standing at attention, looking uncomfortable. But then, he was a nervous sort.

"What's on yer mind, Squivvers?"

"Sir, are you missing someone?"

"What makes you ask that?"

"You're standing at the stern of the ship. Most men of the sea face the bow. It occurred to me that you might be looking for someone."

A rock of truth dropped between them. Bairn dropped his chin to his chest. "Aye, yer right." He would not have expected such a deep thought from a curiously odd, simpleminded sailor like Squivvers. "I had a family. Right there, right in my hands. Everything I'd ever wanted—a family, a woman to love. And I walked away from it."

Bairn's life story spilled out of him, all of it, including that he had thought he would marry Anna and remain with the church. "But with each passin' day, the walls began to close in on me. I started to feel my life narrow down. Everything I had wanted, everything I would miss—opportunities, money, ambition, success. Mostly, my freedom and independence. It was all disappearin'."

Bairn explained how he had thought he could sail away with an easy conscience, or at least that the guilt would quickly fade. But even now his spirit remained troubled.

His heart was not in this journey, but it was too late to turn back.

He gave a sharp look at Squivvers and caught the uncertainty in his one good eye. Almost a frantic look.

"I ken what yer thinkin', Squivvers. I've had those same thoughts."

"No, sir, I was just—"

"Y' dinnae have to apologize. Yer absolutely right. I was on the edge of the Promised Land and turned back to go to Egypt, just like those Israelites. As a boy, listenin' to my father's sermons on Moses, I'd often wondered why those Israelites were ready to turn tail so quickly." Bairn pounded his fists on the railing. "Now I understand. Returnin' to Egypt felt safe. It was known. Even misery felt safe. They preferred the habit of slavery to arduous freedom."

Habits. Egyptian habits. Slavery.

It was a difficult thing to be free.

Squivvers's face had gone bright red. He shifted from one foot to the other, acutely uncomfortable. "Sir, are you finished?"

He glanced at Squivvers. He might have said more than he intended to the sailor, but what did it matter? Perhaps there might be something wise inside of that curiously odd sailor's head. Something profound, something to help him set things straight. "Aye."

"I was just asking in case you had thought your brother might have gone overboard." He tipped his head toward the stern's railing.

"Why? Is the laddie not sound asleep?"

"No, sir. Cook found him rifling through the biscuit tin and locked him in the galley."

Aha. Bairn cleared his throat, mortified. So then, Squivvers hadn't been asking him if he was missing someone on *land*.

Jacob's Cabin

Another day had passed with no sign of Jacob and Dorothea and the infant. Anna could see that Christian, a malleable man with little confidence in his own opinions, had no idea what to do next. Jacob was the one they all depended on for guidance and direction. Josef Gerber felt they should send out a search party, but Christian was fearful that the search party could find themselves lost too. Isaac Mast insisted that the hay get mown, and that was a difficult chore to ignore. It was what Jacob had wanted them to do, and it made them feel like they were doing something. There was no time to waste.

But what, Henrik kept persisting, about Jacob and Dorothea? Did the church not care about their time? About their lives? Of course they did. Of course, they all insisted, but there was no plan of action. The newcomer volunteered to go searching, but Christian and Isaac wouldn't let him go—they needed his strong young back to help sickle the hay.

All they could do was pray, Isaac said, and Christian agreed.

Anna felt a tug at her sleeve and looked down to see Catrina by her side. "Where do you think they are?"

"I don't know," Anna said. "Jacob knows these woods, though. He must've walked everywhere to place boundary markers." It was unfortunate he had not communicated such vital information to anyone. Nobody doubted that Jacob had found a beautiful land for them—they just didn't know where it started or ended.

The newcomer, more than anyone, waxed eloquent over the terrain. "This land Jacob Bauer chose, no doubt it's the best land in all the New World," Henrik said. "Tucked between two rivers—the Schuylkill and the Susquehanna. Excellent irrigation, excellent fertility. Lush soil, dark and moist, like crumbled cake. I imagine it's similar to the first Garden, set between the Euphrates and the Tigris rivers."

As soon as Henrik left to go outside, Catrina whispered, "Where is this garden the newcomer talks so much about?"

"He means the Garden of Eden, in the Bible."

She looked blank.

"It's where God set the first two people on earth, Adam and Eve. They lived in the Garden of Eden, a perfect world, until the devil tempted them to disobey God and they were banished from the Garden. Henrik believes that's what the New World is meant to be. A return to the Garden, he calls it."

"Do you think that could be true?"

Anna didn't know how to answer that question, so she hedged. "It's a nice thought."

"I like it," Catrina said. "But if we really are in the Garden of Eden, wouldn't that mean that we'd all be together? Jacob, Dorothea, and her baby, and Felix."

And Bairn. Don't forget Bairn, Anna thought. She put an arm around Catrina's small shoulders. "Soon," she said. "We'll all be together again soon." That was her prayer.

October 28, 1737

It was a luscious feeling, to do nothing.

While others napped on Sunday afternoon, Anna slipped

quietly away to take a walk down to the stream. She sat down on a bed of marsh grass, stretching her legs out. She took off her shoes and dipped her feet into the cold, clear stream. So cold it made her skin goose-pimply. Then her feet grew used to the cold and she pulled her dress up to her knees so she could dip her ankles in.

It had been a wonderful day, the best day of all for the little church of Ixheim. Today they had their first worship service in the New World. The morning skies had been clear and the air was brisk but not unpleasant, so Christian suggested that they meet outside, under the cover of trees, to worship God and give thanks.

The evening before, Christian had opened his large wooden trunk and emptied it out on the cabin floor. A special hidden compartment in the chest had protected his precious family Forschauer Bible during the trip to America. The Gerbers and the Masts had also brought copies of the *Ausbund*, their beloved book of hymns. Hearing these stories of persecution and martyrdom reminded everyone why they had risked so much to come to a new land. They no longer had to hide their religious practices.

Once or twice during the long service, Anna had let her gaze drift to the newcomer. She wondered if this worship service was very different from those he had known, those inspired by Jakob Ammann himself, but if so, he gave no sign of it. He sat on an uncomfortable tree log as quiet and unmoving as the rest of them. His chin was tucked low in what she thought was reverence and humility, but after watching him for a long moment, she realized he had fallen asleep.

The fellowship meal after the service was served outdoors as well. No cooking was allowed on Sundays since it was a day of rest. But Maria had cooked a venison stew in an iron skillet on Saturday evening, and there was hearth-baked bread to scoop up the stew. There had been no petty quarrels on this fine Sunday, no sharp remarks or jabs. Everyone had gotten along with each other remarkably well.

Wind rattled through the branches of the trees and stirred the grass that limned the creek. Anna took a deep breath and stretched again, letting her numbed toes dangle in the water. She watched a leaf float along the water's surface and closed her eyes, feeling herself drift along like that leaf, just drift along . . .

A soft plop in the water startled her. Eyes open, her heart did a flip-flop. Henrik stood a few feet away from her, skimming rocks into the creek. She remembered her legs were uncovered and yanked her feet out of the creek, scrambling to find her shoes.

Henrik's blue eyes were laughing. "Should I cover my eyes?"

"What?"

"If I cover my eyes, you can put your shoes on so you can stop blushing the color of cherries."

Anna turned away from him as she tucked each foot into a shoe.

He bent down and dipped one cupped palm into the water. He raised it, dripping, to his mouth, drinking noisily. He looked at her as he wiped his mouth with the back of his sleeve, then flashed her a bright smile. "That might be the finest water I have ever sipped." He plopped down next to her on the grass. "Or maybe it's just the company that makes it so particularly fine."

Those words he spoke, they were sweeter than honey. She wasn't accustomed to men who spoke such sweet words; it wasn't their way. And she was embarrassed to discover that she liked it. "This is a nice spot, this creek." She felt foolish. What a silly thing to say. She could feel another flush start to burn on her cheeks.

But the newcomer didn't seem to notice her discomfort. "Indeed it is." He gazed up and down the creek. "It's a fine land. A running creek that abounds with fish. Woods that supply plenty of fresh meat. It's a poor hunter that can't bag a buck or doe within an hour's time."

That was a jab at Christian, she knew. He had taken a turn at hunting yesterday afternoon and returned empty-handed by dusk. Henrik went into the woods and soon returned with wild turkeys that were easily shot, roosting on the lower boughs of trees.

It rankled her, such open dismay leveled at the minister. It wasn't just from Henrik—the others made their own digs and jabs. Christian might not be a dynamic man, but he had always done his best for them. Over the years, in his peaceable way, he was the one who settled disputes, sat by the dying, and wept with the grieving. To be fair, the newcomer wouldn't know such a thing about Christian.

"I mean to catch some ducks and geese soon. We can raise them for eggs."

"And their feathers for pillows."

"A feather pillow. A luxury I'd almost forgotten." His head turned to her and the sun seemed to catch at something in those blue eyes of his, making them sparkle. "First, though, I need to build you a coop."

For me. As if he was building it just for her.

"We need to start building soon. Enough of this hay gathering."

"Christian depends heavily on Jacob. Any day now, they should arrive. Jacob and Dorothea and the baby. And then everything will be as it should."

"From your mouth to God's ears." The newcomer tipped his head back, lifting his chin, closing his eyes to soak up the autumn sun. But even with his eyes closed, Anna felt his awareness of her, like a warm breeze that swirled around her.

13

Ephrata Community
October 28, 1737

Dorothea ached from such little sleep. She sat in a chair next to the bed where her husband lay. Her head nodded as she reluctantly succumbed to a fitful slumber. She jerked awake when she heard Jacob stir, call for her, so she rose and leaned over him. His eyes were haggard and red-rimmed. What had happened to her husband? This strong man was failing before her.

Jacob looked directly in her eyes. Slowly he lifted his head. He seemed to be searching for something to say to her. "Dory," he whispered.

Tears sprang to her eyes. Dory was a pet name for her that he hadn't used since their courting days. "I'm sorry . . . to be . . . leaving you like this." He groped for her hand and she clasped it, holding it against her heart.

"You're not going anywhere, Jacob Bauer."

A wisp of a smile curved his lips. "I have no fear of death." His eyelids fluttered shut.

He may not fear death, but she feared life without him.

Dorothea knew to concentrate on each task, one by one. Get through the morning, then the day. But what to do about the long nights, like this one, remained troublesome.

She sighed and stretched, feeling loose-jointed with weariness. When she checked on the baby in the cradle, she saw his open eyes stare back at her. He asked for so little, this dear one. No sweeter baby ever lived, she was sure of it, and then she wondered if perhaps the Christ child was as docile a baby for the mother Mary. She picked the baby up and held him against her chest, loving the feel of an infant in her arms, so grateful to have a distraction during the endless dark night. She thought it must be only midnight and dreaded the hours until dawn. Somehow those hours seemed twice as long as any others. She took one more slow look around this sparsely furnished room, with its narrow bed, small table, and chair. The mattress Jacob lay on was nothing more than a thin pallet on top of a thick plane of oak. The sheets were of a rough, fibrous cotton. It was not a room designed for pleasure. No books to pass the time. The fireplace was the only concession to comfort.

Silence, thick as wool, wrapped around her.

She heard doors open and close. Then the sound of bare feet pattering down the hallway, the quietest susurration. Even at midnight, this odd community wasn't asleep; something was happening. She heard a faint sound and strained her ears. What was that? It came from somewhere far from her little room.

She went to the small window and unlocked the latch, then pushed and pushed until it opened. She peered out into the darkness and heard the sound again, coming from the next building over. Why, it was music! Voices, men and women. She strained to listen: women's voices sang high, men's voices sang low, separately at first, then joining together in melody before separating into harmonies. The sound of the music swept over her, filling her with a breath-held feeling of utter joy. A joy so intense it brought tears to her eyes—happy tears. And when it ended, she breathed out a long, slow sigh. "Oh, that was such a wonderment."

Her eyes flew open and she looked to see if Jacob might be awake, observing her delight in the music—he would surely disapprove and remind her it was against the rules of their church to have such harmonies. They were to sing in unity, one voice, with no one standing out. No one was to elevate himself or herself, because that would be the start of pride.

Rules. So many rules.

But how could something so beautiful, so worshipful, be forbidden?

Thankfully, Jacob was sleeping, unaware of what went on around him. Tomorrow . . . no, this morning, for it was already the next day, she would try to find out why there was music in the night.

She kept the window open an inch or so and tucked the sleeping baby into the cradle, fed the fire in the clay-lined fireplace with a few pieces of wood, and stretched out next to Jacob on the small bed, ever so carefully so not to disturb him. She listened to his raspy breathing, labored but not unsteady, before turning to her side to face the window. The music that floated in through the crack in the window surrounded her, lifting her thoughts to another world. It thrilled her to the depth of her very soul. She closed her eyes and let the sound fill her. Soon, she slept, curled like a contented cat.

***Lady Luck*, Atlantic Ocean**
October 29, 1737

Felix was fed up with the awful dog. It followed him everywhere, up ladders, down hatches. The only place he could get away from it was if he climbed the mast to the crow's nest, which he could do only at night when the crow's nest, most times, was empty. And even then, the dog would sit on the deck, eyes fixed upward. Waiting.

If Felix didn't know better, it was like the awful dog thought its only purpose in life was to watch over him. And then to tattle on his whereabouts with a bark.

The dog was a combination of Maria and Catrina, all mixed up in one.

He was down in the lower deck, hungry and searching for the apple barrel, because Cook banned him from the galley for the unfortunate bread dough incident.

The captain had sent him to the galley to fetch Cook. Naturally, Felix did as he was told. Cook had even told him to stay out of the galley while he was gone. That was the part that Felix didn't remember. Cook had been in the middle of kneading bread dough and it looked like fun. His mother used to let him knead dough, but that was long ago, way back in Ixheim, before their adventures began. He liked the thought of kneading dough, of thinking of those times in the kitchen with his mother.

So he slipped back into the galley after Cook stomped away to the Great Cabin, poked the dough, once, then twice, then punched it. A few times. The last punch knocked the jar of yeast so it went flying, spilling yeast everywhere before it rolled to the ground. Not such a difficult problem, Felix thought, as he worked the spilled yeast into the dough and quietly slipped out of the galley.

But it turned out to cause quite a kerfuffle.

The way Cook described it—which Felix thought might be a bit of an exaggeration—the dough exploded. Still, there was a chance that Felix might not have been blamed for the ruined dough, but the awful dog gave him away. It had followed him into the galley and was quietly licking clean the floor of spilled yeast. When Felix shut the galley door behind him, he unwittingly locked him in.

And Felix was banned from the galley, once again.

Ephrata Community

Dorothea's eyelids fluttered open but the heaviness of fatigue pulled them shut. For a moment she forgot the anxiety and depression that weighed her down and willed herself to remain in that blissful state between sleep and full consciousness, before reality set in.

A knock on the door interrupted her thoughts. "One moment if you will." She stumbled over the table leg as she moved to pull the heavy door open. Two robed figures with hoods covering most of their faces stood at the threshold; at first, Dorothea wasn't sure if they were men or women. Neither spoke. She looked from one to the other. Then she recognized one of them as the woman who helped her when she arrived. "Sister Marcella."

"Yes. And this is Sister Alice." Sister Alice, small and birdlike, stood behind Sister Marcella, a basket in her hand filled with polished red apples and yellow-green pears.

Sister Alice handed her the basket. "We eat only one meal a day."

One meal a day! *One meal*. No wonder they all looked so gaunt and thin. Different robed figures had brought her meals throughout the day. "I didn't realize there was a famine in this land. We don't have much money, but we can give you what we have, and I'll be sure to reimburse you when we return to our church." She was touched by their generosity. They had been kind and hospitable to her in this time of need.

Sister Alice shook her head. "You are our guest. And there is no famine. Quite the contrary. The Householders have had a bountiful harvest this year."

"The Householders?"

"They are our Third Order."

Dorothea gave a puzzled look. "Third Order?"

"The Brotherhood, the Sisterhood, and then the Householders."

Sister Marcella, the more serious of the two, filled in the missing pieces for Dorothea. "The Householder group are the farming families in the area who provide food and support for us. There is an abundance of food."

"Then, why do you eat only one meal a day?" Why would anyone eat so little if they didn't have to? Food was a great pleasure in life.

"Father Friedsam believes that self-denial brings us closer to God." Sister Alice seemed pleased to tell her more. "Nor does he allow us to partake of meat, either. But no one expects you to limit your intake of food. Please feel free to ask for anything you need. After all, you have a baby to nurse too." She went to the cradle and picked up the baby.

If Dorothea had any doubts that the solemn sisters were

tenderhearted, they vanished as she watched them fuss over the baby. "He is adopted. His mother died on the ship, right after he was born. I took him on."

Sister Alice's eyes went wide. "Oh! We assumed he was a late-in-life child. Like Sarah and Abraham."

Dorothea was startled by that comment. Did she seem so very old?

"What are you feeding the baby?"

"Goat's milk."

"We can help with that. Today is our day of fasting, but I will see if goat's milk is in the kitchen."

"Fasting?"

Sister Alice nodded her head with vigor. "Oh yes. We fast often."

The basket of fruit in Dorothea's arms was looking more and more inviting. "You fast?" She was accustomed to fasting on the morning before her church took communion, but twice a year provided plenty of practice for self-denial.

"We do," Sister Alice said. "Father Friedsam believes that it helps us to see God's presence. Suffering brings us closer to God. Father Friedsam chose the name 'Ephrata' from the Bible. It's a word that denotes suffering."

Suffering. Dorothea knew all about *that*.

Sister Marcella had her eyes on Jacob. "How is your husband faring today?"

"The same, it seems."

"Is he able to eat?"

"A little. He has trouble chewing and swallowing. He's very weak."

"Perhaps I could poach some chicken and shred it into small pieces for him. Add milk to it for nourishment."

"But you don't eat meat."

"We do not judge others for their choices. If your husband has such weakness, it seems meat would provide the best nutrition for him."

"If it would be helpful," Sister Alice said, "we can stay and watch over your husband for you. Or care for the baby."

"Know that I do appreciate your offer. You've all been most kind. But no. Thank you, but no." She looked over at Jacob. "Is it possible to send for a doctor?"

Sister Marcella shook her head. "The closest doctor is in Germantown."

"How far would that be?"

"About sixty miles southeast. It would take days of travel, there and back, assuming a doctor could be persuaded to come, which is quite unlikely."

She looked in the direction of the small window. "Surely, you must grow herbs or plants for medicines. Do you not have anything to bring down fever?"

"Perhaps we can see if Brother Andrew has something to suggest. He has some familiarity with treating ailments."

Sister Alice set the baby back in the cradle and joined Sister Marcella, standing by the door, ready to leave. Dorothea didn't want them to leave. "Do you mind if I ask you a question about this place?"

Sister Marcella and Sister Alice exchanged a look. "We have nothing to hide."

"In the night, I hear singing. Music."

Sister Marcella clasped her hands together. "What you hear is our midnight worship."

Dorothea couldn't hide her astonishment. "You worship, at midnight?" Every night?

"We adhere to a strict schedule. Father Friedsam stresses discipline."

"But I thought I heard . . . harmonies."

"Yes," Sister Alice said. "Father Friedsam writes most of our hymns. There are usually four parts, though sometimes there are even six or seven parts. That's when our choir practices for three or four hours."

"Why . . . at midnight?"

Sister Marcella looked at her as if it was so obvious. "Because Father Friedsam believes that the Second Coming of Christ will occur at midnight." She gave Dorothea a calm smile. "We want to be ready."

A bell chimed and Sister Marcella reached for the door latch. "We must go tend to the Three Sisters."

"Are there others who are ill?"

A giggle burst out of Sister Alice, and Sister Marcella lifted a sparse eyebrow at her, silencing her immediately. "The Three Sisters is what we call our garden."

"But why?"

"Beans, corn, and squash," Sister Alice said. "They're always grown together, helping each other. The squash provides shade for the roots of the corn, and the corn provides a natural pole for the vines of the beans to climb up. The roots of the beans help stabilize the corn. A wonderful example of God's community from the world of nature."

"I'm unfamiliar with corn."

"Soon you will know it well," Sister Marcella said. "It's a plant native to the New World."

"The Iroquois Indians introduced it to us," Sister Alice said. "They're the ones who taught us about the Three Sisters."

Dorothea leaned toward them. "But aren't you afraid of the Indians?"

Both sisters shook their heads from side to side. "God is with us," Sister Marcella said. "We have nothing to fear."

God was with Dorothea too, but she felt she had much to fear.

Almost in unison, the two women spun on the balls of their feet and started back down the long hall. Dorothea stared after them, her gaze moving up and down the length of them, from their hoods to the shapeless robes that covered their bodies. Then she noticed their feet were bare. There was something, she thought, so touchingly human about the sight of bare feet.

Dorothea closed the door with a sigh. What an odd place she was in! She wondered why the old Indian had directed them here, of all places, though she supposed he might have thought they were one and the same—speakers of the same German tongue.

Strange—to have much in common with these people and yet feel so separate from them. Ah, but then there was the music. She hoped she might hear it again tonight. It filled her with a peace unlike anything she had felt before. She went to Jacob's bedside and smoothed out his blanket. He seemed a little better and the thought cheered her. More color in his face, less of that heavy labored breathing.

The two hooded sisters were outside, walking past her open window on their way to the garden, talking as they walked. She paused when she heard their conversation.

"Es geht ihm hinnerlich." *He is doing poorly.*

The other sister's hood bobbed up and down in agreement. "Ich denk der Mann is am Schtarewe." *I think the man is dying.*

Dorothea's shoulders sagged at their assessment.

14

Jacob's Cabin
October 30, 1737

On this sunny afternoon, Anna was alone in the cabin while the others were either in the meadow or down by the creek. She watered her rose and set it by the cabin door to get sun. Soon, it must be planted to survive, though she had no idea where. This cabin of Jacob Bauer's, it was a temporary home for them all. Strange, to realize that Jacob had built it to house his family, yet everyone *but* his family was living in it.

She knelt by her trunk and opened it for the first time since she had left Ixheim, pulling out the sewing bag and extra linens, all made by her grandmother. Memories of her grandparents flooded her. Each piece of linen reminded her of how she prepared for the journey to America. It was difficult to decide what to bring, what to leave behind.

But the most difficult thing to leave, of course, hadn't been a thing at all, but her dear grandparents. She had little hope that Bairn would be able to coax her grandparents to return with him, if indeed he could even get to Ixheim. Her grandfather, an adventurous man, might be talked into it, but her grandmother would squelch the idea.

She held a delicate handkerchief to her face, eyes closed as she breathed in the faintest scent of lavender from her grandmother's garden. Lavender would be at the top of her list of things to plant in the garden. She heard a horse whinny from the meadow and another one nicker in response, and closed her trunk with a sigh. She should get started on supper before everyone returned, famished, annoyed with her for dawdling the afternoon away.

As she cut vegetables for the soup, she cherished this rare moment of solitude. A huge iron kettle hung from a tripod over the fire. The fire burned low. Anna picked up the iron poker and began to nudge the great charred logs.

She poured water into the kettle and set the bucket on the table—made up of four large trunks pushed together—behind her. For a moment, she gazed at the flames dancing through the logs. Bairn and Felix, what would they be doing right now? One moment, she found herself missing them terribly, longing for them to return. In the next instant, she fought a silent battle with Bairn for leaving, almost a seething anger toward him. How could love and anger coexist in her heart?

Before she could examine those thoughts, the cabin door opened and the newcomer appeared with a large bundle of dried hay gathered in a blanket. His face lit up when he saw her. "More hay to squirrel away in the loft to keep the livestock well fed through the winter," he said cheerfully, "though we have very little livestock. Five hens, one rooster, one pig, two sheep, only four horses."

"And three of those horses are borrowed," she reminded

him. They burst into shared laughter, the nonsensical kind that felt good, lighthearted.

Soon, they would need to return those horses and wagons to the farmers in Germantown. That was another matter Christian remained indecisive over—who should return them? When should he go?

"Is that a rose plant by the door?"

"Yes. A rose from Ixheim. I brought it with me."

"You must have taken great care with it, for it to survive an ocean journey."

"Indeed. It was rarely out of my sight." She wondered why Henrik had come to the New World. Why would he not have been with others on the ship? So she asked him.

It was a reasonable question, but Henrik stiffened as though she had stabbed him with it. Instead of answering, he lifted the blanket of hay and said he should get this hay up in the loft before the minister's wife came after him with her broom for messing up her clean floor.

He came back down the loft ladder with the now-empty blanket and sniffed the air with an appreciative look on his face. Steam thick with the smell of bean soup billowed around them.

Henrik set the blanket on the ground near the fireplace and turned around to lean against the table with his arms folded across his chest. As big as the cabin was, he seemed to fill it.

"Are you hungry?" Anna asked.

"Bean soup. Just what my stomach was pining for." But from the way he was gazing at her, bean soup did not seem to be the only thing on his mind.

Anna turned abruptly toward the fire. "The soup is burning." She started to reach for the handle of the kettle with her bare hand, then pulled it back at the last second and used a folded-up dish towel instead. She wiped her hands carefully on the towel before she turned to face him again.

Henrik uncrossed his arms and straightened, filling even more of the room. A strange smile—one that Anna couldn't read—pulled at his mouth. A rakish grin. "So what do you pine for, Anna?"

"Just what you would expect," she said.

"What would I expect?"

Again that strange smile.

A few seconds of silence ticked by before she answered. "A family of my own, to love and be loved." She looked around the cabin and gave him a wry smile. "Though I suppose this church could be considered plenty of family."

"How have you managed, on your own all this time?"

"I had little choice."

He shook his head. "They take you for granted."

He was referring, she knew, to the rude way Maria had spoken to Anna earlier today. It was her turn to rise early to start the fire, but she had overslept. By the time she woke, the few remaining embers had gone cold and the black ash had turned to white. Maria was furious, banging pots and pans, telling everyone that breakfast would be much delayed because of Anna's late sleeping.

"Please don't speak poorly of them. They are the only family I have." Especially with the Bauers gone.

His eyes met hers. "Not anymore."

Her heart warmed by his kind intent, but she looked away from his earnest gaze.

Ephrata Community

Dorothea heard a knock at the door and opened it to find a man in a white robe. She immediately knew it was a man and not a woman because the top of the hood was pointed, not rounded. She was learning much about the community since she'd arrived. This man wore thick eyeglasses and had large, protruding teeth that pursed his lips in a perpetual look of disapproval.

"I was told your husband is ill."

"Yes. Are you a doctor?"

"No. I'm Brother Andrew." He said it as if nothing more needed to be said. He went to Jacob's bedside and examined him—checking his pulse, his fever, listening to his labored breathing.

"Back in Germany, there was a woman we called a Braucher." Anna's grandmother. "She can heal the sick with her touch alone. It's a wondrous gift of God and comes from a faith that runs deeper than the core of the earth." She looked hopefully at Brother Andrew. "Isn't there anyone in the community who has the healing touch?"

"If this Braucher was given a gift from God to heal, then perhaps you should pray to God for the gift of your husband's healing."

As if she hadn't been praying! "And when my husband recovers, then he'll be himself again, won't he?" Dorothea reached out to squeeze Jacob's hand, hoping for some response. "Surely, he'll be well again."

Brother Andrew did not answer her.

"Do you have any idea what causes his suffering?"

"I've seen this once before. It has a ravaging effect. It consumes an individual. Hence the name."

"What is it?"

"Consumption," he declared, and he left as quickly as he came.

❧

Jacob's Cabin
October 31, 1737

Day after day had passed with no sign of Jacob or Dorothea.

Josef Gerber wanted to go searching, but Isaac Mast wouldn't hear of it. Not until the meadow hay was cut, dried, and stacked in the cabin rafters. "If we cannot feed our livestock through the winter, we will have no way to sow crops in the spring, and no harvest next fall." His dark brown eyes gazed around the room. "We do not want to face a starving time," he added, striking fear into everyone.

The sailors on the *Charming Nancy* had told Felix gruesome stories of "starving times" that occurred in the Jamestown and Plymouth settlements, and he relayed the stories to everyone in the lower deck. There were starving times in the Old World that were not easily forgotten—famine, poor harvests, shortages. Mostly, Anna remembered, the starving times came from effects of war.

The newcomer stepped in to fend off Isaac's anxiety-provoking comments, which were becoming a common occurrence. Henrik had a way of evoking calm and hope for the future. "We have no reason to worry," he insisted. "We now live in a land of plentiful supply."

Yes and no, Anna thought, as she listened to Henrik. Their diet was a lopsided one, short on vegetables and heavy on meat. And always accompanied with brown bread made with molasses and baked over the open fire. It was still too warm to butcher the pig and salt it for the meat barrel, so they relied on hunting game as often as they could—venison, possums and raccoons, wild fowl. Josef Gerber was the best hunter in the group. They weren't always sure what they were eating, but so far no one had fallen ill with digestive troubles.

Anna and Catrina had made a daily adventure of foraging in the woods for herbs, tree bark, roots, and edible plants to gather and eat or, better still, to use for medicinal purposes. Some plants Anna recognized from her grandmother's tutelage: lady ferns, which could be mashed up and the juice would ease stinging nettles, burns, and cuts. Tansy to rub on the skin to repel insects. Mint to aid digestion, catnip to stop bleeding. Sage to relieve a woman's aches during her monthlies. Feverfew to cure a headache.

If Anna had doubts about something—and about most plants in these unfamiliar woods, she did have doubts—she fed them first to the pig. If it wouldn't eat it, she wouldn't trust it. The pig turned up its nose at many offerings, for which Anna was grateful.

Henrik volunteered again to go search for Jacob and Dorothea, an act that endeared him to Maria. She was afraid Christian would end up going by default and knew he had a poor sense of direction. On top of that, Catrina had woken up in the morning with a sore throat. She lay quietly on a mat, bundled up, far from the cabin door that was constantly opening and closing and letting cold air swoop in. Even Anna felt concerned about Catrina's health—she was a child who was never quiet, yet today she had said barely two words.

Christian, Isaac, Josef, and Simon huddled together for a conversation, as they often did for matters of grave concern.

Josef held one opinion, Isaac the opposite, Simon saw both sides, and they all looked to Christian to make the decision. Unfortunately, Christian was paralyzed by decision making. He liked to gather all the possible facts before he came to a decision, sift through every detail, then hold off to gather more facts.

"How in the world did Christian ever decide to come to the New World?" Henrik whispered to Anna. "He can barely decide what to wear each day. And he only *has* one change of clothing."

"He didn't decide," Anna whispered back. "Jacob Bauer decided for everyone."

"Most likely," Christian said, "something arose that would make them take shelter for the time being."

"Like what?" Maria, ever forthright, asked him. "What could have possibly stopped Jacob Bauer from forging ahead? You know how that man thinks. Nothing gets in his way."

"Perhaps the baby might have gotten sick. Or Dorothea."

"Where would they have found shelter? We saw nothing along the way. Not a single light or sign of any other farm."

Christian sighed. "Maria, I don't know where they are, but I do know that Jacob has lived here for over a year now. He would know where to take shelter. A cave, an abandoned shack. He would know where to go."

Such reassuring words from Christian, who was prone to fretting, satisfied everyone. The men and women were able to return to their tasks.

The mild autumn days allowed time to cut and dry the hay, then cart it into Jacob Bauer's cabin and hoist it to the rafters. Maria was constantly sweeping the scattered hay. "I can't wait until I have a proper house," she said, frowning as she looked around the cabin. "I feel as if I'm still on the lower decks of that awful ship."

It did seem as if they were still on the *Charming Nancy*, sharing small living quarters with people and animals. Anna looked up to the cabin rafters. "But it is much taller, Maria." Most of the men in the church had had to duck their heads as they walked around the lower deck. "Here, everyone can stand up straight."

Maria swept the last of the stray hay over to the side. "You sound like the newcomer. The cup is always half full." She set the broom against the wall.

Anna almost laughed at that. Maria was right, for once. The newcomer was a cockeyed optimist. He had a way of looking at all of life as if filled with wonder. The time on the ship, he declared more than once, was God's way to prepare the church to endure life together in a small cabin.

And when it came to nature, the newcomer was in complete awe of it. Yesterday, he stopped sickling hay to observe a herd of deer that watched them curiously through a stand of trees at the edge of the meadow. Isaac jabbed Henrik about that all evening, insinuating he would do anything to avoid hard work. But Anna knew his wonder was sincere; it wasn't just deer that captivated him—raccoons, eagles, beavers, even a skunk. If Anna didn't know better, she would have thought he'd never seen wildlife before coming to the New World.

The newcomer's positive outlook was quite refreshing, because oh! how the others grumbled! All of them. Each new experience was approached with complaints or fearfulness. The men complained about the meadow grass they were gathering—too thin, too many weeds among it. And yet had they sown it? Barbara spoke incessantly about Indians.

And yet had she seen any? Not one. Maria made twice daily references to returning to Ixheim; in her recollections, everything was better in Germany and they never should have left.

As Henrik picked up the sickle to head down to the meadow, he stopped and whispered to Anna that he wondered if this was like listening to the Israelites after the miraculous crossing of the Red Sea. The first moment life became difficult and uncertain, they pined for Egypt. "So when you're foraging in the woods this afternoon, please be sure to bring back strawberries and leeks for tonight's supper."

When he saw she didn't realize he was teasing, he grinned and said, "Lach!" *A jest.*

Well, it was true. The little church had already forgotten the cruel landowners of Ixheim and mewled for safety and security. Just last night, she overheard Maria try to convince Christian to move to Germantown.

Anna watched the newcomer follow the other men down the path. The sky had a different look to it and the wind was picking up. She turned and went back into the cabin to check on Catrina. She added another blanket on top of her because she was shivering. Anna felt a blast of cold air and turned to see who had come in from the meadow. Then she stopped abruptly.

On the threshold of the open door stood an Indian. An old Indian, a broad-faced man with snow-white hair that reached to his waist, his leathered face carved with deep wrinkles, his eyes as clotted as milk. And he was wearing Jacob Bauer's red Mutza.

15

Jacob's Cabin
October 31, 1737

The old Indian spoke not a word. He walked into the cabin, looking curiously at everything the immigrants had brought with them, opening up the large wooden trunks, pulling out clothing, blankets, books, examining them, then dropping them back in the trunk. He was drawn to the pots and pans that were grouped on top of a trunk for easy access for cooking, most of which took place outdoors over an open fire. Maria ran toward where Catrina lay, protecting her with her body. Barbara gathered her toddler boys and huddled them against her. Anna remained where she was, watching the old Indian as he lifted up a metal spoon and held it in the air.

"Anna, run and get Christian from the meadow!" Maria hissed.

Anna felt as wary as a deer, but she didn't sense the Indian posed a threat. The last thing she wanted to do was to make an enemy out of this old man. Besides, he must have some answer for them about Jacob and Dorothea. Something. She picked up a loaf of brown bread, recently baked over the fire in a crocked pot, and slowly walked over to the Indian. She held it out to him with both hands, hoping he wouldn't notice that they were trembling. The Indian looked her up and down, staring at the cap that covered her hair. Other than mild curiosity, she couldn't read anything in those eyes.

The Indian took the bread from her, sniffed it. She realized he didn't know what it was, so she pulled off a corner of it and ate a bite. He did the same, chewing it slowly and thoroughly, as if bread was an entirely new thing to him. And perhaps it was.

As he chewed, Anna relaxed a little. Clearly, the old Indian wasn't dangerous. He had no weapons on him, none that she could observe. He was alone. He was hungry—that was obvious by his interest in the bread. She could see that he was missing most of his teeth; no wonder it took him so long to chew. She wondered how old he was—possibly in his seventies or eighties? He wore leather skins for pants and shoes. He had a strong, unwashed scent, but it was combined with another scent—something like animal grease. His chest was bare under the red Mutza.

The red Mutza was big on him, but then Jacob was a big man. The edges of the coat sleeves were dirty, but the coat didn't look worse for wear. She doubted he'd been wearing it for long.

"Do you speak English?"

He ignored her.

"The coat. It belongs to Jacob." She reached out to touch the sleeve of the red coat, but the Indian misunderstood and thought she wanted it. He jerked away from her, backing up until he was out the cabin door. "Wait!" She ran to the door, but he had already disappeared.

Maria had come up behind her and held her arm in a vise-like grip, gasping for breath. "He's killed Jacob and Dorothea. He's killed them all." She lifted her skirt and ran to the meadow where Christian and Isaac and the others were stacking dry hay into the cart.

Anna called out to stop her, to make her wait, but she ran wild down the long path toward the meadow. She could only imagine how Maria would describe the event. Telling the others about him would be like releasing a beehive in a cluster of horses; they'd all be skittish with anxiety. She went back inside to stay with Catrina, and to be a visible contrast to Maria's panic. Everyone would be crowding into the cabin for a full report within a minute or two.

And she was right.

As soon as the men heard the old Indian was wearing Jacob's red Mutza, they organized a search party to find the Indian, or to find Jacob and Dorothea's bodies. The baby too. With Maria's heightened exaggerations of the Indian, they expected a gruesome discovery.

The newcomer was the sole voice of reason. "Anna, what condition was the red Mutza in? Was it bloody? Or ragged?"

"No. Not at all. It looked like it did when Bairn handed it to his father on the docks, just a few weeks ago. It's old, threadbare in spots, but it didn't look like it had been through anything disastrous." She looked to Christian. "I don't think the Indian could have done anything to hurt Jacob and Dorothea."

Relief swept through Christian's eyes. "Why? What makes you think so?"

"He's old, and feeble. And he was hungry. Jacob would have towered over him. There's no way the Indian could have hurt them. And why? Why would he have hurt them?"

"Why wouldn't he?" Maria said. "He came in here, rifling through our things. He was looking for something."

"Or someone," Anna said.

All eyes turned to her.

"He had a curious look on his face as he walked around the cabin. He was alone, and I could see no weapons. I offered him bread and he seemed grateful. I don't think he'd eaten in a while. I just don't think he would have hurt anyone."

Maria saw it differently. "He didn't utter a word, Christian. He was like . . . a . . . an animal. A possessed animal."

"He didn't understand English. That doesn't mean he couldn't talk."

"But you tried to communicate with him!" Maria said. "You pointed to the coat and he ran off. Guilty! He killed them."

"Be logical, Maria. You're letting your imagination run away with you. All that we know for sure is that he came across the red Mutza, and not long ago, by the looks of the coat. It was in good condition. We don't even know if he encountered Jacob and Dorothea. It's possible they had to leave their belongings along the way."

"But why?" Barbara said. "If something happened along the way, someone would have seen a sign of them. I agree with Maria. The Indian must have taken the coat after he killed them."

Josef put a hand on his wife's shoulder. "Barbara, we trust in the sovereignty of God in all things. All things. Jacob and Dorothea and the little one are under God's protection."

Isaac Mast lifted his bearded chin. "Christian, I blame myself. I was the one who insisted that the meadow be mowed. I tried to think the way Jacob would think. I believe we did what he would've wanted us to do, to stay the course and trust that he could take care of himself. But I was wrong. We've waited too long. It's time to find out what has happened to them."

Standing by the door, Henrik chimed in. "Whatever you decide, you'd better hurry. The wind is picking up and the rain is starting." Indeed, rain was pecking at the roof.

"The hay!" Christian said. "We've got to get the last of it in!" He bolted out the door and the rest of them followed right behind.

❧

Anna had heard stories from her Swiss grandparents about flash floods, but she had never lived through one in Germany. The clouds rumbled as slashes of lightning stabbed the sky. Raindrops fell as the group scurried around the meadow to gather armfuls of cut hay and drop them in wagons, then suddenly, with little warning, the skies opened. Rain pelted down upon them in a great roaring current, a torrent so heavy Anna had to hold her head down in order to breathe. So heavy was the sound of rain that she couldn't see anyone, couldn't hear anyone call out to each other.

Struggling to walk, she moved toward the woods to take shelter under a canopy of trees, then felt a strong arm around her waist as Henrik appeared at her side. He supported her as they made their way back to the cabin with the others.

Soaked to the skin, the little group sat in silence, waiting for the storm to pass, listening to the water pound on the roof. Water even poured down the chimney flue, defeating Isaac's best efforts to get a fire going. Outside, lightning shimmered in the ethereal greenish light of the storm, sending weird flashes into the cabin through the two tiny windows.

A few hours later, they stepped out of the cabin into a world scrubbed clean, strangely beautiful. The sky was bright blue, red cardinals trilled in nearby trees. Christian, Isaac, and Josef stared dumbly at the meadow now flattened, soaked and soggy; the remaining cut grass was ruined.

"Nature can be cruel," Isaac said glumly.

"Come now, most of the hay is safely tucked in the cabin's loft," Henrik said. He lifted his hands. "Let us not forget to praise God. We are safe."

Barbara sidled up to Anna. She was a tiny woman whose head barely topped the elbow of her husband. Her high, squeaky voice suited her size. "The newcomer should be our leader," she said. "With Jacob Bauer gone for good, we are going to need someone like the newcomer to survive. He's the one."

Anna glanced over at Henrik. He was close enough to have heard Barbara, but he showed no sign of eavesdropping. His eyes were closed and his chin lifted up, as if praying.

"Jacob Bauer is not yet gone for good, Barbara," she said. Not yet.

Ephrata Community
November 1, 1737

Dorothea knew that the sisters expected Jacob to die; each time they knocked on the door, she opened it to see a cringing look on their faces, expecting her to give them the death message. But they did not know Jacob Bauer. While she couldn't deny that he wasn't improving, he did not yet die. She held on to a glimmer of hope that he would beat this illness, whatever it happened to be. And in the meantime, she was so grateful for this unusual place, for a roof over their head, for wood for the fireplace, for food to eat.

She took a green apple out of Sister Alice's basket and polished it with her apron. While the sisters and brothers ate sparingly, only one meal a day, and although they were not meat eaters, they were generous with their portions for Dorothea and even provided cooked chicken or beef broth for Jacob. And the sisters often reminded her that there was always a bowl in the kitchen full of something to eat, there for anyone to take.

No one expected or insisted that Dorothea abide by the ways of the community. Just the opposite; they were immeasurably kind to her. She had observed their kindness extended to others too. There had been vandalism against a newly constructed building—broken windows. The vandals, two boys, had been caught in the act, but rather than call for the sheriff, the community fed them and sent them on their way.

She found herself easing into the life of the Ephrata Community. There was a strictly adhered to pattern she had observed throughout the days and nights—a combination of work and worship. For the first time in her life, she did not fear the night. No, even better. She looked forward to it. At midnight, she listened for stirrings as the sisters woke and made their way to the chapel for worship. And the singing that wafted through the hallways, it was hauntingly beautiful. So different from the sad, somber music she knew from church.

Dorothea would open the window a crack, because it was hard to hear otherwise. Then she would lie on the small bed next to her ailing husband and let the glorious sounds fill the room. It was the only time she felt complete peace, when that music floated into the room and surrounded her. She felt the music swirl around her, lift her from sadness and anxiety and fearfulness . . . to peace and certainty. And hope.

Jacob's Cabin
November 2, 1737

The sun rose brightly, the sky extended in all directions, an unending canopy of blue. Henrik filled a tin cup with hot coffee and dunked a chunk of bread into the cup. "With your blessing, Christian, today I am going out to search for Jacob and Dorothea. Doing something is better than doing nothing, is it not?"

Christian gave Henrik a look of sheer astonishment. "Today? Any trails would be washed out after the rainstorm."

"I'll head south toward Philadelphia. Someone must have seen them, or some sign of them. You don't need me here, just to sit in a cabin."

Lines creased Christian's wide forehead, and Anna knew he was pondering the motivation behind this plan. Was the newcomer thinking of leaving them?

Henrik had been gracious to them, but on many occasions Anna had glimpsed a look of something in his eyes, or perhaps it was his seeking nature—looking for a better place to belong. He had lived among them for a week or two now, and it seemed he had yet to find his place among them, his role. They certainly weren't the tillers of the Garden of Eden that he seemed to be looking for—petty arguments sprang up, jealousies, irritations.

Henrik didn't wait for Christian to give him his blessing.

He started to pack a sack with provisions—brown bread, a goatskin for water, venison jerky—and rolled a blanket, then tied it with rope around his stomach. Watching him, Josef strode over to take a rifle off the wall. "Take this with you," he said.

Henrik looked at the rifle. "God is the only shield I will need." He patted his leg, where a knife lay in its sheath. "And a little help from this." He glanced around the barn and rested his eyes on Anna, smiling as his gaze caught hers. "I'll soon return—a few days. Perhaps a week. I will have an answer to the mystery of Jacob and Dorothea Bauer." His face was alight with determination. "By God's grace, I will bring them with me."

Ephrata Community

When Sister Marcella came to check on Dorothea in the morning, she asked her to stay. The sister stood awkwardly by the door. "Is there a problem?"

"No," Dorothea said. "I just . . . wondered why you had come to this place." And that was partially true. But mostly she wanted to talk to someone, about anything other than illness.

Sister Marcella's tightly cinched mouth relaxed, ever so slightly. She came away from the door and warmed her hands by the fireplace. "I came from Germany with my husband and son. My husband started a farm and then I heard Father Friedsam preach near the Cocalico Creek. He spoke like no one I've ever heard—about living like the disciples did."

Father Friedsam. Father of peace.

Yesterday, through her small window, Dorothea had figured out which robed figure was Father Friedsam. She heard someone call out his name loudly and saw him stop to wait for the brother to reach him.

"So Father Friedsam's preaching and teaching . . . that was what drew you here?"

"Yes. He taught us that the believer can communicate directly with God, that we can listen and be understood by Him, and achieve a peace and a comfort not available in any other way."

Maybe that was what had been missing in her life, Dorothea thought. She had never received peace and comfort from her faith, only duty. Only obligation. "I can't imagine what Jacob would say to that," she said, more to herself than to the sister.

But suddenly, Sister Marcella let out an unexpected snort. "I know what my husband had to say. He called it heresy. He became so hostile to the community, and especially to Father Friedsam, that I finally moved here."

Dorothea stared at her. "You left your husband and child?"

Sister Marcella stared back, unflinching, her gaze steady and unwavering. "I had to. It was the only way to live a truly righteous life."

Dorothea thought of the kind sisters who had come in to bring fresh goat's milk for the baby or change Jacob's soiled sheets. "And the other women, they left their husbands as well?"

"Some. Not all. Sister Alice, Sister Helga, yes. They were once married. Now we are married only to God. We were lost, but now we have been found." With that, she went on her way.

Dorothea had learned of other odd aspects of the community, but leaving one's husband? That might be the most unusual one of all.

Sister Alice, who was easier to detain with questions than Sister Marcella, had told her all kinds of details about the community: It had formed only a few years ago but was quickly growing. Saturday was its day of worship, not Sunday. A Pennsylvania law prohibited work on Sundays, and some men in the congregation were arrested for violating it. "The prisoners sang hymns and refused food for several days," Sister Alice explained. "It caused their jail keepers so much worry that the authorities decided to release them." The corners of her mouth had lifted in a smug smile. "We haven't been bothered about working on Sunday since then."

The baby stirred from his nap and Dorothea hurried to pick him up before he let out a cry. Jacob's eyes flickered open, then he drifted off again.

What would she do if Jacob didn't recover? Where would she go? She hadn't paid any attention to details he'd told her about the land he had warranted. She looked out the window, over the large green clearing and up at the small orchard. While she was here, she had started to sense an otherworldliness, as if all of material life was suddenly soft and ethereal. This place—it was safe from the dangers of the world, within her and around her. That's all she ever wanted—just to be safe.

But this peace and comfort that Sister Marcella spoke of . . . she wanted that too. Her church . . . Jacob and the others, they thought of themselves as better, smarter, wiser than the Mennonites, the Dunkers. Her church thought they were the ones who had found the true path.

What if they were the ones who were lost?

16

***Lady Luck*, Atlantic Ocean**
November 3, 1737

It was the middle of a windless night. Bairn had ordered the main sails to be furled and slowed the ship to a few knots. In the morning, he hoped, the wind would rise and they could set full sail, but tonight was a good opportunity for the crew to rest. Besides, it was the Sabbath. He would have thought Captain Berwick would observe a day of rest, but he did not seem to fear God the way his cousins, the Stedman captains, did.

Bairn saw something move in the crow's nest, though no sailor was posted. Then he saw the dog standing duty below the main mast. "Felix! Get down here!"

Felix peered over the crow's nest, groaned, then made his way down the ropes that led to the deck, before dropping the last few feet. "Bairn, there's something wrong with the crow's nest."

"Don't tell me about the crow's nest when I told y' to stay in my quarters. It's past midnight!" That laddie! He was wearing Bairn to a frazzle. "Go. Now. Go to bed. Stay there. You'd best pay heed to me."

"But I couldn't sleep."

Felix's lip trembled, and his troubled look scored Bairn's heart. At times he forgot how young his brother really was. "Why cannae y' sleep?"

"Too quiet tonight. Maybe I could sleep if you told me a story."

Bairn sighed. "One story. Then I must get back on watch."

He followed Felix down the deck to the first mate's quarters, dog trotting behind. Felix jumped up on the top bunk and Bairn sat on the floor, back against his own bunk. "What do you want t' hear?"

"Squivvers told me that there were giants in the bilge."

"He's tryin' to scare you. He wants you to stay out of it."

"I'm not scared."

Yes, he was.

"Do you know any story about giants?"

A memory flitted through Bairn's mind like a starling. His father, preaching to the small church in their home in Ixheim. Preaching about the twelve spies that went into the Promised Land to scope things out. A Bible story would be good. The laddie needed some Bible training.

So he strained his memory to pull forgotten details to the forefront.

". . . And when the twelve spies returned," Bairn said, "they reported to Moses all they'd seen—a land of milk and honey. They even brought grapes as proof of the land's abundance. But ten of the spies had more to tell. They spoke of giants in the land and caused great fear among the Israelites. Utter panic."

"Were the spies lying?"

"No. No, they weren't lying."

"So what happened next?"

"God forbade that generation from enterin' the Promised Land. They stayed in the desert for forty years because of their fearfulness."

"That seems a little harsh," Felix said, yawning. "Giants *are* giants."

"The problem, you see, wasn't that the giants weren't real, but those fears became bigger than the other good things they'd seen." Bairn let that settle for a moment. "Fear can be like that, can take hold of a person."

Fear. Bairn ran a hand over his face. The truth was, he had left Port Philadelphia because he'd been afraid. Afraid as he had been only once before in his life. Afraid he was losing control over his life.

He had run away because he did not have the courage to stay. He had run to the sea, to a life that welcomed him. Welcomed him, perhaps, but not saved him. It was a sobering realization.

Abruptly, he rose to his feet and tiptoed to the door, pleased that the laddie had fallen asleep at last.

"Bairn, have you ever seen a giant?"

Bairn stilled, his hand on the door handle. *Just one giant*, he thought. *My father*.

Ephrata Community
November 5, 1737

Dorothea answered the knock at the door and found Brother Andrew standing there, a solemn look on his somber face. "I've come to purge your husband of the sickness."

She looked at the instruments in his hands—a large bowl and a sharp kitchen knife. Oh dear. "Bloodletting?"

Brother Andrew nodded. Dorothea let him pass by her to pull the chair next to Jacob's bedside.

She felt her knees start to sway. "But why is that necessary for this kind of illness?"

"To restore his four humors."

In her nervous discomfort, she tried a poor pun, and instantly she regretted it. "Jacob has always been missing some humors."

Brother Andrew furrowed his large brow and stared at her, unblinking.

This brother might also be missing some humors. "Would you mind if I got some fresh air while you're doing the procedure?"

Brother Andrew lifted a hand in a dismissive wave. She picked up the baby, grabbed her shawl, and went outside. The autumn sun felt wonderful on her face. She felt almost guilty as she wandered around the gardens, enjoying the peace and quiet of the community, while Jacob was inside getting purged.

Dorothea walked around the paths in the center of the community, amazed to see how far it extended in each direction. Nearly two hundred acres, Sister Alice told her. Being here was a haven to her, as close to Germany as she would ever get. The milled lumber buildings spoke to her heart—so similar to the architecture of Ixheim, in the Palatinate near the Rhine Valley. Steep roofs, multiple small dormer windows, central chimneys in each building.

She should never have left Germany. This New World had brought nothing but disasters.

She sat on a bench in the sun and noticed Father Friedsam walk down the path with a young man, a stranger to the community. They walked slowly, not noticing Dorothea, and stopped close enough that she could hear them. The man was no youth, but a certain boyish enthusiasm snapped in his eyes.

"Why are you here, in the New World?" Father Friedsam asked.

"God gave me a vivid dream. He called me out of my old life. Everything had to be left behind in this venture into a life of faith. Complete obedience."

"Yes! Yes, that's exactly the right response to a call from the Almighty. Complete obedience." Father Friedsam gripped the man's shoulders. His long beard ended in a dagger's point, jabbing the air, punctuating his words. "Do not depart from us. Stay with us awhile. We are creating a society that lives a radical faith."

"Thank you." The young man's eyes glowed. "But this group I've joined up with, they are sheep without a shepherd." Silence swelled for a moment, then the young man spoke in a tone of infinite tolerance. "I have come to see—to know, actually—that these people need me. I think that God led me to them, to help them and guide them."

"The people you are caring for—they too would be welcome here. Consider bringing them to the community. There is a place for you here. For all of you."

"Perhaps I'll suggest it to them."

"If there are some married individuals, they are free to live as Householders. And those who are single join the celibate order."

"Celibate order? Did you say *celibate*?" The young man's voice rose an octave and Dorothea had to stifle a laugh.

As Father Friedsam explained the importance of celibacy to him—that it was the only way to free a believer from earthly concerns and enable him to focus all his attention on union with God—the young man's enthusiasm seemed to rapidly diminish.

"I'll have to give this matter some prayer."

Chimes rang, and Father Friedsam lifted his hooded head. "I must go. Godspeed to you."

The young man watched him go, then suddenly noticed Dorothea on the garden bench.

She shifted the baby on her hip and gave him a slight smile. "You are a seeker?"

"I suppose you could say that." He approached her. "I find the Ephrata Community to be an eccentric place."

"Eccentric, strange, odd, yes, all that. But wonderful too." She tucked a blanket under the baby's chin. "It is only strange at first. In time, you begin to see why they do what they do. They long to know God in a deep way, so every part of their life holds meaning to bring them closer to God." She pointed up the hill and explained to the young man that the buildings were set in a triangle because Father Friedsam believed it best represented the Holy Trinity.

"I'm sorry to say I must make haste and leave. I am on an errand." He took off his hat to scratch his head and she noticed an unusual white patch in his hair. "Are you one of the Householders?"

"No," she said. "I am here as a guest. My husband is ill. They've been kind enough to take us in."

The young man stared at her, then the baby, then back at her, and she colored a little at the intensity of his staring. An expression of confusion crossed his face; then a light went on and he grinned. "Are you, by chance, Dorothea Bauer?"

She stilled. "How would you know my name?"

He sat down beside her. "Your people have been worried about you."

Her heart started to pound. "My church? The people from my church? You know of it?"

"Yes." He smiled. "Anna König, Christian and Maria Müller. Their little girl with—" He pointed to the corner of his eye.

"Catrina." She covered her mouth with her free hand. "*Lieber Gott*. You know them? You know where they are?"

"I do. I'm returning there this very day."

"Oh, you must tell them Jacob is ill. He's very, very sick."

"The bishop? He's sick?"

"Yes. Near death. But I am praying for a miracle. Tell Anna and the others to pray too. And my sons—please tell them where we are! Ask them to come for us as soon as they can."

His smile faded. "I'm sorry to be the one to tell you this, Dorothea. Your sons, the tall one and the young one—they left Port Philadelphia on a ship to sail across the ocean."

"What?" The word came out as a tiny squeak. She turned sharply to look at him.

"They're gone."

She lurched to her feet, almost falling, so that the young man reached out to steady her. He said it so easily. *They're gone*. A moan slipped out of her. "Why? Why did they leave?"

"The tall one, he was offered a first mate position on a ship. From what I understand, he couldn't refuse. And then the young one, Felix, he followed him and stowed away on the ship."

Dorothea's eyelids squeezed shut, and her face tightened in pain. The news made her heart ache.

The young man asked if he could get her something. "Water, perhaps?"

She shook her head. "I just need to let it sink in." She was shocked by this news, and yet, in a way she couldn't explain, not shocked at all. She felt the young man watch her, and turned her head to meet his gaze. "He's not coming back, is he?" she said, her voice shaking.

"I don't know."

Dorothea could feel herself hunkering down inside, trying to protect herself from the hurt she felt.

Jacob did this. This wouldn't have happened had he just stayed in Philadelphia with the church, waited until they could all go together. He expected too much of their son, too soon. And Felix—he'd already lost one brother to an early death. She couldn't blame him for not wanting to lose his other brother.

The baby started to whimper, then cry. He was hungry. And then the door opened to the building where she and Jacob were staying, the Bethaus, and she saw Brother Andrew leave with a bowl full of dark liquid. "My husband. He needs me. I must go and return to his side." She grabbed the young man's arm. "Please. Tell Anna we are here."

"Dorothea, would you like to return with me?"

She lifted the infant against her shoulder. The baby only wailed louder.

She shook her head and reached out to firmly grasp the young man's hand. "Jacob is not able to travel. Please—just let Anna know. She'll know what to do."

"Of course. Of course I will. Don't worry about a thing." He whispered the words like a prayer.

Dorothea watched him go, feeling greatly relieved. Soon,

soon! someone would come to get them, to help them get home. *Home*. Wherever home was, whatever it looked like.

It was only after the young man rode off down the bridle path that she realized she had never found out his name.

When she returned to Jacob, she went to his bedside and studied him. A strange hue had overspread his face. She sank into the chair beside the bed and sat for a while, feeding the babe in her arms with sips of goat's milk, thinking.

Weary thoughts. *Jacob did this. He did this to me*. After the baby had its fill and drifted off to sleep, she laid him in the cradle. Though the room was not cold, she was shivering. She added a log to the fire and sat, cross-legged, on the wood planked floor near the hearth.

She lowered her head into her hands and surrendered to the tears that had been stinging her eyes. She could only weep.

She wept for her stubborn, sick husband and the children he had lost. She knew that if she lost Jacob, if she lost any more, she would never be able to bear it. Knowing that she had lost her sons to the sea, she simply could not bear it.

Lady Luck, Atlantic Ocean
November 6, 1737

Felix's feet twitched, wanting to take off running, but he knew he would be found out. It was a gloomy day and dark in the lower deck, with the barest of light coming in through the cracks of the upper deck and the cannon portals. He would have to remind his brother of the need to add oakum to those gaps in the planks. He heard a rustling sound and looked up through the wooden grate above his head, and nearly jumped out of his skin as he caught sight of a long thin tail out of the corner of his eye.

It was a rat.

His blood pounded in his ears and a scream clawed at his throat, but he wouldn't let it out. He hated rats, really hated them, but at the moment their company was preferable to another tongue-lashing by Captain Berwick. He wasn't scared of the captain, exactly, but he'd taken a dislike to Felix for some reason.

Just moments ago, he'd been poking around the Great Cabin and found a detailed map of the western coast of Africa in the captain's bunk, under his bed pillow. He leaned against the wooden frame to examine it. He was proud of himself for identifying the African continent—Bairn had made him memorize each continent by recognizing their shape. He'd like to tell his brother what a good teacher he was, but he didn't want to tip him off to snooping through the Great Cabin.

"Are all little lads as nosy as y', Felix?"

Flinching, he looked up and saw Captain Berwick, standing at the coaming of the Great Cabin. He had been so sure the captain and Bairn had been occupied on the fo'c'sle deck. *So* sure. But then he'd become absorbed with the map and lost track of time. It was always the little things that got him in trouble.

His gaze took in the map in Felix's hands and his horrified expression.

"I'm—I'm sorry." Heat suffused Felix's neck and cheeks as he stuffed the map back under the bed pillow. He was frantic. But sometimes he got his best ideas while in that condition. "I was looking for the cat. To eat the rats."

The captain's sour countenance revealed he did not believe Felix's excuse, and he proceeded to give him a lengthy homily on what happened to boys who made a habit of lying. Felix considered the sermon to be punishment enough, but then the captain told him to go find Squivvers and order him to tie Felix to the rudder as shark bait. Felix backed up to the door and sprinted away as fast as his feet would carry him, down to the lower deck.

And now he sat unmoving on the companionway for the longest while, hardly daring to breathe as his eyes got used to the darkness. Slowly, he craned his head back and peered up through the hatch on top of the companionway again. He saw Squivvers climb up the tall mast to the crow's nest to take a turn on watch. Felix was safe, for now.

And the rat, thank goodness, was gone.

Jacob's Cabin
November 7, 1737

Anna gazed down the path, silvered in the gathering dusk. She had heard something, and then she saw a horse and rider emerge out of the woods. "Christian!" she called. "The newcomer has returned."

Christian and Maria had been standing by the fire pit, warming their hands, and he hurried over to where she stood watching Henrik's horse come up the long path. "Is he alone?" His question put the instant worried look on Maria's face.

"No. No! Someone is with him!"

Christian and the others gathered down the path to greet the newcomer.

And Peter! Peter Mast had come home.

"Look who I found stumbling through the woods!" Henrik said. "Our Peter has had a change of heart."

The teenager looked hungry, filthy, and so grateful to be back among them. He hopped off the back of Henrik's horse and was swallowed up in hugs by Maria and Anna, by Christian patting his back. When Peter saw his father standing by the cabin door, he broke loose of their hold. He took a tentative step forward, then another, until he was walking slowly toward his father. Isaac watched him, first with a stern, fierce look on his face. Then his heart won out, and his face crumbled into a grin and he opened wide his arms for his boy to run into them.

Pleased, so pleased, Anna turned her attention back to the newcomer. "And Jacob and Dorothea? Did you find them as well?"

Henrik slid off the horse in one graceful movement, one breath to the next. With reins in hand, he shook his head. "No sign of them at all. Nothing. It's like they vanished from the earth. Like Enoch. Like Elijah. Gone, without a trace." He took a step closer to Anna and whispered, "I fear they are no longer."

17

Ephrata Community
November 10, 1737

They hadn't come for her yet. Dorothea had thought by now, surely by now, the young man would have returned with Christian, Isaac, or Josef. Even lazy Simon. She wasn't sure how far away they were from the Ephrata Community, but the young man had been gone for five days. What could have happened? Where could they be?

Sister Marcella had spoken to Father Friedsam to ask if he had any information about the young man with the patch of white hair, but he remembered nothing other than his name was Henrik. Perhaps something had happened to him along the way.

She had a terrible dread that they weren't coming for them. For her. Jacob drifted in and out of consciousness. Dorothea lifted a dipper of water to his lips, trying to help him sip some water. Most of the water leaked out the corners of his mouth and dribbled down his bearded chin.

"Keep trying," Sister Marcella said. "It's important that he has water." One sister or another checked on them frequently throughout the day, bringing food for her, goat's milk for the baby, wood for the fire, all for which Dorothea was thankful.

As Sister Marcella straightened the covers over Jacob, she said, "Dorothea, most immigrants come for one or two reasons—to own land or to escape religious persecution. What brought you here? Did you come to escape hardship?"

Not so long ago, Jacob would have answered for her, he would have given Sister Marcella a resounding yes—confident that hardship and suffering was behind them. They had come to a New World, where land was plentiful and they could worship as they pleased. Their son had been resurrected from the dead, like Lazarus from the tomb! Their family was reunited.

But today, Dorothea's life felt as perilous as crossing the ocean waters.

She knew more than Jacob about this topic. She knew you couldn't escape hardship and suffering. Even here there were hardships to suffer, even here in this land of freedom and plenty there was pain, there was loss.

She pushed the thought away and came back to the world. Her gaze returned to Sister Marcella. Her face revealed nothing other than kindness.

"Both reasons, I would say. My husband came a year ago to obtain land warrants for our church. Our church wants to own land and wants to worship God freely, in our own way."

"So when did you arrive?"

Dorothea had lost track of time. Her head felt fuzzy, stuffed with wool. It seemed like months, though it was only a few weeks ago. "The eighth of October. On a ship called the *Charming Nancy*. The ship docked in Philadelphia."

"And where are your church people now? What happened to them?"

"My husband insisted that we go ahead of them to the settlement." She squeezed her eyes shut. "They are probably there, wondering what happened to us."

"Do you know where the settlement is located?"

"Lancaster County. That's all I know." She looked at Jacob. All the knowledge of this New World was locked in his mind. That foolish, brilliant mind. But she couldn't think of her husband in terms of right and wrong anymore, of good and evil.

"Lancaster County is quite extensive. Can you remember any other specific details that your husband might have told you? Any landmarks? A river or creek, perhaps. They're called kills here."

"Why kill?" What a fitting word.

"It's an old Dutch word that means body of water. Schuylkill, Northkill, Catskill mountains."

"Oh! Schuylkill. I think I remember Jacob saying something about the Schuylkill River."

"The Schuylkill River empties into the Delaware River. In Philadelphia."

"Oh . . . maybe that's where I heard of it." Dorothea shook her head. "I don't remember. There's been so much to absorb these last few weeks. I can barely keep up." The baby stirred in his cradle and she reached down to pat his back.

"All right then. Let's try another way to remember. What kind of land would your husband obtain?"

"What do you mean?"

"There's a variety of land in Lancaster County. Would he have chosen flat land? Hills? Deep forests?"

"I don't know. We farmed land in Ixheim. And we had sheep. It was quite hilly."

"There are very few sheep in the New World, only those brought over by English settlers. Do you think he would have chosen land that reminded him of your home in Germany?"

"No," she said softly, thinking of the graves on the hillside that held both of their parents, and also their son Johann. "No, I think he would have wanted to forget."

***Lady Luck*, Atlantic Ocean**

Felix hadn't intended to create such a big problem. It's just that so much about this barque ship was different from the *Charming Nancy*, and he was curious to explore every inch of it. He didn't realize the anchor home was on the side of the bow. He was merely examining a chain, released it from its lock—only to discover he had undone the anchor cable. Down, down, down into the water sunk the anchor ball. The ship was at full sail, and the sailor at the helm shouted for help because the ship was suddenly not handling well. First came a slowing, then the ship leaned strangely larboard, and he saw his brother Bairn bolt down the deck to the helm. For a moment, Felix thought the ship might keel over.

There were other shouts between sailors posted at different positions, shouts to take down the sails immediately. Then came another hard jerking motion—so hard that Felix lost his balance. It was at that point that he thought it might be wise to make himself scarce.

Much later, Bairn found him in the cargo hold. There was a look on his face that Felix hadn't seen before—he looked troubled. Calmly, he informed Felix that the anchor ball had dragged from the ship, caught on a rock, and had to be abandoned. He also told him that a ship without an anchor was in a perilous condition. And then he told him that the captain had fired him as cabin boy and ordered him to remain in the first mate's quarters until they reached Boston Harbor. If, Bairn stressed, he could indeed bring the ship to a stop in the harbor.

Bairn was looking at him in a way his parents had often done, with a mixture of exasperation and confusion and surprise. "Are you very angry?"

"Nae. Not angry. Very disappointed. You've created a great problem for the ship. And y' don't seem to understand that yer actions have a ripplin' effect."

"I'll help. I'll help solve the problem. When do you need it fixed? Tomorrow?"

"We will not worry about that. Don't worry about tomorrow, laddie. This day has brought us more than enough grief. We don't need to borrow from the future."

But Felix had no doubt Bairn would know how to solve this problem. He could fix anything. He was a fine leader, his brother. Even Squivvers said so. The sailor told him that the best leaders were the ones who didn't even realize they were leaders. "Good leaders don't try to grasp it," Squivvers had said. "They live a life worthy of being followed."

That described his brother.

But Felix would have preferred Bairn to be angry with him. Once and for all, get it over with, the way his father would shout and rail, but then it would be over. To be quietly disappointed in him felt much, much worse. It reminded Felix of his mother.

For the first time since the ship left Port Philadelphia, Felix felt a touch of homesickness. He missed his mother.

Ephrata Community
November 11, 1737

Three nights in a row, Jacob had woken in the night, sweating, panting, sucking in great gasps of air like a drowning man and Dorothea thought surely the end of his earthly life was at hand. Her legs were shaking so hard she had difficulty standing upright. She knelt by his bedside and prayed for him, squeezing her eyes shut. She wouldn't look, she couldn't even bear to think of what was coming.

But each time, he didn't die. His breathing settled back to that raspy labored intake of air, and he slipped in and out of unconsciousness. He hadn't spoken a word since the bloodletting, though his eyes fluttered open now and then. He lay in bed with an impassive expression, his eyes like empty windows when they did open. He ate when she pressed mashed food to his lips, he drank when offered a cup. But he did not speak.

Out the window, she saw the tangerine tint of the sunrise. Another day had arrived and Jacob was still with her. Another day, hoping someone would come for her. Another day that she feared would end in disappointment.

She drew in a deep breath, her chest shuddering. What if they weren't coming? What if they couldn't, or didn't want to?

The baby stirred and she rose, unsteadily, to her feet. Dorothea bent over the small bundle in the cradle and rocked it slightly with her foot, watching this little babe drift back to sleep. How she loved him!

A thrill shivered through her senses when his chubby

fingertips touched hers. She drew him into her arms and tipped her face upward. This child had thoroughly captured her heart. "My little boy"—she breathed a kiss in the soft folds of his neck—"you have become my son." She loved this beautiful baby, foolishly and desperately.

This child had twice saved her—he gave her a reason to want to live on the *Charming Nancy*. And he gave her a reason to continue enduring through Jacob's mighty illness.

Lady Luck, Atlantic Ocean
November 12, 1737

The *Lady Luck* would soon reach around the long crooked arm of Cape Cod to head into Boston Harbor. The wooden ship hugged the coastline, and when the rain stopped, Bairn could even see lights at points along the coast. Those lights helped him navigate the *Lady Luck*'s path, though he was long accustomed to using the stars to navigate. In particular, the North Star. Fixed in the sky, a sailor's most valuable friend.

He heard a creaking sound coming from the mast above him—not an unusual sound on any ship, but this one made his spine shiver.

Another creak from above. Bairn froze.

It wasn't the normal creak of boards batted together, it was the sound of a crack starting.

He looked up and saw a small figure peering down at him. "I told you, Bairn. There's something wrong with the crow's nest."

"Felix! Get out of the nest!"

As Felix leaned over to climb out, it put added pressure onto the crack. The crow's nest startled to topple like a treetop. "Jump out, Felix! I'll get you!" Bairn's heart was pounding as he tried to put himself directly under Felix. "Jump! Now!"

Felix leaped out of the crow's nest just as it gave way and crashed to the deck. He landed on top of Bairn, pinning him to the deck. Bairn got the wind knocked out of him, and when he came to, he opened his eyes to find the captain peering down at him.

"What in the world happened?"

The captain faded in and out, then there were two of him—a horrifying thought. Bairn blinked until there was just one of him. "The crow's nest, sir. I think the base is rotted through."

Captain Berwick's face turned purple with rage. He pointed at Felix. "That—that gremlin! He's a curse on us!"

Bairn rose to his feet and helped Felix to his, looking him over to make sure nothing was broken. But from the way he cannonballed on top of Bairn, there was no chance he could've been hurt. "Captain, I dinnae mean to make excuses for the laddie, but he had warned me that there was something afoot with the crow's nest."

"Laddie? He's naught but a *devil* in disguise! He shouldn't have been up there in the first place. I'm wonderin' what me cousin was thinkin'—to recommend so highly a first mate with a mischievous imp for a brother."

Bairn thought that was a bit harsh on both the boy and him. But the captain wasn't finished.

The captain's glare shifted from one to the other. "This is why all ships should have brigs." His glare settled on Felix.

"Keep him locked in yer quarters." Then he stomped down the deck toward the Great Cabin.

"Well," Felix said. "He sure gets huffy." The watch bells rang and his face lit up. "I'm famished. I'm going to go see what Cook is up to."

Bairn was hungry too, but he had a duty to perform first. "I'm sorry, laddie, but you'll be stayin' put in my quarters for now."

❧

November 13, 1737

Felix paced the room. He wasn't good at having nothing to do, and having nothing to do for hours on end was losing its luster. Frankly, ship life as a whole was losing its thrill.

Ever since that unfortunate incident of dropping the anchor, the crew considered him to be a jinx. Bairn explained that they were prone to superstitions, these sailors, and it didn't take much for fear to replace what little logic they had.

If anyone caught sight of him on the decks, he was marched back to the cabin. Even Cook, who had been slightly more tolerant toward him than the crew, glared at him this afternoon, scornful, when Felix paid a call to him in the galley kitchen. "You'll get nothing from me," Cook said, wheeling back into the kitchen. The door swung behind him. And then Felix found himself face-to-face with the captain.

An encounter with Captain Berwick was right up there with having your face slapped until your teeth rattled loose. The captain was peculiar even for a captain. All that sneezing! Bairn said it was because he pinched snuff. He remembered that Maria said snuff was one of the devil's tools. That would explain a lot.

He did not like Captain Berwick. He hadn't liked Captain Stedman either, but at least he was a reasonable man. Captain Berwick had a mean streak. Felix had seen him hit Squivvers once, hard, just because his tea was delivered cold. Worse, he had it in for Felix from the first day. No question about it.

The captain ordered Felix to be confined in the first mate's cabin, after shouting an extremely unpleasant threat to his life if he dared to venture out again.

The thing was . . . if Felix could just find a way down to the cargo hold, he was sure he could figure out something to substitute for the anchor. Gathering rocks from the bilge was one brilliant idea he had, tied up in a spare sail. But Bairn told him that would require so many rocks to drop anchor that the ship would lose its ballast. A solution to one problem would only cause another problem, Bairn said.

And wasn't that the truth about life? That was another thing Bairn said.

Felix jumped on Bairn's bunk and let his feet dangle over the edge. A nudge against his leg startled him. He sat up, looked down, and discovered the awful dog staring up at him, brown eyes full of hope and expectation, the leather satchel in its mouth. "Drop it."

The awful dog blinked, but did not drop the satchel.

"You are the worst dog in the world."

The awful dog wagged its tail furiously, as if Felix had just given him a grand compliment.

"Here's what I don't understand about dogs. No matter what I do or say to you, you still adore me."

The dog blinked.

Bairn walked into the cabin and observed the two of them, staring at each other. "Are you trying to teach tricks to the dog?"

"No. He's too stupid. He doesn't listen to a thing I say. I keep telling him to drop the satchel and he just looks at me."

"Try fetch."

"Fetch."

"You have to think like a dog. Throw something, first, to distract him from that satchel you stole." Bairn threw a balled-up sock against the wall, and the dog dropped the satchel and bolted after the sock in full dog style, all joy and jubilation, overshooting the sock and charging headfirst into the wall, sending him into a sprawl. The awful dog shook his head in surprise and confusion.

Felix burst out laughing. "See? I told you he was stupid."

"He dropped the stolen satchel, though, did he not?"

Felix grabbed the leather satchel before the dog returned to his side. It *wasn't* stolen. It was just accidentally borrowed for a rather long duration, to be returned next spring when he and Bairn sailed back to Port Philadelphia. He hoped *Lieber Karl* wasn't missing it.

18

Jacob's Cabin
November 14, 1737

Peter Mast was the first to hear the sound of an approaching horse galloping up the path. They had just sat down for evening supper in the cabin—the men sat around the makeshift table in the center, made up of immigrant chests, and the women and children sat wherever they could find a space. Peter peered out the small window to see who was coming. "It's a stranger."

Christian sought out Anna across the room. "Come, Anna. To translate." He looked at Maria. "The rest of you stay here."

Of course, they all followed Christian and Anna outside.

The man stopped his horse in front of the fire pit. Christian walked up to greet him. "Friend, you are welcome here."

The man shielded his eyes and scanned the meadow. "You're on my land."

As Christian listened to Anna's translation, his eyes went round in alarm. "There must be a mistake."

"Well, I think you're wrong. I like this spot, near that crick running so clear and clean. This land is free for the taking, and I'm taking it."

"It's been claimed. Our leader has land warrants for this land."

The man looked down at them with a sneer. "You belong to those Mennonites?"

"We are Amish. Similar to the Mennonites." Christian pointed to a bucket of water brought up from the creek. "We have water for you. Your horse, as well. And food, if you have hunger."

The man kept his eyes on Christian. "Sheriff's been told not to let you people sit on a jury. You people acquit the defendant. No matter what the charge."

"Only God can judge a person's heart."

As Anna translated back and forth, it was clear that the man held a personal grudge against the Mennonites. All of them. And any who resembled them.

The man leaned slightly over. "I heard you people have a rule that if someone slaps you on one cheek, you must turn the other."

"Yes, that's true," Christian said.

The man stooped from his horse and slapped Christian sharply on one cheek. With the back of his hand, he struck his other cheek. Christian stepped back, holding his stinging face in his hands.

The newcomer walked up to the stranger on the horse, calm and confident. As the two men stared at one another, the air seemed to acquire a thickness, a heavy weight. "Yes, we do observe that. But we also have another rule. One will receive in like measure as he has been given."

Again, Anna translated, but this time her voice was quavering. You could see the stranger's wheels turning, but by the time she said the last word, the newcomer grabbed the man by his coat collar, jerked him off his horse, set him firmly on the ground, then in another move, swung him onto the saddle so that he faced backward. It happened in the blink of an eye, so quickly and so unexpectedly that the man had no time to react. The newcomer stepped back to give the beast a hard swat on the rump. The animal lurched forward, then stretched forward into a trot, following the path with the stranger hanging on awkwardly to the saddle's cantle to stay astride.

The newcomer watched the horse and man until they were out of sight, then spun slowly to face those who had watched the interaction. "'Behold, I send you forth as sheep in the midst of wolves: be ye therefore wise as serpents, and harmless as doves,'" he said. "That is the advice of our Lord in dealing with such men. Matthew 10:16." He started toward the cabin. "Let's return to our meal. The stranger won't be back."

In his wake remained a considerable silence.

Isaac and Josef slowly turned their gaze at each other. "Well," Josef said. "An unexpected solution."

"A brilliant solution!" Peter cried with a happy grin. His father turned and stared until Peter's eyes dropped. Isaac stomped on ahead, but Peter held back with Anna. "Did you see that?" he whispered. "How could they argue when Henrik jams Scripture in their face? He's a genius!"

Anna had to admit that the newcomer was full of surprises. Everything set Henrik Newman apart. His looks, those piercing blue eyes, the shock of white on his curly dark hair; his personality, curious and open and responsive. He could read moods as easily as dry soil absorbs rain. And then, just as smoothly, use that information to persuade others to his point of view.

Peter looked around him, at Maria comforting Christian, and leaned in closer to Anna. "Henrik Newman should be our leader."

"Jacob Bauer is our bishop."

Peter lifted his eyebrows. "Not if he's dead."

Anna resisted that thought, though as the days passed and not a word or sign emerged, she was starting to wonder if it could be true. Most in the group shared Peter's assessment, and grieved it. Jacob and Dorothea were much loved, and the little church felt their absence deeply. Jacob, especially. They were like a ship without a rudder.

Later that night, after supper and devotions, the men gathered to discuss what to do next.

"But it's such an obvious answer," Henrik said. "Let's do the most important things first. Winter's coming won't hold off for long."

This very morning, frost had covered the hay in the meadow like a layer of snow, melting quickly as the sun rose in the sky.

"There's the problem, right there," Josef said. "We can't agree on what are the most important things. I think we should plow the meadow to get ready for spring planting."

"And gardens," Barbara said, affirming her husband. "We must get a garden ready."

"Barbara is right," Maria said. "We have no neighbors to borrow from and getting provisions takes more than a few days' journey. If we don't get a garden ready for spring planting, we don't eat. If we don't eat, we'll starve."

Her husband frowned at her. "We won't starve, not as

long as we have livestock. That's why I think we should build fences to guard the livestock. Using a tree branch as a gate for the animal pen won't suffice for long."

Isaac shook his head. "Peter and I want to start felling trees to build cabins."

"Not me," Peter said, though no one asked for his opinion. "I want to build snares to trap marauding beasts."

"Marauding beasts?" Barbara said, alarmed, as her hands reached out for her toddler sons. "What marauding beasts?"

"The woods are full of panthers," Peter said. "Haven't you heard their screams in the night? They sound like a dying woman."

Barbara grasped her children against her as if a panther had just slunk into the cabin, but everyone else ignored Peter.

"If we plow the meadow first," Josef said, "then we get two benefits—a field ready for spring sowing, and gathered fieldstones that can be used for cabin fireplaces. Plowing is the most essential thing we should do, before the ground freezes."

People looked at Simon, a man not overly burdened by ambition. "I just want to stay warm this winter."

Maria's voice carried over the buzz of conversation. "Henrik, what would the followers of Jakob Ammann do in this situation?"

All eyes shifted back to the newcomer. "Ordain an additional minister," he said. "To support Christian and divide the heavy burden of leadership. 'Without counsel plans are disappointed.' Proverbs 15:22."

Isaac, Josef, and Simon looked at each other in alarm. They did not want to risk getting ordained and accepting a lifelong responsibility for the group. Maria, though, was delighted by the suggestion. Her husband was beat hollow, worn out. She beamed at Henrik. "He's right. He's absolutely right. Isn't that a fine plan, Christian?"

Christian nodded. He always bent to the will of a stronger influence. Most often, that of his wife's.

Peter left the table to go fill up a cup with hot water from the kettle on the hearth. Anna poured it for him. He lifted the cup with both hands and breathed over the surface of the water to cool it. "Whenever Henrik quotes Scripture," he said softly so that no one else but Anna could hear, "it has the effect of shutting everyone up. They all know he knows more Scripture than they do."

While it was true that the newcomer did quote many Scriptures, Anna noticed he often lopped off pieces of Bible verses, tailoring them to fit his views. That one about taking counsel, for example. Her grandfather often quoted that verse, but always included the next part: something about the wisdom of having a multitude of counselors.

Isaac rose from the table and stretched. "I don't think we should add another minister until we know what has happened to Jacob. We owe him that. And in the meantime, Peter and I are going to start work on our cabin. Tomorrow, first thing. The rest of you can do whatever you want to do."

Josef lifted his hands in exasperation. "But you can't get started. Not yet. We don't even know where the boundaries lie."

Arms crossed.

Eyes rolled.

Brows furrowed.

Lips tightened.

Fingers tapped.

And round and round they went.

***Lady Luck*, Boston Harbor**
November 15, 1737

The seamen were full of praise for Bairn's ability to bring the ship into harbor despite the lack of an anchor ball, but he was quick to point out that credit must be given to experienced seamen who carried out his orders.

It was a much trickier maneuver than Bairn let on. He did not want to remind anyone of his younger brother's mishap with the anchor ball. But his heart was pounding like a drum as he brought the ship into port, shouting at sailors to shift one sail, reduce another, open yet another, to slow the vessel and steer her around anchored ships, then to glide gently to a stop in Boston Harbor.

He had a bit of luck with the whole thing—and of course, decent weather must nonetheless be given its due. A light cross-course breeze blew in from the sea, gently helping the ship along with minimal sail. As soon as the ship came to a stop, the breeze dissipated. The day grew utterly windless, and the *Lady Luck* stayed in position while four seamen took the longboat and rowed to the wharf to seek out a ship chandler shop and return with a new anchor ball before the tide changed. It wasn't until the men returned and the anchor ball was securely fastened to the anchor home, then dropped, that Bairn took his first deep lungful of air since the ship entered the harbor.

There was no time to appreciate a moment of success. The captain had sent word to bring in the cargo, rowed in by stevedores on longboats. Bairn went straight to the capstan, a type of winch, to insert long bars in the fitted holes. By pushing on the bars, stevedores would haul the rope wound around the capstan and could move the load up or down. As soon as he was assured that the cargo could load efficiently, the captain arrived and told him that he would supervise the hold.

"Are you sure, sir?" It was unusual to have a captain spend his time supervising the unloading and loading of cargo.

The captain gave a nod. "I want ye t' turn yer attention toward tasks to complete while the ship's in port."

"Aye, sir. I'll get to them."

There was much to do to ensure the *Lady Luck* was prepared for the upcoming ocean voyage. She was an aged ship, worn and creaky, leaky as a sieve. He set sailors to work putting oakum into gaps between boards on the upper deck. By midnight, Bairn collapsed in his bunk, exhausted.

Felix's head appeared, upside down from the top bunk. "The land of Boston looks nothing like Philadelphia—there are fewer trees here."

Bairn yawned. "Aye. Now go to sleep."

"I can't sleep. There's something I'm puzzling over."

"What?"

"All the tobacco that came on the ship in Virginia was taken off today."

Bairn shifted on his bunk. "The captain sold it t' purchase new goods. 'Tis not uncommon to use one cargo to barter for another."

"I thought the cargo hold is where goods go that the captain wants to sell in England."

Bairn closed his eyes, drifting, drifting, drifting to sleep. "Aye."

"So then . . . ," Felix said in a loud voice and Bairn startled awake. "Why was he loading so much in the lower deck?"

There was just no quit in Felix when he had something on his mind. "No doot they're goods that'll bring in a higher value. He wants t' keep them protected."

"When I tapped on some of the barrels, I heard something slosh inside."

"Water. We watered the ship."

"I don't think so. Squivvers told me to stay away from those barrels because they cost the captain a heap of cash."

Bairn was wide awake now. *Rum*. Boston was one of the largest producers of rum in the world. But Bairn didn't want Felix to know about rum, not at the tender age of eight. He could imagine what his father would have to say on the subject.

"Bairn, what's a rum runner?"

Bairn groaned. "Where did you hear that term?"

"Squivvers said that the captain is a rum runner."

Rum was a highly profitable market, especially when sugar or molasses was brought in from the Caribbean. So profitable that it raised the attention of parliament. The British enacted the Molasses Act of 1733, slapping a tax of six pence per gallon on rum runners. The colonists did not appreciate such taxes; most ignored the tax to smuggle Caribbean molasses in and Boston rum out.

"Squivvers said that the captain isn't going to sell a lot of the things stored in the cargo hold."

Bairn rolled over, rising on an elbow, scowling at his younger brother with all the annoyance he could muster. "Felix, what are you talkin' aboot?"

"I heard the captain say you would be needing them."

"What?"

"He said you were going to re-outfit the whole lower deck."

Knowing full well that Felix had an answer to this question, Bairn asked anyway. "Did you happen t' see what was in *those* barrels in the cargo hold?"

"That's what I can't figure out. Link chains. Fetters and manacles, like the kind farmers use to hobble oxen."

He saw Felix open his mouth to ask another question and lifted a hand in the air to stop. "Sleep, laddie. Dinnae trouble yerself. I will see to it in the mornin' and sort it all out."

Felix let out a sigh and flopped back on his bunk.

As Bairn punched up his pillow, the awful dog trotted into the room, swaying and staggering. He went right over to Bairn and started hacking, coughing, then emptied the contents of his stomach.

Bairn jumped out of bed. "Felix, what have you done? Did you poison your own dog?"

"I didn't do anything. Honest, I didn't!"

"Now there speaks a guilty conscience if ever there was one." He touched the boy lightly on the shoulder. "Go get a bucket and mop and clean up your dog's mess."

Bairn laid his head back down but did not rest. Darkness filled the quarters and pressed against his open eyes. He was much troubled in mind by Felix's news.

19

Jacob's Cabin
November 16, 1737

On a windy afternoon, Anna was searching for edible plants in the woods. These were the times she especially longed for her grandmother, who could identify any plant by sight and know if it could sustain life . . . or take it away. Some beneficial plants, like wild carrot, looked nearly identical to deadly poisonous hemlock. More than once Anna had berated herself for not paying closer attention to her grandmother's lessons.

Catrina's shouts startled her. "Papa wants you to come," she said, when she reached Anna. "Two men have come on horseback. He needs you to translate."

Anna followed her out of the woods and up to the cabin. The two men looked quite different from Englishmen, and soon she realized why. They spoke only French, and were insistent that this land, *this* land, belonged to the French and that the church was trespassing. They finally left, promising to return with the law to evict them.

Henrik came into the cabin with an armload of firewood

and saw Christian and Isaac and the other men talking in hushed voices by the fireplace. "What's happened?"

"Two men were here today. Frenchmen. They said that we are on French land, not land owned by the London Company." Christian rubbed his forehead. "I don't know where we will go."

"We're not going anywhere." Henrik dropped the firewood in the box next to the hearth. "Did you show them the warrants?"

An uneasy silence followed, until Christian admitted he had not thought of it.

Fingers drumming on the table, Henrik fixed his eyes on him. "So where *are* the land warrants?"

Christian looked at Isaac, then at Josef, then Simon. Each man, in turn, shrugged his shoulders.

"Surely Jacob Bauer spoke of getting land warrants."

"He did, he did," Christian assured him. "We just don't know where he put them. Jacob had surveyed the land and set out boundary markers using either boulders or notched trees. But those boundary markers are hidden in a wilderness of ten thousand acres. And where the warrants happened to be, Jacob did not tell me."

"Christian, they must be found. Without those warrants, we have no legal right to be on this land. These strangers who ride in—there will be more and more like them." The newcomer slapped his hands on his knees and stood. "I think we should go through Jacob Bauer's belongings and look for them."

No one moved. For a while there was no sound in the room but the hiss and sizzle of wood in the fireplace.

The newcomer looked around the room. "From what I can

surmise about your bishop, if the situation was reversed, he would have torn apart your trunks to find those warrants."

Still, no one moved. Anna was the first to speak. "He's right. Jacob Bauer was a man of action. He would think us foolish to not move forward." She went to the far corner, where Jacob's trunk lay, and pulled things off that were resting on top of it. Henrik came to help her, and soon, a few others joined them.

With the trunk lid open, she turned to Henrik. "What do land warrants look like?"

"Papers." Henrik dropped to his knees to reach into the trunk. "If he is a well-organized type, they would be kept separate and protected from the elements. If not, it might be a collection of scraps of papers." He stopped riffling through the trunk to turn to Anna. "He could read, couldn't he?"

"Of course. He's our bishop."

"Was."

A prickle started at the nape of her neck. She couldn't believe that Jacob Bauer was dead. Not yet.

Henrik turned his attention back to the trunk. Nothing that pertained to land warrants could be found. Maria went through Dorothea's trunk as well. There was no indication that they had a claim to the land. Nothing at all.

Christian sat on the bench, hands clasped together in his lap. "Wouldn't the London Company take our word for it?"

"No, Christian." Henrik leaned his hands on the table. "Without them, there is no proof that Jacob Bauer actually claimed the land. Anyone could take it."

No one would dispute that. While waiting in the Court House back in Philadelphia, Isaac had heard a story of a German farmer who had built his log home and cleared acreage to farm on the wrong land—an easy mistake to make in the unsurveyed wilderness. When the legal owner arrived, he was pleased to see the improvements made on his land, then had British soldiers arrest the German farmer for squatting.

"Something will have to be done," Henrik said.

Christian tapped his fingertips together in a meditative rhythm. "It seems you've more experience in dealing with legal matters than the rest of us. If you are willing, we would like you to go."

Henrik dipped his head in a gesture of compliance. "Most likely, I will need to make some kind of payment on the warrants. For the patent deeds." He winced. "If I had any money to my name, I would offer it, of course. But alas . . ."

Christian went to his trunk and opened it, taking out a purse full of money. "This is all we have left." He handed the leather purse to Henrik, who took it reverently and put it in his coat pocket. "What if those Frenchmen return to claim the land before we can get this resolved?"

"We have God on our side," Anna said.

Christian dropped his hands to look straight at her. "Those men do not know our God."

Henrik had a three-word answer. "Then, they will."

Shawl in hand, Anna scurried out of the cabin toward the horse pen, where Henrik was brushing down the mare, brush in hand. "So, it's settled, then? You're leaving for Philadelphia in the morning?"

"Yes. I'll see if I can get copies of the land warrants. If not a copy, then some kind of confirmation."

She came around to the mare's right side and petted her

velvet nose. "Henrik," she said slowly, "you don't speak English. How will you—"

"Don't worry, Anna." His gaze met hers over the horse's head. "If there's any problem, I'll find someone who can translate for me. I've had some experience with legal matters. Don't you worry yourself over it. I'll be back with those land warrants. For *this* land." He gave her a broad wink.

She smiled, relieved. She looked up at the cabin, at the curl of smoke coming out of the chimney. "I've been meaning to thank you," she said. "I don't know how we would be managing without you."

She watched his hands move the brush over the glossy chestnut hide of the mare.

Their eyes met. "Anna, do you believe in dreams?"

"How so?"

"Do you think God speaks to us in our dreams?"

"I don't know that I do. But I don't know that I don't, either. I guess I just haven't had that kind of experience with God."

"I left the Old World because of a dream. God called me out."

"He called you?"

"Yes. He told me to leave my country, my people, my father's household."

"God told you all that."

"Yes. In a dream. It was very vivid. When I woke, I had this white patch." He pointed to his head.

She'd often wondered about that unusual shock of white hair. When she first met him, she'd thought it odd. Such a young man to have white hair. Yet the more she knew of Henrik, the more it seemed to suit him.

"God called me out of a corrupt land, filled with idolatry, and told me to separate from loved ones, to forgo my old habits of sin, of living in darkness."

"But I thought you said your grandfather was a disciple of Jacob Ammann."

Henrik looked blank, for just a split second, then he gave her a soft smile. "Even so, the tentacles of the world creep in. It was important to take stronger steps of separation."

So *that* was why he had come to the New World alone.

"When God gives a command, even in a dream, we must not refuse." He looked at her earnestly. "Don't you agree?"

"I think . . . that we will only be blessed if we are obedient to the Word of God."

"Yes, yes, of course. But doesn't God speak to us in many ways?" He looked out toward the setting sun. "Through nature's glory, for example. As for dreams, He spoke to many Old Testament prophets through dreams. Why should we limit God's ways?"

Anna stared at him in wonder. Imagine having such a clear word from God, like an Old Testament prophet. Her shoulders came up and she rocked forward on the balls of her feet. What a wondrous thing! She sucked in a deep breath, feeling almost dizzy.

"You believe me." He whispered it like a prayer.

"Shouldn't I?"

Those dazzling blue eyes sparkled as he leaned in toward Anna. "What if you were given a similar word from God? What if someone was given a command by God for you?"

Looking into those intense eyes of his reminded Anna of how she felt during summer thunderstorms while tending her grandfather's sheep in the steep hills of Ixheim. It was like that first instant after lightning strikes and the air is dancing, and you wait with prickles on your arms for the explosion of thunder that was soon to come, and then the pouring rain. They were mesmerizing, those blue eyes.

"Anna, I have no doubt," his voice was breathy, but insistent, "no doubt at all—that God has a special plan for you—"

Before he could finish, Peter Mast arrived with an armful of hay for the horses. "Maria is looking for you, Anna. She wants to know where you've hidden her skillet."

And the intimate moment between Henrik and Anna was broken.

As she walked up the path toward the cabin, Henrik's comment kept rolling around in her mind. What plan would God possibly have for *her*? It was an odd thought. Odd and pleasing, both.

Anna was halfway up the path when Peter caught up with her, brushing bits of hay off his shirt. "So what are your plans?"

"My plans?"

"After the newcomer returns and land gets parceled out, where will you go?"

She looked up the path toward Jacob's cabin. "I'll stay right there. I'll stay waiting for Dorothea and Jacob to return." And Felix. And Bairn.

He shook his head. "There's no chance that they're still alive."

She stopped, annoyed. "Peter, your babe is with them. Lizzie's son."

He looked away so that she couldn't see his eyes. "When

my Lizzie died on the ship, I stopped thinking of the child as mine. Dorothea saved the baby. He is her son now." He took a deep breath. "Was. He was her son. I can't imagine how any of them would still be alive. Haven't you heard the howl of those wolves in the night?"

She had heard. Just yesterday, in broad daylight, a fox slipped up close to the cabin and flushed out a laying hen pecking in the grass—not ten feet from Maria, standing at the fire pit.

He took his hat off and scratched his head. "Well, my offer is still good."

"Your offer?"

"On the ship, I told you I wouldn't object if we were to be married, you and I."

She had to bite her lip not to burst out with a laugh. "Thank you, Peter, for that heartfelt proposal, but I'm much older than you." Only three years separated them, but with Peter's acute immaturity, it felt like a dozen.

"Lizzie was a month older than me."

"Peter, you must know how I feel about Bairn. About all the Bauers."

He gave her a pitying look. "I can guarantee the ship's carpenter is never going to return."

Anna felt as if she'd been slapped. "What makes you say such a thing?"

"Every day in Philadelphia, Bairn walked the docks. I saw him with my own eyes. He isn't one of us. He belongs on a ship. He's not coming back." His gaze shifted to the newcomer, down by the horses. "Anna, the way I figure things, you've got three chances to marry before you're an old maid. Me, but you think I'm too young for you. My father, who's definitely too old for you. Or the newcomer. And personally, I think you'd be crazy to miss your chance with Henrik Newman. He's worth two of that ship's carpenter."

He waited for a moment to see how she would take it.

She straightened, looked directly at Peter, and declared with defiance, "I'll thank you to keep your opinions about my future to yourself."

He shrugged and started on the path.

But as she watched Peter lope up toward the cabin, her eyes grew teary.

❧

The firelight wavered over Henrik's features. "Are they asleep, Anna?"

"Shhh." She pointed to the small sleeping figures next to her. She had promised a bedtime story to the Gerber twins tonight, and they had fallen asleep in her arms before she finished.

"We didn't get to finish our conversation down by the horse pen this afternoon. I wanted to say that I believe God has a vision for the church of Ixheim."

"Our church?"

"Yes. God has called the church to a new, radical faith." He looked at her intently. "A holy experiment."

"Our church?" she repeated dumbly. She looked behind him to see Maria scolding Barbara for laying clothes too close to the fire. Christian was propped up against a wooden chest, nodding off. Catrina was teaching Peter Mast to play checkers and slapped his hands whenever he made a mistake. Isaac was arguing with Josef and Simon about which tree wood to use for his cabin. "You think God wants to make our church a holy experiment." A holy experiment of what?

"I do. But it's lacking leadership."

"Jacob Bauer provides strong—"

"He's gone, Anna," he said sharply, decisively.

He met her gaze, and in his eyes she saw something that looked like nervousness. Here and then gone.

"This church needs to face that fact. Jacob is gone. Someone needs to stand in the void."

Anna looked again at Christian, yawning and scratching his round belly that hung over the waistband of his black breeches.

"Anna, God has revealed what my purpose here is." The words came from his lips in a ragged whisper, and traces of wonder glimmered in his vibrant blue eyes. He was staring at her hard, his face fierce and intent. In a subdued voice brimming with wonder and awe, "He wants me to be a minister, to lead the church of Ixheim."

"But you would need to be marri—" Oh wait. She saw where this was going.

"Yes, yes, I would." A silence gathered between them; his breath was ragged.

She stared at him, momentarily tongue-tied. Light from the fire glimmered over his strong face and his eyes glittered with determination.

"God has given us work to do. Together." Reaching across the space between them, he put his hand over hers. "Did you hear me? God has given *us* work to do."

With an effort, and without waking the twins, she pulled her hand out of his grasp.

"I know you love another," he said, startling her with his

intuition, "but this ship's carpenter—he is never going to return. He's enraptured by the sea. That's where he belongs. His first love will always be the sea. Always." He crouched down beside her. "He had his chance, did he not? If he truly loved you, why would he have left you?"

Anna lowered her eyes. He spoke the words that were already on her heart.

"How could a man ever leave a woman as lovely as you?" He lifted his hand to her cheek. "Anna," he whispered. "I am here. He is not. Trust me. Have I ever given you reason not to believe me?"

Anna lifted her eyes, but before she could answer him, she realized Maria had been watching them, an appraising expression on her face.

20

***Lady Luck*, Boston Harbor**
November 17, 1737

First thing in the morning, as soon as he saw the cook return to the galley with the captain's breakfast tray, Bairn met the captain in the round house. Captain Berwick welcomed him in, delighted to see him. "Ah, Bairn. Yer early. Good. I want to discuss charting the ship's plot."

"Sir, 'tis already plotted. North, then east, following the stream of warm water."

"Not northeast. We've had a change of plans. I want t' head here." He pointed on the map to the western coast of Africa.

Bairn took a deep breath. This, he had been expecting. "Captain Berwick, sir, I signed up for this ship under the assumption that the *Lady Luck* was heading to England. To sell goods from the colonies and return with Germans. You said so."

"With all yer worryin' and frettin', ye've convinced me of the hazards of mid-winter sailing. I want you t' chart *Lady Luck* t' go south 30 N latitude."

Aye, to reach the trade winds. Bairn had to tread carefully. "Sir, as you ken, winds and currents have a powerful influence. 'Tis easiest to use the westerlies in a northeasterly direction, not to fight them."

The captain ignored him. "During the trip, I want you to re-outfit the lower deck."

"In what way?"

"Some hardware has to be added."

Bairn braced his forearms on the small table. "Captain Berwick, have ye gone into the man-stealing trade? Is that why you've purchased rum? To trade for slaves in Africa?" The Triangle Trade. Rum. Slaves. Molasses.

The captain blinked. "It's just business."

Bairn's tone was purposefully polite. "Not to this first mate." He said it mildly enough, he thought, though the whole notion made him livid. "I dinnae think Captain Stedman would have a cousin who was in the rum-and-slave trade. I have heard him say, on many occasions, that man-stealing was the work o' the devil."

The captain gave him a hard look. "My cousin dinnae have the financial pressures that I have. There are investors to please, debts to pay off. I'll thank you t' keep your moral high horse in check and follow me orders."

His moral high horse? Not so long ago, Bairn might have turned a blind eye to the rum-and-slave trade, thinking only of the riches that awaited him.

Not so long ago.

But Anna had changed his thinking about . . . everything.

"Not I," he could hear her say in her soft, gentle voice, as sweet as an evening bird. "It is not I who has changed you. It's the work of God, stirring your conscience."

That, too, troubled his mind. In fact, Bairn hadn't felt a

peaceful moment since he had left the docks at Port Philadelphia.

It was no wonder the lower deck was not filled. And now Bairn understood Captain Berwick's enthusiasm to promote a ship's carpenter to first mate. He would be employed to drill shackles and chains into the walls. He had walked right into this mess.

"And another thing. That brother of yours has to be put off ship in Boston."

"Put off? An eight-year-old laddie, alone in a city?"

"He's hardly an innocent laddie. He's a rascal, a gremlin, a scalawag. I dinnae care what ye do with him. Sell him as an indentured servant. Just get him off me ship."

"Then I'll go with him."

"Nonsense. Ye'll be a rich man by this journey's end." He gave him a lopsided grin. "And I'll be even richer."

"Sir, I'll find you another first mate."

The captain's grin faded. "May I remind ye, Bairn, that ye signed a legal contract. If ye jump ship now, I'll have you arrested and sell yer little scoundrel of a brother t' the first redemptioner who has the misfortune to bid on him. And dinnae think I won't."

They locked eyes. Then the captain flicked his wrist toward the door, dismissing Bairn without another word.

Jacob's Cabin
November 18, 1737

As the sun rose over the tops of the trees around them, Anna was already tending the hearth. She pulled a pat of resting dough from the bread crock, mixed together last night before she went to bed. She was kneading it when Maria's hand dropped onto her shoulder. "I think your grandparents would approve."

"Approve of what?"

"The newcomer, of course. He is the kind of man your grandfather wanted for you."

Anna punched the dough.

"You have a destiny, Anna. You are meant to serve God with your life."

Her hands clawed at the dough. "That destiny belongs to all of us. We are all meant to serve God."

"Exactly. And nothing is more pleasing to God than to marry and bear children who will grow up to serve and please Him."

Anna refused to look at her, refused to respond to her. The silence stretched between them. Maria always spoke with such certainty, even concerning things she knew nothing about. She'd hardly had time to form her own impressions of this newcomer, and here Maria was trying to persuade her to bind herself to him for life. So was Peter. So was the newcomer himself!

After mixing the dough with leavening and shaping it into fist-sized balls, Anna put them in clay vessels around the edges of the fire. They would be ready in time for breakfast. She noticed how much gray ash was piling up under the fire, so she scooped it into a bucket and started toward the door, but Maria grabbed her arm.

She looked down, watching her own fingers tighten around the bucket handle.

"Listen to me, Anna. He wants you, that newcomer. He

wants you, he does. There's no little fondness in his gaze as he looks at you. He's positively besotted. I know the look of passion in a man's eyes."

Anna's mouth sagged open. "*What?*" Maria's words shocked her. Women did not speak aloud of a man's desire. They never even acknowledged the existence of such a thing.

Christian came into the cabin. He sat slowly and heavily in his place at the table, moving as if he carried a log on his big shoulders to round them and weigh them down.

"You would do well for the church," Maria whispered. "Marrying you would keep Henrik with us. Keep him from leaving to find another church."

"What makes you think he wants to leave?"

"Before he left for Philadelphia, he asked Christian if there were other settlements nearby, any that he knew of. Why else would he ask? He must be thinking of leaving."

"What did Christian tell him?"

"That he would have to go to Germantown to find other like-minded people." She continued to clasp Anna's arm. "You must encourage him to stay with us."

"Maria, our church rests in God's hands, not in man's."

"He's not just any man. We have seen the hand of God working in his life. Think of the wolf that was coming after my Catrina. Think of the flash flood." Her grip on Anna loosened, but Maria's eyes were on her weary husband, who sat with his head in his hands. Christian looked utterly spent.

They needed a leader, that was clear.

Anna's mind spun. She wasn't sure what to think.

Ephrata Community

Of all the months of the year, Dorothea had always loved November best. Sunlight was soft and golden, slanting low as the days shortened. It could surprise you, November could. One day, there'd be cold snaps and frost, and you'd think here comes winter! But the next day would dawn mild and sweet.

Another surprise from the month of November: Sister Marcella, who had at first seemed a woman stingy with her words, started to linger in Dorothea's room after bringing the day's fresh supplies. She even had the longsuffering Brother Andrew haul in another wooden chair, so the two women could visit together by the fire in the late afternoon.

Today, the solemn sister had the baby on her lap, playing peekaboo with him, getting giggles out of him.

"Does he remind you of your son?" Dorothea asked.

Sister Marcella's smile faded and Dorothea regretted that she brought up the sister's child. It haunted her, though. To think of a mother who willingly left her child. Dorothea's sons might have left her, but she had never left them. Not willingly.

She wondered if she should apologize to the sister, but before she could, Jacob stirred and she hurried to his side to see if his eyes were open.

"You give your husband very tender care," Sister Marcella said, her gaze on Jacob as she came to the bedside.

"For all of Jacob's faults, I know he would do the same for me," Dorothea said. "A promise is a promise, after all. That's what marriage is meant to be. A promise to the end." In the silence that followed, she realized what she had just said, and to whom. "I'm sorry. It's not for me to pass judgment."

Sister Marcella seemed to come back from somewhere far away. "I must go." Her eyes grew glassy as she handed the baby to Dorothea.

"Please, don't be upset with me. I spoke without thinking." Had she gone and ruined it? Such a fragile thread of friendship—had she snipped it? Brother Andrew would come and haul away the extra chair. The days would grow so long again.

Sister Marcella gave her a mild smile, sad and sweet. "I'm not upset. Not with you, anyway. Not at all." But still she left the little room.

When Dorothea heard the latch click shut behind Sister Marcella, the room seemed especially empty.

***Lady Luck*, Boston Harbor**

Squivvers came looking for Bairn and found him in the carpenter's shop, fitting the crow's nest with a new base. "The captain sent word that you're to meet him in the ship agent's office right away. A longboat is waiting for you." He winked at Bairn. "The captain's got a lady with him. A mighty fancy lady."

"Let me go get my brother."

"The boy is to stay here, the captain said. Cook was put in charge of him."

Squivvers followed behind Bairn as he started down the rope ladder of the ship.

Bairn paused and looked up the ladder. "What are ye doin', Squivvers?"

"The captain gave me orders, sir. I'm to accompany you."

Aha. The captain was worried Bairn would jump ship. "Then would you at least wait until I reach the longboat so the rope ladder stops swaying? Yer apt to kill us both."

Squivvers froze. "Yes, sir. I'm sorry, sir. Just following orders, sir."

They rowed the longboat to the dock, tied it, and went to the agent's office. A fancy woman stood talking to the captain, just as Squivvers said, as well as an elderly man, leaning on a cane. Both were very well-dressed, with a polished air. The captain lifted his head as Bairn entered the office. "Bairn, these two are from Germany. They intended to arrive in Port Philadelphia, but the ship encountered some difficulties and took shelter in Boston Harbor."

Bairn nodded at them, unsure of why that would be of any concern to him.

"They have booked passage to Port Philadelphia on the ship *Friendship*. A Quaker ship." The captain smiled grandly. "And they have graciously agreed to allow your charming brother to accompany them."

Bairn took in a deep breath. "Then yer serious. You meant what you said."

"Serious as a snakebite." He leaned close to Bairn so the woman couldn't hear him. "He's bad luck. He's making the seamen as nervous as a scalded cat. And the repairs we've incurred because of his mischief have cost half your wages."

Bairn glanced at the woman. She held herself as if she had a rod down her back, reminding Bairn of the baron's wife in Ixheim. "Do you speak English?"

"Indeed," she said. "I am Magdalena von Hesse. My father is the Pfalzgraff of the Palatinate."

A Pfalzgräfin. *The daughter of a count*. That explained

her stiff back. Bairn's response was reflexive and courtly: straighten up, heels together, eyes downcast.

She was a striking woman. She had a creamy complexion and raven-black hair, and her eyes were perfectly matched by the violet silk she wore. Her English was cultivated, charmingly accented by her German heritage.

"And this is my manservant." She lifted her palm in the direction of the silent elderly gentleman who stood behind her.

"Yer emigratin' to the New World?"

"No. We are on a mission to find a man who we believe is in Philadelphia, or nearby."

"Yer lookin' for a needle in a haystack."

"Perhaps, but I think it won't be difficult to find this particular man. He is a distinguished man. He has a way of making a reputation for himself."

"An Englishman?"

"No. German."

"Why are you looking for him, if y' don't mind my asking?"

"He is my husband."

Bairn and the captain exchanged a look. These kinds of stories were not unusual. While the New World provided an opportunity for a new life, men often used it to desert their old life. And old wife.

"And you want him back?"

"It's a rather complicated story."

"I'd like to hear, if y' don't mind. I know yer doin' me a grand favor, by accompanying my wee brother, but I would like to have a peace of mind, knowing whose company I am puttin' him into."

"Have you heard of a morganatic marriage?"

"Aye." He had. It was a marriage of a noble to a commoner. Any children of the mixed marriage could not inherit any privileges of nobility. He also knew that the one of noble birth had the privilege to put away the partner of common birth and marry another, whenever he or she desired to.

"Our marriage was in the process of dissolution. But after Karl left, I had a change of heart. When I went to his village to tell him, I discovered he had left for the New World."

"So he does not know that you have come for him."

"No."

"And y' think he will be pleased to learn that you had a change of heart?"

She smiled. "Of course."

Bairn wondered. He did not envy this poor chap. But he did feel an approval to let Felix be with this woman and her manservant. She had a mission on her mind and much to contend with; Felix would be of little nuisance. So he hoped, anyway. "Have you a plan to track this man down?"

"No, we haven't gotten that far. Any suggestions would be most welcome."

"Start at the Court House. They will have a record of his name."

"His name is Karl Neumann." She gave him a confident smile. "I suspect he will be rather easy to track down."

"I don't mean to discourage you, but there are hundreds of German men, fresh off the ships, flooding into Philadelphia."

"My husband is a memorable man."

"How so?"

"Karl is never a stranger to anyone for long. He has the happy talent of being at ease in any company, from princes to paupers. I suppose his most notable trait is that he has the ability to attract people who want to help him." She glanced away. "He has a habit of exploiting that particular charm."

The manservant, who appeared rather hard of hearing, seemed to suddenly realize what the conversation was about. He pointed to his head and said in a raspy voice, "Weisskeppich."

"And then there is that," the countess added. "He has a patch of white on his dark hair."

Bairn stilled. A wispy nagging thought that had been floating in the back of his mind, for weeks now, suddenly came into focus as a full-blown image.

Neumann. Newman. New man.

21

Ephrata Community
November 19, 1737

Though her years with Jacob had resulted in several challenging encounters, the time at the Ephrata Community was the one God used to bring Dorothea to herself. And in the most unexpected way.

She had heard God speak.

Not in the way He spoke to Abraham or Moses. Not in a thundering way. No, God spoke to her in the way He spoke to Elijah—a small, still whisper. His voice came to her in the night, through the midnight music in this place, filling her soul with a peace she had never known. For the first time in her life, her entire life, she was not afraid of God.

"There is no fear in love; but perfect love casteth out fear: because fear hath torment. He that feareth is not made perfect in love." She had memorized that verse as a child, had heard it spoken in church. But now she understood it, now it became her way to view her circumstances. Perfect love casteth out fear. And God was the author of such love.

It was a metanoia for Dorothea, a sweeping change in how

she thought. She had always considered her relationship to God as one of duty, of burden, of fear and unworthiness. Thoughts were more important than feelings.

Here, at the Ephrata Community, she observed the longing these faithful ones had to know God, to experience Him. Not to fear Him, never that. Even in their austere lifestyle, they had a deep hunger to draw close to God. These robed men and women, so sincere, had been strongly influenced by the mystics and the Pietists of the Old World, people her own church disavowed. They emphasized emotional and spiritual experiences over liturgies and creeds. Feelings were more important than thoughts.

She knew what Jacob would say, if he could. He would warn her away from those radical zealots. He would insist that Father Friedsam had let his own thinking create his own theology. And imagine what he would have to say if he knew some of the more peculiar parts of his theology—the concept of God being both genders, male and female. That a believer's relationship to God would be a kind of marriage. Only through celibacy, Father Friedsam believed, would the believer be free to focus on the path of a "spiritual marriage" with God.

Her husband would be outraged. And yet here he was, and she was, benefiting from the kindness and generosity of these sincere believers. Day after day, they displayed practical care and support for the Bauer family, expecting nothing in return.

Was that not the way of Christ?

It felt strange to have opinions that were separate from her husband's. Strange, in a good way. Jacob was such a strong personality that his opinions invariably became her opinions. But in this time of solitude, she was forced to think for herself.

He awoke sometime later, the room still moonlit. He had slept just long enough to wake up disoriented. The awful dog stared at him, unblinking, tied to his bunk.

He glanced at the bunk above him. Felix was not there.

❧

Bairn knew he was stalling.

It was that strange and silent time just before dawn when the stars were most bright and the sky was most black.

Darkness. Utter darkness.

Bairn clenched his hands. He closed his eyes for a moment. How he missed Anna at moments like this. He must go search out Felix before the captain found him, and tell him he would not be sailing across the ocean on the *Lady Luck* as he had hoped. Instead, tomorrow the lad would be put on another ship that was sailing down the coastline, accompanied to Philadelphia by the countess and her manservant. What else could he do? He had no choice. He had to get the boy off this ship, far away from Captain Berwick. He would not let his brother face a dangerous and uncertain future.

To desert would be unthinkable. Captain Berwick reminded him once again of his legal obligation to complete the journey. The captain made plans to head out at full tide tonight, assuming the wind held up. *"I only took you on because of my cousin's strong recommendation, Bairn. I trusted your word to be good."*

He stared down at his fisted hands. What did Bairn have to offer besides his word? To himself, to Felix? To Anna?

Bairn lifted his head to see a sky thick with stars, swirling in silence. On the *Charming Nancy*, Anna once said that she always sensed a word from the Almighty when she was stargazing. He could chart a path across the mighty oceans using those stars, but they'd yet to tell him anything other than how to get where he was going. They could not tell him how to get back again.

How to get back. To his family. To Anna. This exile of his, it never seemed to end.

His eyes intuitively sought the polestar, the fixed point. That was the place to begin, to chart a navigational path. The fixed point.

Mayhap that was the problem. What *was* his fixed point?

Anna's, he knew, was a faithful love for God.

That was why she could be the same person in every setting—in Germany, on the *Charming Nancy*, in the New World. Her fixed point had never changed. Her belief that God was with her, that her life had purpose and meaning.

It dawned on him that his exile would never end, wherever he was, not until he found his own fixed point. His eyes lifted again to the stars, illuminating the dark sky. Mayhap they did talk, after all.

Felix held the lantern high as he went down the companionway that led to the lower deck. On the bottom step he stopped, letting his gaze roam over the barrels that the stevedores had brought to the ship today. No, wait. That was yesterday. It was already a new day. He had heard the captain give the crew the night off, with orders to return to the ship by high noon. The captain planned to lift anchor at high tide. So he waited in Bairn's quarters until he knew the ship was empty of crew. Nearly empty. The captain remained in his Great Cabin; Bairn was asleep in his bunk. The time was right. Felix slipped out to investigate, taking care to leave the awful dog behind.

There was an odd smell down below, different than the usual dank odor. He walked around the barrels, breathing deeply, trying to figure out what the smell reminded him of. Then he remembered a bottle Anna's grandfather used to keep hidden in the sheep shed, back in Ixheim. For medicine, he would tell Felix.

Rum! This must be the cargo Squivver told him about. For the captain's rum-running.

His foot splashed in a puddle, and he lifted the lantern to see that the floor around him was wet. Some of the barrels must be leaking.

And then Felix got an idea. A fine idea. A way to help his brother.

Bairn was in a strange mood of late, quiet and thoughtful and sad. Felix would report the leaky barrels to his brother, who had coopering skills to fix them. He was a fine carpenter. He could tighten the lashes on those leaky barrels so the captain wouldn't lose so much valuable rum. His brother would save the day. The captain would be greatly pleased. And maybe Felix could get a reprieve. He was tired of being locked in the first mate's quarters.

It seemed as if so many of Felix's good ideas went sideways. But this might offset the regrettable events that often trailed his life.

Felix set the lantern on the ground as he crouched to count the leaky barrels: one, two, three . . . and suddenly a rat scurried right in front of him. Right in front! He jumped up to get away from the rat and his foot knocked over the lantern. He hated rats.

Then the strangest thing happened. You would've thought the lantern would be snuffed out when it knocked over. Just the opposite happened. The puddle by the barrel was on fire.

Felix stood frozen, as if caught in a dream, watching the flames travel along the puddles' paths, licking the barrels. From somewhere, he heard a dog's relentless bark. His heart started beating at what felt like twice its normal rate.

And then there was his brother, peering down the companionway hatch. "Felix Bauer!" Bairn's words were jagged in his throat. "Felix," he said again, with that whipcrack emphasis he could sometimes produce that sounded so much like their father. "*What* have y' *done*?"

Felix's eyes widened and he backed up from the flaming puddles, swallowing hard. "I don't know!"

22

Jacob's Cabin
November 23, 1737

The slop bucket had sat by the hearth since breakfast, waiting for someone to take it outside. If Anna didn't take care of it, the cabin would stink only worse, and Maria would scold.

Clouds had moved in since supper, low and dark and heavy, and the temperature had dropped. Anna emptied the bucket in the pig's trough and was hurrying back to the cabin when she heard the sounds of horse hooves. She stopped and peered down the path to see a horse and rider galloping. Her heart lifted. Was it Bairn? Had he come?

The man took off his hat to wave and she saw the color of his hair. Black, with a shock of white.

The newcomer. He had returned from Philadelphia.

"Anna!" Henrik hurried his horse toward her and swung off it as he reached her, a bright smile on his face. "The land warrants," he said, slightly out of breath. "Everything got sorted out." He turned his head slightly. "And we have some company for supper."

Lagging far down the path came two British soldiers

on horseback. While Maria prepared a meal, Anna translated for the soldiers. They had accompanied Henrik on the return trip, he explained, for two reasons: to assure the church that the land warrants were valid and also to secure the borders.

"The French are trying to encroach beyond the Blue Mountain range," one of the soldiers said. "The matter is now in the hands of the king's army."

Christian turned to Henrik with a sad look. "They are men of war. There will be bloodshed on our behalf."

"But Christian," Henrik said, "by enforcing what the law says is right, peace will prevail."

The soldiers left soon after eating a meal. Henrik motioned to Anna to come outside with him, so she wrapped her shawl around her shoulders and followed him to the fire pit.

"I think it might snow tonight," she said. The first snow of winter. She shivered as a gust of wind swept past.

"Anna," he said, his voice somber. "There's something I need to show you." He pulled a newspaper out of his pocket. "Wasn't the name of the ship that the Bauer brothers sailed on called the *Lady Luck*?"

"Yes. That's right. Why?"

"I have some news." He held the newspaper out to her and pointed to an article on the front page with the headline "LADY LUCK GOES DOWN IN FLAMES IN BOSTON HARBOR."

Time stopped. A shard of lightning rent the sky, illuminating the dense clouds as if a lantern were lit behind it. Her scalp started tingling. The rush of blood pounding in her ears overwhelmed all other sounds. Tears pricked her eyes as fear for Bairn and Felix gripped her, and she had the strangest sense that this would be a moment that split her life into two parts, before and after. *Please, no. Please, God, don't let it be.*

When Henrik spoke again, his voice was quiet and careful. "Anna," he said. She risked a look up at him and saw that his face had gone soft. "The newspaper said there were no survivors."

She squeezed her eyes shut against the burn of tears, but they came anyway. Tears poured down her face. Poured and poured and poured, flooding her heart, her soul. Henrik gathered her into his arms and let her weep.

He was really gone. Bairn was gone.

Jacob's Cabin
December 1, 1737

A subtle change occurred after the news of Bairn and Felix and the burning of the *Lady Luck*. The church stopped waiting for Jacob Bauer to return. They just gave up. And they stopped looking to Christian as their leader. When there was a question or a disagreement, they sought out the advice of the newcomer.

Maria sensed it first. She withdrew from the others and kept to herself. Anna kept trying to bring her back into the circle, but she refused. "They don't want us anymore."

"That's not true. Each one of us is needed."

Maria shook her head. "We aren't wanted here. Everyone wants Henrik to take Christian's place."

"That's not the way our church works. We don't pick and choose leaders on a whim. We let God choose our leaders."

"Christian thinks we should leave. Go to Germantown in the spring and wait for another church to arrive by ship."

"You can't be serious." Anna was stunned. "We are your family."

Maria looked back at Henrik, shoveling ashes from the hearth into a bucket. "Not any longer." She grabbed Anna's forearm and looked at her with desperation in her eyes. "Come with us. You must come."

A long shuddering shiver ran through Anna. What was happening to them? Where was the sweet unity they experienced during that first Sunday worship? They seemed splintered and separated—she to her silent grief, Maria to her easily hurt feelings, Christian to his wounded ego. Sometimes Anna thought the only thing they all had in common anymore was a discontent leveled against poor, earnest Christian.

Anna covered Maria's hand with hers as a curious, tingling shock numbed her limbs. She had to get out of this cabin, away from Maria, away from this heavy burden she couldn't carry any longer.

Without giving an answer to Maria, she went outside to hack at the frozen soil in the garden area that Josef Gerber had staked out, tearing at the dark earth as if it were filled with memories. As her hoe cut into the dirt, she wondered how she could move forward without Bairn, without Felix. Without Jacob and Dorothea. And now . . . without Maria, Christian, Catrina. She felt overwhelmed by so much loss. She, who had always been so sure of who she was, felt as if her life had become a confused tangle.

That night, as Anna lay on her sleeping pallet in the loft, needing to sleep but unable to, she could feel the Pennsylvania sky loom over her, big and black and brutal, pressing down on her. Crushing her.

Her scattered and weary thoughts turned to Dorothea.

On the *Charming Nancy*, she had watched grief reach out and cover Dorothea like a heavy cloak, to the point where she became a burden to others.

Anna could not, *would* not let herself fall apart. She would not let her faith crumble in the valley of sorrow.

She wished she could talk to her grandfather. He would know how to help her get through this dark period. She tried to imagine herself back in Ixheim, sitting with her grandfather at the worn table as she had done so many times, with the morning sun shining through the window. She could hear his deep voice rumble, "*We are blessed to be a blessing.*" It was the way he started each day.

She pressed her hands against her eyes. What could that possibly mean to a tiny church in the Pennsylvania wilderness, one that was splitting apart at the seams? *Blessed to be a blessing.*

Her eyes flew open. She did not understand why God had brought them here, only to allow so much suffering. She never would. But she still had life, she had strength, she had determination. She could use her life to honor those who had tried so hard to preserve the little church of Ixheim. She would not let this church splinter apart and disappear. She would do what she needed to do to hold it together. She sighed, resolved. *Whatever that looks like.*

Jacob's Cabin
December 6, 1737

The British soldiers who had accompanied Henrik back to the settlement had warned there was talk of men in the area who were making off with horses. One quiet Friday evening, they woke to a stirring in the night—the sound of a horse's whinny far off in the distance. The horses penned near the cabin whinnied in response, giving away their location. Henrik put on his coat as Peter grabbed the musket above the cabin door.

Henrik stopped him. "No violence."

"Henrik, don't be a fool."

"Violence only begets violence."

Peter surrendered his rifle to him and Henrik returned it to its spot above the door.

"I'll come too," Isaac said.

"Lock the door behind us," Henrik said, then they slipped quietly outside.

Anna watched out the small window as the three men put harnesses on the horses and led them out of the pen and into the woods. Then there was silence. Finally, Anna returned to bed.

An hour later, she woke again to the sound of horses circling the cabin. Christian peered out the small cabin window. "It's them." He was literally shaking in fear. He looked at Anna. "What language are they speaking? Are they natives?"

She strained to make sense of what words they were shouting to each other. "No. French. I am sure of it."

"What shall we do if they try to enter the cabin?"

"We trust in God's protection," she said firmly.

Catrina started to whimper and her mother held her close.

"Shhhh . . . not a word," Anna said. Mercifully, the Gerber twins slept through the entire event, though their mother and father did not.

The horse thieves circled the cabin a number of times, then gave up and rode off. There were no horses left to steal.

At dawn, Henrik, Peter, and Isaac emerged from the deep woods leading the horses, tired but relieved.

Anna would have expected Maria and Barbara to be relieved, grateful, but when they all went out to greet them, the two women proclaimed that it would have been better to die in Ixheim than in this frightening, terrible place. "With nobody but wolves and savages for neighbors!" Maria wailed.

Oh, how these people complained! Divided by conflicting opinions, the group had made little progress in the settlement despite accommodating weather. Each spent their days doing what they thought best—Isaac and Peter Mast hunted in the woods for fallen logs to build a cabin, Josef Gerber sharpened his plow and oiled his tools, Christian split rails to build a fence to protect his two little sheep, Simon built animal traps.

Perhaps Henrik was tired after being in the woods all night, perhaps he was fed up from listening to Maria stir up discontent to leave this land, but he spoke to everyone with a firmness in his voice that verged on threatening. "You say you want to be God's people, but you run away from any hardship or suffering that comes along with that. We must remain determined. Strong and full of faith. Do not listen to those who are full of doubts." He cast a sharp glance in Maria's direction.

There was a long pause, and then Christian, in a quiet, wounded voice, shocked everyone by saying that his family had plans to leave the settlement. They would go to Germantown and wait for more ships to arrive in the summer, to join up with another church that had a bishop. If anyone wanted to, they were welcome to go with them.

Henrik walked around the small circle, making eye contact with each one. "For those who are committed to face the rigors and rewards of frontier life, for those who seek to be blessed by God in this endeavor, I hope you will stay."

Josef Gerber spoke aloud what everyone was thinking. "If Christian leaves, what are we to do without a minister?"

All eyes went to Henrik. An expression of satisfaction crept over his features. Anna found herself watching him, wondering at the cause of his joy.

And then all eyes shifted toward her.

❧

Jacob's Cabin
December 9, 1737

Anna had gone down to the creek to get a bucket of water for supper. She walked beside the tumbling creek, a golden glow in the sunlight, and watched the water shift and adjust to rocky barriers in its path. Startled by a flash of indigo, she lifted her eyes to see a blue jay catch the sun's rays. She recognized the bird's proud crown of feathers from birds in Germany. Not her favorite bird, blue jays, as they raided other birds' nests, but they were the only bird to cache food and she had to admire such intelligence. Her own church could borrow a little wisdom from the blue jay.

She tucked away that piece of information for next year: blue jays don't migrate south. *Next year.* The thought surprised her. What would her life look like next year?

She heard footsteps behind her, moving over the crunch

of fallen pine needles. She turned and saw Henrik coming toward her, his stride so fluid and elegant. "I thought you could use some help."

As she bent to fill the bucket, Henrik watched the sun set behind the tops of the trees. "Take a moment, Anna. God's daily gift." So she stood, and they watched it together, in silence, soaking up the beauty. The sky was streaked with reds and gold, a sign of tomorrow's good weather. A hawk hung like a snagged kite in the sky, then suddenly swooped down on an unlucky field mouse.

Now and again, she felt Henrik's gaze on her profile. As the sun dropped, long shadows covered the woods. "You are unique, Anna. Any other woman would have collapsed in grief."

"How could I collapse in grief when I know God holds all things in His hands?"

"You are a true daughter of God." He took the bucket from her and began to walk briskly toward the cabin.

"Henrik . . ." She took a deep breath, filled with the pungent smell of decay and earth, so much a part of the forest's spongy floor, and wondered if she would always associate that scent with this moment. "Henrik, I was wondering if you might be willing . . ." Her voice drizzled off.

There was a tone in her voice that made him stop and turn toward her. "Willing?" He set the bucket down. "Willing?" he repeated.

"To marry me."

He stared dumbly at her, as if he was not certain he had heard correctly.

"I didn't mean to go and blurt it out like that, but with Christian leaving soon . . . Well, it seems wise to take the long view. To consider the future. Our church needs us. You and me both." She couldn't look at him anymore, but she could feel his gaze hard on her, and she felt breathless all of a sudden, the way she got when she was running.

"You want to marry me?"

"Please take time to think about what I've asked. To pray."

"I will. I'll do just that. I'll pray, I'll seek God's wisdom, and I'll give you an answer in the morning."

But she didn't really expect him to turn her down; she could tell by the way he was looking at her, with possessiveness and a bright expectancy, and something else. A desperate eagerness.

Jacob's Cabin
December 10, 1737

Early the next morning, Anna took the slop bucket to the pig and found Henrik digging a hole in the garden staked out for the cabin. Beside it was her basket that held her rose. *Her* rose. The one Bairn had given to her. "What are you doing?"

"Maria has often said that Jacob and Dorothea considered you to be a daughter. Your rose needs to be planted. You need to know this is where you belong." His gaze took in the meadow down below. "I am confident that Jacob Bauer would have wanted you to have this cabin. He built it for his family. And no one is left. So this . . ." He looked up at the cabin. "This is your home."

She knew he meant well, but the thought brought little comfort.

He gave her a wry smile. "This is my rather feeble way of letting you know that I do not shy from a challenge."

"What is the challenge?"

"To make you love me as you loved him."

Her eyes went to her rose, her beautiful rose—the one that Bairn had dug for her when he was only eleven years old. The rose she had brought all the way from Ixheim. The rose that continued to survive, despite all odds. "I am fond of you, Henrik." And she truly was. Wherever he went, it was like lights were on, fire blazed. Was that love? She wasn't sure. "But I can't promise to love you the way you might want me to. The way you deserve to be loved."

"Give me a chance, Anna." He brought her hand up to his mouth and pressed his lips to the inside of her wrist. "Just give me a chance. That's all I ask." He looked up at her with those beautiful, mesmerizing blue eyes. They had a way of capturing you, those eyes of his.

He pulled her against him, gathering her in his arms with the same tenderness he showed her after she learned of the *Lady Luck*'s fire. She pressed her face into his jacket. His chest was so strong, so solid; he was someone to lean on, to depend on.

She leaned back to look at him and smiled, feeling curiously shy. "Christian has to be the one to marry us. Before he leaves."

A small, admiring smile crossed his face. "Consider it done."

23

Up the Schuylkill River
December 12, 1737

Felix collected the reins some, slowing down so that he could listen over the clatter and rattle of the horse and carriage as the countess droned on as she did, drifting far off the point of her story. My, she did talk. She did the talking for all four of them. Even more than Maria and Catrina, combined, and that was saying a lot.

Talk, talk, talk.

And the countess did not like to listen. Many times Felix had tried to interrupt her to share a story of his own, but she would look him up and down in that way she had of seeing straight through him. "You are not to speak first to nobility. You wait until you are spoken to." And then she would rap him on the knuckles with her fancy gold-tipped walking stick.

How well he knew that rule. That was pretty much what every adult told him for as long as he could remember. When he said as much to the countess, *Rap!* Again, his knuckles were whacked. After traveling with her for two weeks now, both hands were red and sore.

And she wasn't done with her lessons on noble etiquette. Another thing she had insisted on, with more than one whack to his backside, was to "never turn tail on nobility."

That took some doing on the ship from Boston to Philadelphia. He had to walk backward when she dismissed him, which happened quite regularly. It was a good thing she had grown so fond of Bairn on this journey, smiling at him with that wintery smile of hers, because there was a time or two when Felix thought the countess might have dispensed with him altogether. Even her old butler seemed impervious to his charms.

You never laid eyes on a person as old as the countess's butler. His droopy face sagged . . . and his chin waggled! It wiggled. The countess seemed oblivious to her servant's elderly status; she bossed him around like he was a dimwitted boy. Much the way she treated Felix.

Nevertheless, Felix felt quite important in this role, guiding the bossy countess and her aging butler to his father's frontier settlement. Especially important to have a solemn British soldier follow behind them on horseback, assigned to oversee the countess's welfare by Governor Patrick Gordon, who had been quite pleased to learn that German nobility had arrived in Philadelphia. He even loaned the countess his best carriage.

Now and then, when the trail was clear, Bairn let him handle the reins, as he did now. It almost made up for his brother banning him for life from any and all ships.

The *Lady Luck* had caught fire like a dry leaf. Felix, Bairn, and the captain barely escaped with their lives. Of course, the awful dog followed along, jumping right into the longboat with them, uninvited.

The longboat was within yards of the dock by the time the masts were in flames. The captain hardly even noticed Felix or the awful dog, he was in that much shock. They watched the ship disappear, as if a giant hand from the sky reached down to erase it.

Embarrassing, but these things happen.

On the longboat, as Felix started to unfold the unfortunate sequence of events that led to the ship catching fire, Bairn clasped a hand around his mouth to silence him. He bent down to rest his chin on Felix's head. "I dinnae want to ken if you had a role in startin' that fire," he whispered. "Dinnae tell me if you did, dinnae tell me if you dinnae. Either way. Sometimes, laddie, the devil gets his due."

It was strange that Bairn was not angry with him. Stranger still, the captain was not angry.

Later, Felix heard the captain explain to the shipping agent how fortunate it was that he had taken full insurance on the ship, and that his man Squivvers would testify the cargo hold was full of goods bound for England. Which, even Felix knew, was a bold-faced lie.

By the time the sun was rising, Bairn had located the countess and her old butler to tell them there was a change of plans. They would be joining them on the hunt for her missing husband.

Walking back to the docks, Felix had asked Bairn about the countess's husband. "How do you think we'll be able to find him?"

"Do you remember there was a fellow who arrived in Port Philadelphia who joined our church? He had a white patch of hair."

"Oh, I do remember him." Felix tilted his head. "The man who couldn't stop staring at Anna."

With that mild remark, Bairn had grown sullen and distant. What had Felix said?

That was the problem, right there. Felix never could understand what was all right to say and what wasn't. It was a continual riddle to him.

Take right now, for example. The countess was yammering on with another boring story about dukes and damsels, when a puzzle fit together in Felix's mind.

"Bairn!" Felix burst out, interrupting the countess, who was quite miffed. "I just figured it out. The man who joined our church, the one who's sweet on Anna—he's the countess's missing husband!"

From the silent reaction Felix got in the carriage, he realized he might have said something he shouldn't.

But there was a bright spot. The countess stopped talking.

Jacob's Cabin
December 13, 1737

It would be dawn soon.

Anna lay on her sleeping mat and stared at the ceiling. She had not rested well. Bizarre images and disturbing sensations troubled her sleep, causing her to toss and turn on the thin sleeping pallet. At one point she awoke, completely alert, and sat up. So many emotions were surging through her chest; too many thoughts whirled in her heart.

Today was her wedding day.

Now that the moment had come, she'd lost some of her assuredness. Her heart felt like it was clubbing in her chest, and she kept blinking back tears. As she thought of standing beside the man she was to marry, it was someone else's face she envisioned. She could still see Bairn's gray eyes, shining warmly with humor and admiration.

She must have dozed off, because the next thing she knew, Catrina was shaking her awake. This was the first wedding the girl had ever attended, and she couldn't wait for it. "Are your nails clean?"

Anna smiled and held up her hands. "They are." She rose from the sleeping pallet and rolled up her blanket to set aside.

"Your hair—did you rinse it with the scented lavender water Mama mixed for you?"

"I did. I did everything you and your mother told me to do."

A little later that morning, Anna stood in front of Maria for inspection. The minister's wife's keen gaze traveled from Anna's leather shoes to her brown flax dress to her scented hair, looking for anything out of place.

Anna studied Maria's face, her expression still sharp and assessing, and then their eyes connected and affection softened her countenance. Maria had been especially kind to her the last few days, despite how especially unkind was her opinion about Henrik. "The newcomer will be the envy of every man today."

Anna looked away as a blush crept up her cheeks. "Won't you reconsider and remain with us? Christian will do what you tell him to."

"My husband might not voice strong opinions often, but once he fixes his heart on something, he won't bend until the thing is done. We must go. After the fellowship meal, he said." Their possessions were packed; last night the men had loaded the trunks on the wagons. Christian planned to return the borrowed horses and wagons to Christoph Saur in Germantown.

Already, the cabin looked larger. But that was a cold consolation.

The wedding service would be held indoors. Earlier, right after breakfast, Henrik had left to wash in the creek. Now he was waiting outside with the men.

"Ready?" Catrina said.

She opened the door and blinding sunlight poured into the dim cabin. Anna didn't see Henrik at first. He stood at the door, limned by the sunlight.

"Anna." He said her name like a lovestruck adolescent.

When her eyes met his, her stomach flipped right over. Perhaps she might be able to love him, after all.

Though it was midweek, Christian led a church service. The wedding ceremony took place after the sermon, and at the end, there would be Henrik's ordination as the new minister. Under normal conditions, lots would be drawn. But last Sunday, when Christian asked each person whom they would recommend to draw a lot, everyone voted only for Henrik, except for Maria, who refused to vote.

Anna couldn't concentrate on Christian's sermon, his last one. When he finally came to a conclusion, he asked Anna and Henrik to stand before him. Her legs shook as she rose to her feet.

I must do this. This won't be so hard after all, she thought. *I know the words, I've heard them all my life, all I have to do is say them*. But her chest felt too full, her throat too tight to speak. She could only manage a nod when Christian asked her if she promised to remain faithful to this man who stood beside her. Henrik was beaming, positively beaming.

Suddenly, the solemn ceremony was over, they were married, and then Henrik was ordained as the new minister. One fell swoop.

The room was hastily converted into a place for a shared fellowship meal. All day yesterday, Barbara and Maria had worked hard to make a tasty wedding meal. There was a succulent roast turkey seasoned with herbs, biscuits, and a sweet potato pie.

Too soon, Christian motioned to Maria that they should be off. Shivering, Anna drew her shawl more closely around her shoulders, dreading this goodbye. Before Christian climbed onto the wagon, he turned and said, in a voice that was strangely bold for a man who was not at all bold, "May God have mercy on you in this impossible calling."

The little church of Ixheim stood by the fire pit to wave and wave at the Müllers' wagon train, until they could no longer be seen. Tears streamed down most everyone's faces, even stiff Isaac's.

Henrik stood behind Anna and put a hand on her shoulder to give it a light squeeze. "Why in the world," he whispered, "would he leave us with such a dark foreboding?"

Anna looked around the fire pit. Wasn't it obvious? Since they had left Germany, filled with such high hopes, the little church had been reduced by half.

Up the Schuylkill River

Bairn was out of the wagon, trying to move a large fallen tree out of the narrow trail, wondering why the somber British soldier who trailed behind them on horseback could not volunteer to assist him, when he heard a clatter and rumble.

He stopped hacking at the tree's branches and waited. Through the woods he saw two horses and wagons, one after the other, with a bay horse tied behind it. He climbed on top of the log to see and stood in the middle of the trail until the lead wagon stopped abruptly. Bairn shielded his eyes against the low-lying winter sun. The minister? "Christian? Christian Müller?"

"Bairn . . . der Zimmermann? Bist du?" *The carpenter? Is it you?*

"Aye! And I've brought Felix too."

Christian stood in the wagon and turned to shout behind him. "Maria! You won't believe it! It's the ship's carpenter! And he's got our young Felix with him!" He climbed down from the wagon and hurried to shake Bairn's hand. "We thought you were dead. We read the newspaper account about the ship going down in flames in Boston Harbor. It reported no survivors."

Bairn was stunned. "You think I'm dead?"

"Yes! You and Felix, both. We've all grieved deeply for you."

This was distressing news. "The newspaper got it half right. There were no survivors because no one was on the ship." He looked at the wagons, filled with trunks. "Christian, where are you goin'?"

The older man's round face sagged. "We are leaving. We're on our way to Germantown."

"But why? Why are you leavin'?"

"We are no longer needed. Or wanted."

"What do you mean?"

By now Maria had climbed down from her wagon to join the two men. "Oh Bairn, so much has happened while you were gone. So much has gone wrong."

"Maria," Christian said in a warning voice.

A trickle of foreboding snaked up Bairn's spine.

Maria gave her husband a look. "He'll find out sooner or later." She turned to Bairn. "Your parents have gone missing—"

"They're *what*?"

"You remember how they left Philadelphia ahead of us, back in October. They've never been heard from since."

"Did you not go lookin' for them?"

"We did," Christian said. "We did our best."

"And there was no word from them? No sign?"

"Just one sign. The red Mutza. Anna saw it on an Indian who came to our cabin one afternoon. We haven't seen him again. Your parents . . . are presumed dead."

Catrina slipped up beside her mother. "We have some good news. Anna has been married."

Maria frowned at her. "Not everyone thinks that is such good news."

Christian looked at him in bleak disillusionment. "This very morning."

Twin waves of emotion struck Bairn at once. Fear that he had come too late; fear that he knew whom she had married. "Who? Who did she marry?"

"Henrik Newman."

It was. It was him.

Bairn's mind whirled. Anna—his darling Anna—had not waited for him after all. The news struck him like a kick in the gut.

She had gone and fallen in love with Henrik Newman. Married him? Slept with him?

He looked up the trail. "How much farther to reach the cabin?"

"Not far at all. We left not long ago. Right after the wedding ceremony."

Bairn glanced at the large tree that blocked the trail. Behind it he could see the top of Felix's black hat. Then he turned to Christian's horses. "Which is the fastest horse?"

"The bay, but why?"

Bairn untied the bay from the back of the wagon. He swung a leg up over the back of the horse and held the reins with a relaxed grip. "Christian, return to the cabin with Felix and his passengers. Help Felix move the log so he can follow."

Christian looked flabbergasted. "But . . . I . . . we are headed . . ."

"To Germantown," Maria supplied. She glared at Bairn. "And we'll do nothing of the kind."

"Do as I say!" Bairn commanded, frowning thunderously.

"Well, I never," Maria huffed, arms akimbo.

Bairn kicked the bay to get it cantering. He didn't have time for Maria's injured feelings. "Felix will explain everythin'," he yelled.

All the way up the winding trail, the horse's hooves beat a pounding rhythm: *Too late, too late, too late . . .*

Jacob's Cabin

Even on a wedding day, the animals needed tending, the dishes needed washing, the water buckets needed filling. It had been

Catrina's job to feed the animals, so Anna took armfuls of hay out to the pen. She heard the sound of galloping hoof steps and, alarmed, squinted her eyes to see who was coming up the path. Her heart started to race. She'd never forgotten Bairn's remark that the natives were always watching. Now and then she thought she had seen a few, filtered by the trees, but hadn't told the others so as not to frighten them.

But the man on the galloping horse was not a native. He wore English clothing, a black hat, knee-high boots, and he stood tall in the saddle, so very tall . . .

"Bairn," she said, inhaling a sharp breath.

She flung herself out of the animal pen so fast she bumped her hip on the tree branch that served as a gate and cried out in pain. The wind had come up hard, whipping her apron and skirt and capstrings as she ran down the path to meet him. When he saw her coming toward him, he reined the horse to an abrupt stop, leapt off, and opened his arms to her. She threw herself into those arms and was lifted up, up, up in an embrace. One hand closed over her head, crinkling her prayer cap; his arms wrapped her so tightly against his chest that she could feel his heart beating, fast and steady. *Bairn's heart.*

She didn't know how long they stayed that way, how much time had passed. It was a soft nose bump from the horse he rode in on that pulled them apart.

"I thought you were dead," she said, choking over the words.

"Nae, not dead at all, darlin'." With tender care, he set her feet on the ground, still holding onto her waist with a firm grip.

She looked up at him, at that face so dear to her, the one

she thought she'd never see again, and had a hard time talking around the knot in her throat. "The *Lady Luck* burned and sank. I read about it in the newspaper. No survivors, it said."

"Aye. Nae survivors because nae one was on the ship."

Tears welled in her eyes and she squeezed them tightly shut, trying to hold them back, hold them back. If they started now, she feared they wouldn't stop. Her eyes flew open. "But where's Felix?" she asked. "He's with you, isn't he?"

"He's comin' up the road. He'll be along shortly."

Bairn didn't move, nor make a sound, but Anna could feel something change in him. She looked up, into his eyes. "What?" she said. "What is it?"

"Anna, you cannae marry that man."

Henrik stood watching them, just a few feet away, hands on his hips. "Oh, but she can." His mouth thinned into a tight smile. "She already did."

Bairn glared at him. "It matters not what she just did. A man cannot be married to two women."

Strange, fleeting thoughts darted through Anna's mind, like birds spooked from their roost. Bairn's use of the dialect had improved dramatically, she noticed. She still heard his Scottish accent color the words, but his speech was smooth, fluid, confident. And then the meaning of what he actually said settled in for a stay and she felt a chill run up her back. She flinched and stepped away from him.

"Bairn—that's absurd." She looked at Henrik, who was staring at Bairn. "Tell him so, Henrik." She clenched her fist among the folds of her dress.

"She's right. That's crazy talk." He smiled, though his blue eyes went cold and hard, like pond ice reflecting a winter sky.

Bairn seized her by the arms. "Anna, you must believe me."

"Get your hands off my wife."

"Yer wife?" Bairn let go of Anna and turned to him, his large hands clenching and unclenching rhythmically. "*Which* wife? Does the name Countess Magdalena von Hesse ring a bell to you? Because she'll be coming up the path here shortly."

A change came over Henrik's features, a sudden shock of realization. Surprise siphoned the blood from his face and the defiance in his eyes gave way to alarm. Anna felt the truth all at once, like a tingle in the pit of her stomach.

"Henrik, did you lie to me?" she said, almost eerily calm.

With a wince, Henrik pressed one palm to his chest and took a single stumbling step toward her. "Anna, it's just a misunderstanding. I can explain everything."

He *had* lied.

He had left Europe, not to find a new world, but to escape the old one. She clapped her hand over her mouth and heard herself breathing hard through her nose. She would be sick in a moment, spewing her wedding supper all over the ground.

For a long moment there was a silence so loud that it stifled all sounds, even breathing. Then the sound of a horse whinnying traveled up the long path, and the bay lifted its head from grazing to turn, flicking its ears. Soon, the rumble of wheels signaled the arrival of Felix. At first glance, Anna thought he was alone, but then she realized that he had passengers with him.

Henrik's arms fell to his sides. "Oh no," he whispered. "Dear God, no."

24

Jacob's Cabin
December 13, 1737

Felix pulled sharply back on the reins, and the light carriage he was driving slued to a stop, nearly running into Bairn and Anna. The horse shied and bucked in its harness, and he had his hands full for a moment getting it back under control. Overall, he had done a fine job, he thought, though the countess fussed and complained at every bump and jolt. Mostly, she raised a stink about his awful dog too, but for that, he could not blame her.

Anna ran to the carriage, arms flailing, which set the awful dog into a barking frenzy. "Felix! Oh, merciful heavens, Felix! You're here! You're safe!" As soon as he set the brake and jumped down, she grabbed him into a tight hug, then just as suddenly, released him, gripped him by the shoulders and gave him a shake. "Do you know the worry you caused? We were frantic, searching for you all over Philadelphia. You had the thought to tell the printer that you were leaving . . . and no one else!"

A commotion down the path, the arrival of Christian and Maria's wagons rumbling along, gave him a reprieve from Anna's scolding. Too soon walleyed Catrina appeared. She jumped off the wagon and marched over importantly to Anna's side, grinning foolishly at Felix. "You are filthy," Catrina said, boring into him with her beady eyes. One of them, anyway. "You need a bath."

He looked down at his clothes. He didn't think he smelled so awful bad, but it was true he couldn't remember the last time he took a real bath. He made a mouth at Catrina and looked away.

Bairn helped the countess climb down off the wagon, and then her prehistoric butler. By the time the countess brushed the dust off her fancy clothing, the sound of pounding horse hooves caught everyone by surprise.

No one moved. It was like everyone had frozen stiff while watching a man disappear into the woods on the bay horse. The man with the white spot on his head, the very one who seemed to have caused quite a commotion, was gone.

The countess screamed at the British soldier to go after him. "Go! Go get him!"

The British soldier remained stiffly on his horse and gave a brief shake of his head. "I cannot. The governor gave me orders to not leave your side, Countess."

Exasperated, the countess turned to her old butler with a cry. "Geh un holl mir mein Mann! Geh!" *Go get my husband! Go!* He looked at her helplessly, but she was insistent. She handed him his cane and he took it; his old, milky eyes in their saggy sockets gazed at it as if he thought it might turn into a horse and carriage.

How in the world could the countess expect an old man

to chase after a speeding horse? Felix almost laughed at the thought, but wisely for once, he hung back in silence.

"I'll get him back here." Bairn started to unhook the carriage horse, but Anna stopped him.

"Let him go."

Bairn looked at Anna, shocked. "But what he's done to you. To the countess. 'Tis not right."

Anna had a distant expression on her face, one Felix couldn't read. "Let him go."

Bairn slowed, then dropped his hands. For the longest time, everyone stood there quietly, as if their bodies felt too weighted down to move, eyes fixed on the deep woods.

Then Felix had a fine idea. "Say, we'll all feel better after we eat."

❧

There was a great cry and show of tears from the countess when she learned that her husband had just married Anna, despite Bairn's assurance that it held no legal status. Barbara led the woman up to the cabin to rest, and the older man who accompanied her followed behind, slow as molasses in January, carrying her bags. The British soldier followed along and stood guard outside the cabin door.

"I just knew there was something fishy about the newcomer," Maria said. "Right from the start. I always thought . . ." Her words trailed off as she peered at Anna. And then she reached over to hand her a handkerchief.

Anna waved it off. Little good it would do her now. She swiped at the tears dripping down her cheeks. She couldn't say what exactly she was crying over: the shock and joy at seeing Bairn and Felix again when she had thought they were dead. Or the utter humiliation of discovering Henrik was not whom she believed him to be. Who was he, really? She had no idea. A man who disappeared into the woods like that was a man who had reason to hide.

Christian looked as baffled as Anna felt. "Rather extraordinary, really. Imagine that."

"I suppose he did have a certain winsome charm," Maria conceded.

"He was *so* comely," Catrina said.

"And don't think he didn't know it," Maria added.

Isaac and Christian unhooked the harnesses to take the horses to the pen. Maria started handing Felix and Catrina items from the wagon to take up to the cabin. Anna's mind was still in a muddle, unsure of what to do next. She turned in the direction of the cabin as Bairn grabbed hold of her elbow. "Anna, please. Come with me a moment."

They started toward the fire pit, but her legs wouldn't work right and she had to stop walking.

"Darlin'."

She raised her head. He was looking down at her with such tenderness in his eyes. He spoke to her in English now, and she was grateful because Maria's ever listening ears would not be able to understand them. "It was deplorable of me to leave y'. I regretted it the moment the ship left the dock. I should never have left." He paused as he swallowed. "I ken I failed y' miserably."

Somewhere an owl hooted. Dusk was coming.

She glanced from his face down toward his hand, which had fixed itself to her sleeve.

He let his hand drop. "Will y' say nothin'?"

She could say nothing at all, only look at him, and it was so wonderful to look at him. But it hurt as well. It hurt so much that she had to look away. Her throat was hot and tight, full of the things she wanted to say but couldn't seem to express.

"Why him? Of all men. Why such a scoundrel?"

"I didn't *know* he was a scoundrel." The thought of Henrik Newman made her feel ill again. She had *married* him! She had *believed* his silky lies. What a fool she was.

"I asked y' to wait for me. How could y' have married another man?"

"We thought you were dead, Bairn. *Dead!* The newspaper said there were no survivors."

"And a scant four weeks later, yer marryin' him? Y' could not have mourned me any longer than a scant four weeks?" He took a step closer to her. "Anna, darlin', did y' love him? The way y' loved me?"

Tears pricked her eyes and spilled down her cheeks. She hated to cry. Tears made her feel weak and she needed to be strong. "Bairn, I can't talk about this with you. Not now. I need to sort it out for myself."

"I hoped you'd be more glad to see me."

She shook her head and the tears splattered. "What do you want me to say? That I'm glad you're here, that you're alive? Because I am. Truly, I am. But so much has happened here. We can barely catch our breath between one disaster after another. Bairn, your parents—"

He touched her lips with his fingers. "Christian told me." He glanced toward the woods. "They are not dead. Jacob Bauer would not die that easily. They are out there, somewhere, and I will find them." He turned back to her. "I know, in my heart, that my father is not dead. But what I dinnae ken—and what I need to ken—is if y' can forgive me?"

"Of course," she said. "Of course I do," her voice rising, firming, the words coming from her heart like a prayer. How could he even think it possible that she could not forgive him?

He took her hands in his. "Then, darlin', cannae we find our way back to each other?"

She looked him in the eyes, willing herself to remain immune to the pull of their deep gray depths. Did he really think he could return, without warning, out of the blue, and assume everything to be the way he wanted it to be? Her throat had been getting tighter and tighter, closing up on her, and she wasn't sure she could answer him. She was trembling, as she did when she was very cold or very angry. Right now, it was both.

She took a breath as deep as she could and let it out slowly. Back in control, she wrapped her shawl tightly around herself and said, "That, I don't know," in a voice almost too soft to hear.

Jacob's Cabin
December 14, 1737

The countess was a curiosity to Bairn. As much as she irritated him with her imperious, opinionated, often blunt ways, her lightning quick mood changes, and her endless tedious chatter, despite *all* that, he had to admit she was one of the comeliest girls he'd seen on either side of the Atlantic. Raven-black hair, deep violet-blue eyes, a heart-shaped face, and a slim little nose. Queenly, that's what she was. He stood beside her carriage, waiting to help her get on.

From the trees came the sough of wind. "It's quite remarkable, this place," the countess said, her face wistful as she surveyed the meadow ringed by red cedar, pitch pine, and white oak. An eagle soared on an updraft, hovering on the wind before peeling away toward the Blue Mountains. "Such wilderness. It stuns me. Words fail to capture it."

Bairn held the same opinion. No one in their right mind could fail to appreciate the beauty of this land. He understood why his father had chosen this place, close to God, far from civilization. It made a man feel as if all of creation was spread out before him. A spring-fed creek nearby for year-round fishing. Otter, beaver, and muskrat for the fur trade. Skies filled with fowl. It was a fine place. "Yer welcome to remain with us." He meant it, but he didn't expect her to accept. She did not belong here, not in the wilderness, not with them.

"Thank you, but we must carry on to Germantown. I feel quite certain that's where Karl will be." And it was true, east was the direction he had headed.

Karl. Karl Henrik Neumann. Anglicized, like so many names, at the Philadelphia Court House to Henrik Newman.

The countess could not be dissuaded from leaving in the morning, convinced she was close on the trail of her husband, like a determined dog on the scent of a fox. She might be petite, but she was doughty. And remarkably insistent.

Maria had woken at dawn to refresh the fire and fry last night's potatoes for a tasty breakfast. She put together a dinner packet of salt pork, biscuits, and dried apples for the countess, her manservant, and the grave soldier as Bairn and Felix harnessed the horse to the carriage.

Bairn held the countess's offered hand lightly—he might have captured a small bird. She had one boot raised on the iron footplate as a question stopped her.

"Why do you pursue him?"

Bairn's head whipped around to see Anna approach the carriage.

Slowly the countess turned her head to look at her, as if she had not noticed her before that moment. Perhaps it was true, in a way, for Anna had gone straight to the loft yesterday afternoon, skipping supper.

"The rule is that nobility always speaks first," Felix whispered in a loud voice. "Trust me on that."

Anna ignored him and persisted, moving closer to the countess. "Why?" she repeated, looking only at the countess. "Why do you want to find him?"

A little malicious smile flickered on the countess's mouth, and a trace of color rose under her skin.

Bairn didn't think the countess would answer, but she did. "Foolish girl, you of all people should understand." Her mouth curled a little. "I love him. And he's mine." She turned away abruptly, and Bairn helped her climb into the carriage.

No sooner had the countess and her manservant started on their way, British soldier trailing behind, that Felix stood in front of him, hands on his hips. "So then, what's our plan to find Mem and Papa?"

"I am giving that matter serious thought, Felix. For now, first things first."

"Why isn't finding Mem and Papa the first thing?"

"Because I am certain they would have found some kind of shelter to last the winter months." It was a strange thing, not to have any sign, not any word of their whereabouts. Even in a vast wilderness, news traveled. Even on the ocean, news traveled.

First things first was . . . Anna.

"We need to talk," he said to her. But she wasn't listening. She had caught sight of something off in the distance and was peering at the woods.

She did not stop to explain, but set out with a quick and confident step. She was walking so fast she had to lift the skirts of her dress above her ankles. As Bairn followed behind, he couldn't help but notice how lovely those ankles were.

She stopped down by the creek and turned in a slow circle, but he saw nothing unusual. A thicket of bayberry shrubs directly behind them rustled with activity and a young cottontail scrambled from beneath.

"What are you lookin' for?" Bairn said.

"I thought . . . I saw something. A red something."

The water bent slightly in the breath of the wind, but there was nothing at the water's edge.

"What was it?"

Her eyes went round. "Not what. Who." She pointed behind him to an old Indian who had emerged from behind a tree.

Bairn turned to stare at the Indian, wondering just what he wanted of them. The Indian stared back at Bairn, watching him carefully, purposefully.

In the Indian's arms was the red Mutza. He walked slowly up to Bairn and held it out to him.

Bairn took the coat from him. "My father's coat. Where did y' find this?"

The old Indian's watery eyes, vague and trembling, creased in a slight smile, as if giving Bairn a message though he didn't say a word. He stepped away, then slipped into the woods.

Bairn started to follow, but Anna called him back. "I don't think he wants you to follow."

"Who is he?"

"I saw him once before, wearing your father's coat. He came into the cabin and looked around as if he had something very specific on his mind. He left as suddenly as he came, and I haven't seen him since."

Bairn looked at the coat in his arms. He thought of that slight smile in the Indian's eyes. "My father, he is not dead."

She put a hand on the coat. "We don't know anything for sure. All that we do know is that the Indian knew your father."

"Then why did he come here to return it? How would the Indian have known I was Jacob's son unless he'd been told to look for me?" His heart started to race. "There's a reason this coat has been returned." He looked inside it, shook it, then ran a hand along the bottom hem. Then he reached into his boot and pulled out his knife. "There's something in there."

Bairn slit the threads that held the seam together. He reached his hand under the coat's lining and pulled out papers. He handed the coat and knife to Anna and opened the papers.

"What are they?"

"That sly old dog."

"Who?"

"My father." Bairn leafed through them, then looked at her. "These are Jacob Bauer's land warrants."

Jacob's Cabin
January 5, 1738

Christmas came and went, quietly and solemnly celebrated, as was the custom of the church of Ixheim. Nature gave its own rowdy celebration: six inches of snow fell on Christmas Day.

But as the days passed, to Bairn's disappointment, Anna was having naught to do with him. She was polite but distant, welcoming but cool. She said she needed time to sort things through.

And what was there to sort through? She'd been rescued from a loveless marriage to a lying bigamist.

When Bairn told her as much, she gave him a look not dissimilar to those often given to Felix. And then she said, quite crisply and definitively, that she had not asked for his opinion, and that she needed time without it.

Time. It was a funny thing. Time could be short, and it often was. But there was always time enough for the important things. That was true too. Right now, time was the one thing Bairn had to give Anna. It was the only thing he could offer to prove to her that he was not going to leave again.

Now that the land warrants were in hand, he turned his attention to the settlement, if you could call it that. He was shocked by what little progress had occurred at the settlement over the last few months, especially with the blessing of a mild winter. It was time to move forward, together.

On the table made of trunks, Bairn laid out the deerskin on which he had drawn a map of the area. After examining the land warrants and surveying the land, he decided each family would choose lots of eighty rods sprawling out from Jacob's cabin, land to build their permanent homes.

Bairn had to admit that his father had made a fine choice. Most of the building materials to erect cabins would be available right on the land. Ten thousand acres of rich, loamy soil; gently sloping hillsides covered with eastern hardwoods—

oaks, maple, hickory, elm, cherry, beech, poplar, and the hardy chestnut.

Best of all, there was walnut. That was Bairn's favored wood—for making furniture as well as cabins. It hewed well and planed easily, was lighter to handle than most other hardwoods, and the wood most resistant to rot.

After each family had chosen a tract of land and found a suitable clearing for a building site, it was time to work together to construct the log cabins. Eventually, they would build more substantial houses, with root cellars below and a large chimney in the center, but for now, crude bark-covered log cabins would suffice. In the spring, they would help each other clear twenty acres or so for fields. But for now, everyone's efforts went to building cabins. One by one.

The first cabin to be built was for Christian and Maria, Bairn announced. They deserved it, and no one objected. It pleased Maria mightily to be singled out.

Each day, the men set to work finding fallen logs and felling trees. Bairn showed the men how to chop off the bark around the middle of the trunks of suitable trees. As soon as spring arrived and the sap started flowing, the trees would soon die and drop on their own accord. Those logs could be used for other cabins.

The men labored from dawn to dusk until their muscles ached and their hands were raw. The horses dragged logs to a cabin site, then the logs were notched, rolled into place, and fitted tight with wooden pegs. "Rolling up the walls," Bairn called it. Each person had tasks to do: Peter notched logs. Anna mixed wet clay, grass, and lime to fill in the cracks between the logs. Barbara and Maria wove harvested meadow hay to provide a temporary thatched roof. Felix and Catrina hunted for stones in the meadow to build a fireplace. Bairn built sturdy carts to haul the stones to the construction site.

Within a few short weeks, men and women working side by side, and with accommodating weather, the first cabin was completed. Bairn knew that the first cabin would take the longest, the one they'd made their most mistakes on. They'd figured out a few tricks as they went. All in all, it was a solid cabin, snug and watertight.

When moving day came, everyone helped unload the wagon and settle Maria and Christian and Catrina into their new home. And then the celebration began. Back at Jacob's cabin, a shared meal was prepared over a blazing fire in the pit: they speared rabbits and turkeys onto long sticks and arranged them over the flames.

Bairn had never seen Maria Müller look quite so pleased.

And then a very unexpected visitor arrived.

25

Jacob's Cabin
January 31, 1738

A light snow was falling, large soft flakes that covered the ground like a dusting of confectioners' sugar. Anna and Felix were outside, watching Felix's dog try to catch flakes in the air and look ridiculous trying, when suddenly the dog stopped, pricked his ears, and made a dash down the path, barking as he went. A warning—someone was approaching. Felix ran after him to call him back, then stopped and pivoted.

"Judas Iscariot!" he cried. "It's the printer from Philadelphia!"

"Felix! Don't curse."

But naturally he paid no mind to Anna; he was already halfway down the path to greet the printer. She sounded more bothered than she was. That boy had a mile-wide smile and it did her heart good to have him home. She picked up her pace and hurried to join them.

"How did you ever find me?" Felix said.

The printer looked just as surprised as Felix and Anna. "I smelled something delicious and my stomach steered me here." He climbed down from his horse and shook Felix's hand. "Young boy! I did not expect to see you again. Certainly not for many more months. What are you doing back from your sea adventure?"

By this time, Bairn had walked down to join them. "It's a long story," he said, pumping Benjamin Franklin's outstretched hand. "In the meantime, won't you come in and get out of the cold? We're havin' a bit of a celebration, and we'd be pleased if you'd join us." He turned to Felix. "Take the printer's horse to the pen and give him food and water."

Benjamin Franklin was delighted to sit down to sup with them. He was very impressed with the choice of land, the cabin, the improvements that were under way. As was Anna, for she knew credit belonged to Bairn's leadership.

While she felt strong reservations about Bairn, she'd been learning new things about him these last few weeks. He showed a surprisingly strong drive for harmony and unity. He could not bear if someone was upset, even a child. Or to know that another was chafing under some offense. Though he could be quick with his commands—sounding as if he were ordering sailors about the ship—he would catch himself and apologize to make amends.

"So what brings you up this way?" Bairn asked the printer, after they sat down to eat.

Anna asked Felix to act as interpreter to the group, which made him preen with pride. His language skills had improved in the last few months. Another credit due to Bairn, no doubt.

"It's a bit embarrassing," Benjamin Franklin said. "I was attending to some printing business at the Ephrata Cloister and thought I was on my way back to Philadelphia, but I seem to have gotten a little lost."

Amusement filled Bairn's eyes. "Yer a long way northwest of Philadelphia."

"Well, you see, I've never had a stellar sense of direction. My Deborah won't travel with me any longer. Once I took her to see her niece in New Jersey and we ended up in Maryland." He filled his plate with roasted rabbit, a large turkey leg, and potatoes. "This is a feast I never would have imagined to partake in while wandering the frontier."

"I met a man from the Ephrata Cloister," Anna said. "Brother Agrippa. But he called it Ephrata Community. Not Cloister."

"Brother Agrippa? Yes, Peter Miller, a learned man." Ben Franklin winked at her. "As for calling it the Cloister, that's done only behind the brotherhood's back. It's something like a monastery, and the construction that's going on is quite significant, though Father Friedsam would say they are only there temporarily."

"Where are they going?" Felix asked.

"To their eternal glory. They're waiting for the Second Coming of Christ."

Anna could see Felix struggle to grasp that thought. He chewed and swallowed hastily, squirming in his chair as another question worked its way to the surface. He wasn't going to quit, she could see. Bairn must have had the same thought, because he reached past Felix for the plate of biscuits and offered them to the printer, asking if he'd like more to eat.

Benjamin Franklin was an appreciative guest. And a hungry one. He filled his plate with biscuits and gravy, and reached for another turkey leg. "Come to think of it, I should ask you people if you might know anything about this. Father

Friedsam asked me to run an advertisement in the *Pennsylvania Gazette* about a group of Germans who had gotten separated from other immigrants. He's hoping there might be someone who could connect them to their people."

"How large is the group?" Bairn asked.

"Let me get my notes." Ben Franklin reached for his saddlebag by his feet and riffled through it to pull out a paper. "A woman, late forties, early fifties. A man, same age. Quite ill, from what I heard. The man, that is. Near death's door." He squinted through his smoky spectacles to read his writing. "And a baby. Aged five months."

Anna and Bairn locked eyes. Her heart pounded so hard in her ears she feared she would faint. "It's them," she said.

Jacob's Cabin
February 1, 1738

By the time the first kiss of sunrise lit the eastern treetops, the matter had been settled. Bairn set out on horseback at first light, as did Benjamin Franklin. But the printer was on his way to Philadelphia and Bairn planned to reach Ephrata Cloister by day's end—if the horse could endure the forty-mile journey through rugged wilderness, including a few inches of fresh snow. He had his sharpened ax by his side, at the ready to clear a path in the bush.

Felix begged to go with him, but Bairn squashed the laddie's pleading. The boy would only slow him down. Same with the printer, who had offered to show him the way to Ephrata—but Bairn had more faith in his own ability to navigate correctly than the kindly printer's.

Bairn left clear instructions for the group to carry on work in his absence. He had no idea how long he would be away, nor had he any idea what he would find when he arrived at Ephrata Cloister. Benjamin Franklin said he was under the impression that his father was nearing death. He hoped, he *prayed*, that his father would hang on until he arrived. They had things to settle, he and his father.

The sun was nearly gone by the time he arrived at Ephrata Cloister—he must remember not to call it that moniker. Ephrata *Community*. It was not unlike the sailors referring to the Amish people as "Peculiars." A bad habit. He patted the neck of the bay, a fine horse, who handled the day's long journey in stride.

He saw a group of hooded people walk slowly, ghostlike in the gloaming, heading into a large clapboard building. He called out to them before they disappeared, and one robed figure turned and waited as Bairn hurried over to him. "I was told there was a German woman staying here, along with her ill husband. And a babe."

The robed figure, a man, it turned out, nodded impassively, as if he'd been expecting Bairn. "Follow me."

Ephrata Community

Dorothea liked watching the sunset from the window in her room, holding the baby against her chest. It had become a daily routine for her, watching that large orb drop behind the ridge of trees. There was something about a sunset that made her feel closer to God, though it would seem as if a sunrise would hold more promise.

But the sunset seemed a reminder that God had carried her through another twenty-four hours. He had been faithful; a day was completed. All was well.

She heard a knock on the door and set the baby in his cradle—soon, it would be too small for him—and went to open the door, expecting to see Sister Alice with a supper tray. She could identify most of the sisters now, and many of the brothers, just by sight or mannerisms.

Brother Andrew stood at the door, and behind him was a tall man, so tall he had to bend his head in the hallway.

Tall, so tall.

Her breath caught. Could it be?

"Mem," he said, his voice cracking with emotion. "It's me. Your son. I've come to get you. I've come to take you home. You and Papa."

Dorothea stood at the threshold, trying to absorb the news. "Hans? My Hans? My son? You've come for us!" In her voice was relief and joy, and then an anguish barely expressible. "Oh Hans, you've come just in time. Your papa . . . he is not at all well." She moved away from the door so he could enter the room. She could see the shock on her son's face, the way his jaw sagged open, as he took in the sight of Jacob lying in that bed, a wisp of his former self.

Her tall son knelt by his father's side. "What is wrong?"

Brother Andrew stood by the door. "Consumption."

Her son picked up Jacob's hand, then turned it over. His skinny arm was riddled with bruises. "What's happened to him?"

Dorothea sat on the chair next to Jacob's bed. "That bruising—I noticed the bruises in Port Philadelphia, when we first arrived. He had bruising all over his arms and legs.

And he'd lost so much weight. He wore extra coats so no one would notice. And then—"

Her son looked up. "Then what?"

"He had the swoons a few times while we were in Port Philadelphia. He made me promise not to tell anyone. But that was the reason he wanted to leave and return to the settlement. He was feeling weak."

"What other symptoms has he had?"

"He complained of bone pain. Shortness of breath. You can see the yellowing of his skin."

"Moodiness?"

"Oh my, yes. But that's not so unusual. And he's been under such stress."

"What's he been eating?"

"His teeth have been hurting him, so the sisters have ground up his chicken and beef. That has seemed to help him eat."

He glanced up at her. "No vegetables? No fruits?"

"The sisters thought he needed meat for strength."

Over his shoulder, her son directed a question to Brother Andrew. "Have you any oranges here? Any lemons or limes?"

Brother Andrew looked startled. "It's winter."

"Then, vegetables? Broccoli? Peppers? Mayhap, winter kale?"

Brother Andrew approached the bed. "The Householders keep us supplied with vegetables. I'll go see what I can find in the kitchen. I think I saw broccoli earlier today."

"Why broccoli?" Dorothea asked.

"There is an illness I've seen on ships that looks similar to this. It's caused by a poor diet."

"But your father has had good food to eat. An abundance of meat."

"Aye, but probably very little vegetables or fruit. This illness is called scurvy." He rose to his feet. "If it is scurvy, we'll soon know."

Dorothea reached up and gripped his coat sleeve. "Have you ever seen someone get well again?"

"I have. It takes a bit of time, but the condition can be reversed. On the ship, citrus juice is added to the grog that sailors drink to prevent this scurvy."

"You think he caught this disease on the ship?"

"Not caught. 'Tis not something you catch. But the disease started on the ship. A seaboard diet has little variety."

"But that was well over a year ago."

"Most likely he arrived in the wilderness and subsisted only on hunted game, as most pioneers do. The disease would have progressed. Scurvy takes two years to kill." Her son's eyes were glued to his father. "But, God willing, it does not take that long to recover."

Dorothea felt a great peace well up, filling her inside until it was nearly spilling over. Not only had her son come for her, but he had given her a glimmer of hope that Jacob might not die. Perhaps it was hoping for a miracle, but then . . . did she not just witness a miracle when she opened the door and found her son standing there?

And then it dawned on her that her son had been speaking the dialect nearly like a native Palatinate. Wonders never ceased.

February 3, 1738

A day passed at Ephrata Community, then another, without any significant change in Jacob's condition. It was difficult to get him to eat—when he was conscious, he was confused and refused food. Bairn mashed the vegetables into a puree and spoon-fed him. He was able to get him to swallow by rubbing his throat. It was a slow, tedious process.

Bairn was leaning toward the notion that his father might indeed be suffering from consumption. His breaths were so labored, short and shallow, the way consumption wormed its way into a man's lungs, slowly suffocating him. But the racking cough that was the telltale sign of consumptives—that was missing. He stayed close by his father's bed, standing vigil. By the afternoon of the second day, a hooded sister shooed him and his mother, and the little babe, outside to get some fresh air.

"The air is sweet today and the sun is shining," the sister said. "Please, go outside. I will watch over Jacob."

As they walked to the garden bench, his mother's favorite place, she told him the background story of that particular sister, known to all as Sister Marcella, an immigrant named Maria Saur who was married to Christoph Saur of Germantown, and then deserted him to live here as a celibate. "A strange thing, to hear of a wife deserting her husband."

Her son turned in a circle and stopped when he saw the robed figures walking cautiously on top of the new building, up the hill a short distance. "'Tis a strange place, this Ephrata Cloister."

"That it is. Very." Calm and tranquil, yet buzzing with industry. Sounds of building filled each day, music filled each night. She closed her eyes and listened to the drumbeat of hammers as the brothers shingled the roof of the new building. *Tap tap tap BANG! Tap tap tap BANG!*

She opened her eyes. "What I find most puzzling is that

they seem to take delight in suffering. They even sleep on wooden planks, when, in fact, they do actually sleep. They rise in the night to sing, then they sleep only until dawn. They eat one meal a day."

"Ah. 'Tis no wonder they all look so thin and pale."

She smiled. "They put more weight in a spiritual reality beyond the physical. I have felt . . . intrigued by their desire to join with a sacred power so alive in this world. Their joy is conveyed in their faith. I've missed that joy, somehow, despite a lifetime in church. Being here, it may sound odd, but I've come to know God in a way I never knew was possible. I can't explain it, but . . . all fear is gone. I can face the future, whatever comes to me. I don't think I've ever felt that way before." She laughed. "Does that sound crazy? Your father would say so."

"Nae, I think I understand. Certainly the part about fear being gone. And I can see the change in you. Yer not afraid, as you used to be." He gave her a sympathetic smile. "It must have been a rather frightening thing, to have your husband take sick in the middle of the wilderness, with no one to help."

"That time was . . . terrifying. But that night began this spiritual journey. I found I wasn't alone. God sent someone to help us, and that man brought us here."

"I believe that. I have seen God work in mighty ways lately."

Her eyes searched her son's handsome face, looking for changes in him since she had last seen him in October. What did she see when she looked at him now? A new confidence animated his features, a gentleness she had not seen in Philadelphia had come over his chiseled face. He looked very young, she thought, and . . . surprisingly, the words that came to her mind were at peace. He looked at peace. His face was no longer the one of a wounded man—and she knew that he had suffered greatly—but the calm countenance of one who walked with God.

The baby let out a yawn and Bairn reached over to put a finger out for him to cling to. "He seems a sweet babe."

"Oh, he is. He never cries. Well, hardly ever. And he's always smiling, this one."

"What have you named him?"

"Do you know, I haven't given him a name yet? I suppose I was waiting for your father's input. I just call him . . . baby."

"That will only go so far in a man's life."

She smiled.

"I think you should call him Hans. Hans Johann. After the boys who are no more."

It was a tradition from the Old World—to name a new baby after one who had preceded him on to death. She looked up at him. "This is your roundabout way of telling me that you want to be known by Bairn."

He smiled. "I do. I truly do. That's who I am." He looked down at his clasped hands. "Bairn Bauer. I am still my father's son. I returned to finish his work."

She looked around her at the Three Sisters' Garden, with the loamy beds waiting for spring planting. "Then, Hans Johann it shall be." In a thick voice that betrayed her emotions, she added, "Or do you think we should call him Jacob?"

"Jacob Bauer is not gone yet." Bairn dipped his chin to his chest, then lifted it again. "If you are willing, I'd like to take us back to the settlement."

"If you need to return, don't hesitate. I will send word of his passing." She looked over at God's Acres, the cemetery. "They told me Jacob could be buried here."

Bairn gave a slight shake of his head. "I don't want to wait. I think he is lingering for a reason. I think he wants to go home." He wrapped his arm around her shoulders, clumsy and yet tender. "We all do. We need to be together again. All of us."

Her chest tightened with a bittersweet ache when she thought how proud of him his father would be.

Jacob's Cabin
February 4, 1738

Felix tore into the cabin where Anna and Maria were weaving hay for the Gerbers' roof, shouted that there was someone coming up the path, then blew out again, leaving the door wide open. Roar in, roar out, that was his style. And Anna loved it. She grabbed her shawl and went outside. Maria followed behind.

There was a shift in the wind. Huge clouds the color of fire ash had piled up on the far horizon. The smell of rain, cold rain, was in the air.

"Are you sure, Felix?" Anna shielded her eyes to see down the path. "Who could it be?"

"Hopefully not another of Henrik Newman's wives," Maria said.

Anna cast her a dark look. Her hope was that it was Bairn who was coming up the path, returning with his parents. But then she saw them—two men, clearly English by their cloaks and their hats—well-worn and flat-crowned—on horseback.

One of them asked if he could speak to their husbands.

"The men are working an hour's walk from here," Anna said. "Shall I send the boy to fetch them?"

The one who spoke shook his head. "No time. We need to keep going." He swung a leg over the saddle, slid down, and handed Anna a paper. "We're land agents, sent by the London Company. We're here to post notice of eviction."

Anna felt Maria at her elbow, wondering what was being said, so she gave her a brief translation. "But we have the warrants," Anna said, skimming the notice. "Jacob Bauer received land warrants in 1736. Ten thousand acres."

"A new owner took out a blanket warrant for the land. I'm sorry, but you'll have to vacate soon or risk prosecution."

"But . . . how could that be?"

"The new owner holds the patent deed to the land. He paid the London Company in full and superseded the original land warrants."

Anna sucked in a breath and nearly choked. "But that isn't right. It isn't fair!"

"Perhaps not fair, but it is legal."

Anna thought it over. "What if we don't leave?"

"I must warn against that. You could be evicted for trespassing. And then the new owner, if so inclined, could have all of you prosecuted."

There was silence for a time. "You are welcome to rest your horses and take some nourishment for yourselves," Anna said, her voice low and controlled.

"Thank you for the kindness, but we have a ways to go before the rain hits." He swung up into the saddle, tipped his hat at Anna, and the two land agents cantered away.

"What does this all mean?" Maria said.

"Druwwel," Felix said, scowling, hands on his hips, as he watched the land agents disappear. *Trouble.*

She gave him a soft smile. Their Felix was growing up.

"Wahr. Unne Druwwel hot mer nix." *True. There is nothing without trouble.* She took a deep breath and straightened her shoulders. "Awwer mir aaghalden." *But we will persevere.*

Ephrata Community
February 5, 1738

As the hooded brothers settled Jacob into the wagon that morning, Bairn's mother said her goodbyes. Bairn checked the bit on the horse and made sure the borrowed wagon was properly secured. This would be an arduous, bumpy trip for his father and he prayed he would survive it.

Sister Marcella had come out to bring them food for the journey. She was his mother's favorite, and by the way the two women clung to each other, the feeling was returned. He tried not to look as if he was listening, but he heard Sister Marcella tell his mother that she had inspired her. "As I observed your constant care for your husband and child, it caused me to . . . reconsider my decision to leave my family."

"You're leaving here? You're going back to your husband?"

"Yes. I've told Father Friedsam and sent word to Christoph to come for me." She grabbed Dorothea's hands. "I pray we meet again, my friend. Knowing you has changed me."

Bairn had a hard time keeping a smile off his face as he heard those words to his mother. She held herself straighter, stronger than he'd ever seen her. It was a kind and good thing for Sister Marcella to leave his mother with such affirming words. He knew his mother had received few of those in her lifetime.

Over the head of the horse, across the large grassy area, he saw a group of robed brothers come out of a building and walk up the path to the construction site. One brother trailed behind the others, and there was something about the way this man walked that caught his attention. The other brothers walked slowly and solemnly, head down. This one's chin was lifted. This one . . . he had a swagger. "Do you happen to know that one's name?" he asked Brother Andrew.

He lifted his head and squinted. "That's Brother Mose." He handed a woolen blanket to Dorothea to cover Jacob. "He's a new convert."

Bairn stilled. "How new?"

"A few weeks."

He turned to his mother. "See that Papa is comfortable. I'll just be a moment."

He crossed the grass to catch up with the brothers, but quietly, so he did not draw attention to himself. When he had caught up with them, he reached a hand out to Brother Mose's shoulder. Startled, Brother Mose turned to Bairn, then tensed. Bairn had never seen a person's face change so fast. He caught a glimpse of something in his eyes, a slight panic, then there was nothing. He looked as relaxed and easy as a man could look.

"Henrik Newman." Bairn forced his words through clenched teeth. "Or is it Karl Neumann?" He glanced up at the brothers, who had continued walking ahead, unaware of what was going on behind them. "Perhaps now I should call you Brother Mose."

"I have joined the community. I've seen the error of my ways and have chosen a path of repentance."

"Hiding from yer wife, is what you mean."

Henrik's gaze slid past Bairn to Dorothea, waiting at the wagon. A wariness returned to his eyes. "Where is she?"

"Not with us, if that's what you're worried about."

He studied his folded hands, held at his waist. "Do you happen to know where she went?"

"On a hunt to find you. She won't give up."

For the briefest moment, the mask of bravado dropped off. "Don't I know it. God's truth, she's a terror."

Aye, the countess was a true termagant. Not unlovely, but a termagant nonetheless. "Yer an ambitious man. Are you sayin' you won't put up with her, even for a German title?"

"I'm a commoner. She's the one with the title. Three times she started to dissolve the marriage. Three times! And then, like a cat playing with a mouse, she would have a change of heart and send her loyal manservant to retrieve me. Cold to her core, that woman."

"Was it all lies, all smoke and mirrors? Slipping into our church, was it just a game? Finding the weaknesses, marryin' Anna?" Henrik had set his eyes on her, right from the start.

"No," he said, ever so softly, and there was no bluster to be seen or heard. "No, it was not a game to me. It was a new beginning, a fresh start. Magdalena and I were young when we met. We fell wildly in love and ran off to marry, despite the heartache it brought to our families. We were very immature, and both of us strong-willed. Our marriage had difficulties right from the start. It wasn't long before she took up with another and had me sent away. So when she said she was dissolving the marriage for the third time, I thought she meant it. She had fallen in love with a Danish duke. Each time it happened, my conscience to remain faithful grew quieter. How much can a man bear?" He shrugged his shoulders in a helpless lift. "Es is net gfogt meh zu duh as mer kann." *A man can do no more than he can.* "I ask you, is that so wrong?"

Bairn shook his head. *No. Of course not.*

"I had a vivid dream, an awakening. I made a promise to God that I would lead a straight and narrow life in the New World. No more selfish ambition." He lifted a palm toward Bairn. "And it seemed to be a blessed beginning. After all, you found me on the docks that day. God cleared a path for me, guiding me to your church. And then I met Anna, the sweetest, loveliest woman I have ever known. I thought this was my new destiny, to serve God as best I could with a new life, a new wife."

Bairn's eyebrows raised. "But the countess chased you down all the way to the New World." He jabbed a finger at his chest. "And you ran away from her. Like a rat to the sewer."

"I retreated," Henrik said reasonably. "I came to this place to seek a time of refuge." He swept a hand toward the building. "Magdalena does not share my newfound spiritual fervency. I fear she never will."

"Newfound? I thought you'd said yer grandfather was a disciple of Jakob Ammann."

"Oh, *that*." His dark brows rose coolly above his eyes. "Stories are meant to improve some with the telling."

Bairn stared at him. With a jolt, he realized that a part of him had started to feel sorry for this man. He was that smooth, that silver-tongued. *That* fascinating a tale-teller. He spun a web and pulled Bairn right into it.

"Lach!" *A jest*. "Some of it's true, mostly. My grandfather knew someone who was a disciple. Or maybe it was someone in the village who knew someone. It was a long time ago."

How could a man do so well by doing so little, by living on lies? That's what Bairn wanted to know.

Then Henrik's smile slipped away. He threw back his shoulders and drew a deep breath. "If you happen upon Magdalena, I would like to rely upon your discretion of my whereabouts."

So, that was his plan. To hide here until the countess gave up the hunt and sailed back to Germany. "Why should I do you any favor?"

"Because I did many favors for you when you went off to sea. I searched for your brother in Philadelphia. I went out to look for your missing parents. I tried to help your church survive. I comforted Anna when she thought you were dead." He jammed a finger right back at Bairn's chest. "I filled *your* place. *Your* empty place. A place you left wide open." A twisted smile crossed his lips. "And then there is this: 'He who is without sin may cast the first stone.'"

Aye, there was that.

"She didn't love me."

Bairn looked up sharply.

"She only married me to save the church from collapsing."

"You didn't mind being married to a woman who didn't love you?"

"Given time, she would have loved me. Had Magdalena dissolved the marriage like she had said she would, and had you stayed away like you were supposed to—" he sighed—"I would be a very contented man. Another opportunity, lost."

In that moment, Henrik Newman revealed himself. He was a charming opportunist, nothing more, nothing less.

Bairn turned to see his mother waiting for him by the

wagon. He looked back and met Henrik's eyes. "It is a surprisingly crowded place, this New World. Take care that our paths do not cross."

Henrik nodded, as uncertainty crept into his expression. "I'll try to keep that in mind."

26

Jacob's Cabin
February 7, 1738

It was long dark when they arrived at her husband's cabin, this land Dorothea had heard so much about. She hardly recognized her own boy when he ran to greet them. "Felix!"

He helped her down from the wagon, then spun her in a dizzying circle as he held her. The arms that held her were thicker now, she noticed, and defined with muscle. Laughing, she pulled out of his embrace to better examine him. She could find few signs of lingering boyishness in him.

But then she saw the boy still within. When Felix caught sight of his father lying in the back of the wagon, he burst into tears. "Is he dead?"

"No, no." Dorothea touched her son's tear-streaked face. "He's sick, that's all."

Felix led the horse down to the pen to care for him—a horse must be well cared for, he declared with the instructive confidence of an eight-year-old boy, sounding so like his father that it brought tears to her eyes. Bairn and Isaac gently lifted Jacob into the cabin, setting him on a pallet close to the fire to keep him warm. Anna fussed over the baby, how big he'd grown, and then handed him to Peter to hold while she prepared a supper for them to eat. They were famished from two long days of traveling, exhausted.

Sister Marcella had sent along a bushel of broccoli from the Householders' provisions, so Dorothea pureed the broccoli for Jacob while the others gathered around the fire, eager to share news of the settlement. The Gerber cabin was nearly done, and with the weather so mild, no snow or rain, they went ahead and moved in. Work had already begun on the Mast cabin. "It gets easier with each one," Isaac said and, clearly, Bairn was pleased with their ability to work together to achieve such progress.

Tomorrow, Dorothea planned to pay a surprise visit to Maria at her new cabin. She could just imagine the look on her face when she saw Dorothea. And then they would go visit Barbara.

She watched her two sons, Bairn and Felix, sitting together on a bench. Across from them sat Anna, with the babe on her lap. Her eyes took in the full measure of the cabin her husband had built for them. How hard he had worked—to the point where his health was jeopardized. Gently, she brushed Jacob's hair back and bent down to kiss his forehead. Her heart felt full, nearly overflowing.

"Something's happened, Bairn," Isaac said.

The gentle atmosphere of the room shifted. Dorothea straightened up with a start, bracing herself. The only sound came from the fire's pop and crackle.

"We had a visit from land agents sent by the London Company. It seems there's a problem with the land warrants."

"What kind of problem?"

Isaac looked to Anna to explain further. "Someone has taken out a blanket warrant on the land your father claimed."

"That isn't possible. We have proof. Dinnae you show them the warrants?"

"I tried, but apparently they've been voided. The new owner finalized the claims by paying them in full."

"Yer telling me that someone has paid off the land? But who?"

"We don't know," Anna said.

"But it must have happened recently," Isaac said. "The newcomer returned from Philadelphia just a few weeks ago and said everything was settled."

Dorothea was confused. "Who?"

Ever eager, Felix spoke up. "The man with the white spot in his hair."

"What?" Dorothea turned to Felix. "What did you say?"

"Weisskeppich." He pointed to his head. *White-headed.*

"His name is Henrik Newman," Bairn explained. "He came off a ship and joined our church."

"I met that man."

"I do not think so, Mem. You and Papa had already left Philadelphia by the time the newcomer joined the group."

"No, not there. It was at the community. A few months back—mid-November. He knew my name. He said he was staying with all of you. He told me about Bairn and Felix going off to sea. He promised he would tell all of you our whereabouts. But . . . no one came. Not until Bairn arrived. Did this man not tell you where we were?"

All eyes turned to Anna.

"No," she said, shame and disgust in her voice. "No, he did not."

❦

Bairn stood, made up a feeble excuse about checking the livestock, and walked outside. He needed time to think. He paced for a while, his thoughts as tattered and frayed as an old rope. At the fire pit, he added a log to its glowing embers, then watched the fire grow. After a while, Anna came out and stood beside him, offering him a tin of hot coffee.

He took a sip. The warmth of the cup in his hands helped him feel more settled. "I am going to Philadelphia to get this sorted out. The sooner, the better."

She glanced at the cabin. "Your father . . . it doesn't seem as if he'll last long."

"I'm surprised he survived the journey. I was hoping Brother Andrew was wrong about the consumption, though it appeared he was more knowledgeable than I. But I have no doot Jacob Bauer would rather be here, on his land, surrounded by his loved ones."

"Are you sure you don't want to wait . . . for—"

"For my father to die? Nae, I think he would be quite upset if I let the mischief with these warrants slip away." He pushed the end of the log into the fire. "There are some things I would like to tell him before I go. Just in case he does not last much longer. I thought, perhaps, I should leave a letter. You could read it to him."

"I could. But I think it best if you speak to him from your heart."

He glanced at her profile as she stared at the flames. He loved her dearly. All the way back from Ephrata Cloister, he had thought of Henrik's remark, that she married him to save the church. It made perfect sense to Bairn; she would do such a noble thing. Anna König was the most fearless person he had ever known.

"Your mother seems quite well. Surprisingly . . . ," she searched for the right word, ". . . sturdy."

"Aye. And that is not a word I have ever heard ascribed to her. It seems as if her time over at Ephrata Cloister helped to ground her. I suppose that's one thing we could thank Henrik Newman for—not letting anyone know he knew where they were." He was glad she couldn't see his face in the darkness, for he knew a trace of hostility toward the man shone in his eyes. "Anna, what happened to my mother over at Ephrata—a similar thing happened to me on the ship these last few months. A grounding, deep inside." A vanquishing of fear. "I have no doot where I belong. Not any longer."

She was listening, but her eyes were fixed on the flickering fire. "It's that time of year when ships start coming and going, is it not?"

"Darlin', will you nae trust me again?" He put an arm around her shoulder. "Will you always question my comin' and goin'?"

She shook her head, stepping back, moving out of reach of his touch. "How do I know that you won't leave again when life gets difficult, or when you have that itch to go, or when the sea calls your name?"

He turned her full around to face him, so that she could look into his eyes and know him for what he was. "I don't deserve you, Anna. I ken that. But I'm not leaving this time. I'm stayin'—for you, for my family, for the church. I'm not leaving. You must believe me."

"I want to. But I just don't know if a man can change who he is. Henrik Newman couldn't."

He felt a stain of color spread across his sharp cheekbones. To be compared to that rogue! It was humiliating. "Well, then, lassie, I'll just have to prove it to you."

That night, Bairn hardly slept. He knew the trip to Philadelphia to sort out the land warrants might take a long stretch, so he spent time writing specific instructions for Isaac, Christian, and Josef to carry on with their work in his absence. Simon too. He always forgot about him, he was such a lazy man. He tried to sleep for an hour or two, then gave up and prepared to leave for Philadelphia.

He crouched beside his father's sleeping pallet. He needed to take the first step and his heart thumped hard. He picked up his father's aged hand and held it between his, startled by the sight. This was an old man's hand, webbed with wrinkles and liver-spotted. "We have some things to settle between us, Papa," he whispered. His father's eyes fluttered open, but Bairn was not at all sure he would be heard or understood. Still, Anna was right—it was best if he spoke from his heart.

"Those years, when I was lost to you . . ." He stopped, his voice cracking. This was hard, so hard, to speak so frankly. It didn't come easily to him. "They were not lost years. I learned a great deal, and grew to be a man. I forgive you, Papa. I forgive you for leaving me when I needed you the most." He took a deep breath. "And I ask you to forgive me for leaving you, you and Mem, when ye needed me the most."

To his surprise, his father reached up with his other hand and placed it on top of Bairn's, all four hands together, and gently squeezed.

Bairn's eyes stung with tears. He hadn't known how badly he'd needed to make things right with his father, and it was doubly sweet and doubly painful because he was sure this was the last time he would see his father alive.

Jacob's Cabin
March 6, 1738

Two weeks passed without sign or word from Bairn. Then three.

Almost four weeks later, Felix heard the sound of an approaching wagon. He dashed through the forest where he had been trimming logs and ran to where Anna hung laundry on a taut rope hung between two trees. "It's him! Anna! It's *Bairn*! He's coming! Up the path, now!"

He squinted his eyes. "And he has someone in the wagon. Wait. Two people!"

"Who's with him, Felix?" Anna said, shielding her eyes from the sun. "Can you see?"

Felix couldn't believe his eyes. For the first time in his life, he knew he should think before he spoke. In a wobbly voice, he said, "Anna, I think . . . I think you'd better see for yourself."

Anna stilled, then cried out a shout of joy, and in the next instant she was running down the path to meet her grandparents. Felix took off after her, quickly bypassing her, with the awful dog at his heels.

"Bairn!" he shouted as he ran. "Bairn, Papa lives! He lives!"

Anna had to pinch herself. To think that her grandparents had made that long sea journey, all by themselves! Bairn, they told her, had written to them last fall, asking if they would meet him in Rotterdam in February. And when he did not show up, "We just went on ahead as planned," her grandfather said. They joined a group of Mennonites and came over on the first ship that left from Rotterdam for the New World. A small ship, and they were blessed to have calm seas and steady winds. Her grandfather said the entire experience was a dream; her grandmother was far less approving. "Some dreams turn into nightmares," she said, and Anna could not stop smiling.

But her grandmother was a resilient woman. First thing tomorrow, she told Anna, she wanted to take them into the woods to seek out plants. And her grandfather, a man with an extraordinary facility for languages, had plans to become fluent in Indian tongues. They would be a wonderful, valuable addition to their church. Just being here, they already were.

That evening, a celebration was held at Jacob Bauer's cabin for everyone to welcome the arrival of Anna's grandparents, and for Bairn to share in the joy of his father's improved condition. It was just a short time after Bairn left for Philadelphia that Jacob opened his eyes and recognized Dorothea. Day by day, they witnessed noticeable improvements. Slow, but steady. Now, four weeks later, he was able to sit up in bed for short periods. He had a long way to go before he was restored to what he once was, but he was a man with a determined spirit and he seemed to be gaining strength each day.

Bairn had been correct in his assessment. Scurvy was the culprit to blame, after all.

After the meal of rabbit stew, the talk turned to what Bairn had discovered in Philadelphia. "It turns out that the person who took out a blanket warrant on the land is Henrik Newman. His name is on all the warrants. All of them. He paid what was due on them to the London Company. As far as the land agents are concerned, it is his land."

"Maybe it was the best option," Peter said, still holding out hope that Henrik Newman was a good man. "Maybe having the warrants redrawn in his name was the best solution. So he could pay what was due on them. Maybe . . . there's a chance he was trying to do a favor for us."

Bairn gave him a pitying look. "No chance at all. A month ago, Henrik Newman contacted the London Company and ordered them to evict us."

Unable to believe her ears, Anna stared at Bairn. Finding out Henrik wasn't who he pretended to be was one thing, discovering he had lied and stolen from them was quite another matter. He had twisted God's words to suit his purposes. He had used their kindness as a weapon against them.

Christian tented his fingers together. "Do you think he would truly evict us?"

"Maybe he would do nothing at all," Josef Gerber said, hope in his voice.

"I think he will wait a few years until the land is greatly improved," Isaac said, "and then come to claim it."

"And then he would start a community of his own converts here," Maria said. "He was always chattering away about finding the new Garden of Eden."

Anna shuddered. This, this was the man she nearly wed. She *did* wed him! It was only by the grace of God that the marriage was annulled. It still made her sick to think of him.

"A land agent at the London Company said that Jacob Bauer might have a legal right to challenge Henrik Newman.

But it would be a long, costly effort without any guarantees." Bairn rose and filled his mug with hot water from the kettle. "I do not think we should expend any more effort on a man like him. It's not our way. We must let God do the reckonin' for us."

Our way, she heard him say. It's not *our* way.

"I agree," Christian said. "We could go to Germantown. We could wait for more ships to come in this summer. Join up with another church."

"I don't think that's the answer." Bairn remained by the fire, his hands wrapped around his mug. "I think we should settle near Lancaster."

Christian blinked. "That land has been settled."

"Not all of it. I checked." Bairn sat back at the table. "There is land to purchase, good land. It's farther from the frontier, but that also provides more security from clashes between the British and the French."

"And the Indians," Barbara said.

Felix added his two cents. "I've seen them in the woods."

"He's not lying this time," Catrina volunteered and Felix scowled at her. "I've seen them too."

Bairn set the mug of hot water down and placed his palms on the table. "Listen to me. I can purchase land out west, near Lancaster. Plenty of land for everyone to have a homestead, a farm. I'm able to buy it outright because I'm a British citizen, and I have savings from my years at sea." He went to his father's bed to crouch down beside it. "Papa, I think it's time to let this land go. I think we need to be further south. We are too close to the frontier. Too close to the Indians beyond the Blue Mountains. It does not bode well for the future. Not with the way the British and French are constantly agitating each other."

"Walk away from all this?" Dorothea said. "Leave what your father began?"

Bairn turned his head to face her. "Start new. Start fresh. Closer to the trade routes. Closer to established farmsteads."

Christian pressed his palms together in a worried way. "But it's also closer to the Mennonites. To the Dunkers. They will influence our young."

Anna's grandfather tapped his cane lightly, a signal that he wanted to speak. And when he spoke, everyone listened. "There is always something to fear. There always will be. But God will be with us, wherever we go."

"Even still," Christian said, "we've lost so much time."

"Nae, Christian," Bairn said. "There is time enough."

Everyone looked to Jacob. He was still their bishop, after all. He was lying in bed but paying attention. The thin line of his mouth clamped tight for a moment, and his throat bobbed once as he swallowed. In a voice like a rusty hinge, weak from lack of use, he said, "We will do as my son thinks best. We will go."

Later that evening, as everyone said goodnight and headed back to their cabins, Bairn lingered by the fire pit outside, and as he had hoped, Anna stayed behind. He was silent for a time, but then he turned and took both of Anna's hands in his own, calmer and more sure of himself than he had been in a long time. Ever, perhaps.

She gave him a shy look. "You kept your promise to me. You brought my grandparents to me."

"I would like to take full credit, but most of it goes to yer plucky grandfather. He made it happen. He said that after everyone left last spring, Ixheim was a dreadful place to be. When my letter arrived, he started packing that very night. And then we have to give God a great deal of the credit for providin' western gales that carried them over the Atlantic in only five weeks. It's practically unheard of to make that kind of a crossing."

"But how did you ever find them in Philadelphia?"

"Everyone within a few blocks of Penn's Landing hurried to meet the first ship in for the season, the ship rumored to have sailed on angels' wings over the waters. And there your grandparents were on the upper deck, waving furiously at me, like they fully expected me to be there." He grinned. "I think they had me confused with my father."

It had been a glorious moment for Bairn. He wasn't sure he could even put into words the indescribable joy he felt when he saw Anna's grandparents on that ship. And to think he had nearly missed it! For he had planned to leave Philadelphia that very morning but had one more errand to run. The thunder of cannon and the ringing of bells signaled the arrival of the first ship of the season. A month ahead of anyone's expectations! The citizens of Philadelphia rushed to the docks to welcome the ship with a hearty reception, Bairn among them.

He still felt such a wonderment, how this had happened, that God would deliver these two beloved people to his Anna in such a timely way. They had not seen the end of God's provision.

Bairn had one more story to share with Anna. It had to do with that last errand. He had paid a visit to the savvy printer, Benjamin Franklin. He wanted to let him know he had been most helpful to his family in pointing out the whereabouts of his missing mother and father.

And Bairn left him with a paid advertisement to run in the *Pennsylvania Gazette*: If anyone comes across a German countess, Magdalena von Hesse, searching for her husband, be sure to direct her to Ephrata Cloister.

Gazing at Anna in the flickering firelight, he changed his mind. Perhaps tomorrow he would tell her, perhaps he never would. All he could think about now was how lovely she looked tonight, and how long he'd waited for this moment. "Anna." He took hold of her face gently, made her eyes look up into his. "My life is with you, wherever that may be. You believe that, dinnae y'?"

Anna smiled at him, a smile that started from her heart. The first true smile she'd given to him since he had returned with Felix and the countess. "It seems . . . you'll have to dig up the rose yet again. For our new home."

Her words warmed his heart. She'd spoken of their new home, of a time when they would be married. He hadn't lost her.

Bending down, he kissed her lips, tenderly at first, then with all the feelings he had held at bay, and her answering kiss let him know he was home, truly home, where he belonged.

Martin sat awkwardly on his horse, his ill-fitting clothes hanging on him as if he hung on a hook. His pants were too short and his coat sleeves were too long. He wore no hat and his hair was unruly and wind-tossed, flying in all directions. He was a rumpled mess. Rumpled Martin.

"Is your father in the shop?" Faxon Gingerich said, not bothering to look at Tessa as he spoke.

"No. My father hasn't returned from the frontier yet," Tessa said. "My mother's expecting him back any day."

After Bishop Jacob Hertzler had been injured in a fall two years ago—the only Amish bishop in all the New World—her father had traveled by horseback to the frontier twice a year to act on his behalf: marrying, burying, baptizing. The trip usually took him two weeks, but he'd been gone for three.

Faxon's glance shifted to the stone house before resting on Tessa, the wind tugging at his beard. "Do you know which direction your father headed?"

"Up the Schuylkill River."

Faxon stared at her, his face settling into deep lines.

Tessa felt the first ominous tickle start up her spine. "Have you news? Has something happened?"

Faxon's bushy eyebrows promptly descended in a frown, no doubt thinking she didn't know her place. It was a common complaint fired at Tessa. Who did she think she was, asking bold questions of an elder?

Worried about her father, that's what she was. Tessa stared

back at him, her head held high, erect. "Is my father in danger?" Tessa looked from Faxon the Saxon to Rumpled Martin and caught their concern. Something *had* happened.

Faxon ignored her question. "Where's your mother?"

"She's gone to a neighbor's to take a meal. They had a new baby. You know how she loves babies." Everybody knew that, everybody except for Faxon the Saxon. He wouldn't know that about Anna Bauer because he wouldn't care. He did not hold much regard for any Amish person apart from Bairn Bauer, for whom he had a grudging admiration.

Faxon swung a leg over his horse to dismount. "Has he made progress on the wagon?"

"Some. It's not finished though."

He stood, feet planted, and she knew exactly what he wanted. To see the wagon. Faxon Gingerich had come to her father last summer with a request for him to build a better hauling wagon. Faxon made frequent trips to Philadelphia to sell and trade products and was fed up with wagon wheels stuck in mud. The provincial government was abysmally slow to cobble roads, so he had decided there must be a better design for a wagon. He just couldn't figure one out.

Tessa wasn't sure her father would want her to show the unfinished project, but she was proud of his ingenuity and she could tell Faxon would not be dissuaded from seeing it. "I'll show it to you if you like. I'll try to explain the design."

Rumpled Martin jumped off his horse, and she was startled to see that they were now about the same height. He noticed that she had noticed and gave her a big goofy grin. *Appalling.*

She led the way to her father's carpentry shop in silence. Hand tools hung neatly along the walls, but most of the shop was taken up with the enormous wooden wagon, eighteen feet from stern to bow. She opened the door and held it for Faxon, enjoying the sight of his bearded jaw drop so low it hit his chest. It was not a common sight to see Faxon the Saxon look nonplussed, and Tessa relished the moment. Savored it.

She inhaled the scent of wood shavings, linseed oil, and wax. Smells associated with her father. Worry circled her mind like bees around flowers. Where *was* he?

Faxon's gaze roamed slowly over the wagon; he peered into it, then below it. Its base set on wooden blocks, as her father hadn't made wheels yet. "A rounded base? What could he be thinking?"

He had immediately honed in on the most noteworthy improvement that Tessa's father had made—the one that set it apart from all other wagons. "It's like the keel of a ship. My father used to be a sailor. He said that the curved bottom would keep barrels and goods from shifting and tipping and rolling around."

"If he can pull that off, it will be a miracle," Faxon muttered. He and his awful son walked around the wagon, crawled under it, bent low to examine each part of it, murmuring to each other in maddeningly low voices.

"My father said this wagon will be able to haul as much as six tons of freight."

Faxon Gingerich shot up from a bent position so fast that his long, wiry beard bounced against his round belly. "*How* much?"

"Six tons. Assuming, of course, that you've plenty of horsepower to pull that kind of weight."

With that piece of information, everything changed. Faxon's countenance lightened, he continued inspecting the wagon but without the constant frown.

"It's not meant for people to ride in it," Tessa said. "Strictly a freight wagon. The teamster walks along the left side."

The frown was back. "No place for a teamster to sit?"

"There's a board for him to sit if he grows weary." Tessa bent down and slid out a wooden board.

"How many oxen would be needed to pull six tons of freight?"

"Quite a few. At least six."

Faxon's forehead puckered.

"Or horses could be used too."

"Not possible," Faxon said. "They're not strong enough. Has to be oxen."

"My uncle Felix has bred a type of horse that can pull the kind of heavy freight the Conestoga wagon can carry."

Now Faxon's bushy eyebrows shot up to his hairline. "The Conestoga wagon?"

"That's what my father calls it. To honor your valley. He said you gave him the idea for it. Credit goes to you."

Faxon the Saxon's chest puffed out and he very nearly smiled. It often puzzled Tessa how men needed personal significance to see things clearly. Their secret pride.

"Looks nearly finished to me. Just missing wheels."

"Wheels, yes, but there's still quite a bit of hardware to be made," Tessa said. "Plus pitch will be needed to make the seams watertight. And my mother and Maria Mueller will sew canvas cloth to cover the wagon bows, front to back."

Rumpled Martin regarded her thoughtfully. "You seem to know a lot about it."

Sarcasm. He may be taller now but he was just as rude. She ignored him and spoke only to his father. "You can find out more about it after my father returns."

Faxon's pleased look instantly faded. He exchanged a look with Rumpled Martin, whose misgiving showed plain on his face. A dark cloud descended in the carpentry shop. Something *had* happened along the frontier. "Tell me what's happened."

Faxon's face flattened and he went stone still for a full minute. "Trouble has come to our brethren in the north. There's been another Indian attack on families who settled along the Schuylkill River."

Tessa felt an unsettling weakness in the base of her stomach. These stories had become too common. "Did you recognize any names?"

"Just one. Zook. William and Martha Zook. The parents were found dead, the children were taken captive."

Tessa's heart started to pound. "Betsy Zook?"

"A girl said to be about your age. Smaller than you, though." His eyes skimmed her from head to toe. "Much, much shorter. Blond hair."

Tessa gave her chin a slight jerk. *That's her, that's Betsy.* The Zooks had immigrated to Berks County from Germany just about a year and a half ago. Tessa had met Betsy when the Amish churches gathered for spring and fall communion. Betsy was a beautiful girl, beloved by all, kind to the core. Tessa disliked her.

Betsy was everything Tessa wasn't. She was petite while Tessa was tall. She was curvy while Tessa was a table—flat with long thin arms and legs. She was perpetually kind while Tessa had touchy feelings.

But Tessa's dislike had nothing to do with Betsy. It had to do with Hans Bauer. From the moment they met, Hans fancied Betsy Zook.

A sick feeling roiled in Tessa's middle. So often, she had wished Betsy's family would just move away, go west. Go east. Go somewhere. She had even prayed for it! Especially after she learned that Hans had gone to visit Betsy numerous times.

But she had never wished for Betsy to be a victim of an Indian attack, to be taken captive.

Faxon Gingerich swept a glance over the large stone house her father had built, strong and sturdy. "Your father did well to bring you all down here, so many years ago, although your grandfather wanted to stay north. The frontier has become a devil's playground."

Faxon and Martin walked back to the horses and mounted them. "I will pray your father returns safely and soundly," Faxon said, before turning his horse around and starting down the lane.

"Don't worry, Tessa," Rumpled Martin said. "I'm sure he'll be home soon." He gave her a reassuring smile before cantering off to join his father.

Until that moment, it had never occurred to Tessa that her father might not return at all.

Discussion Questions

1. Even though there were three characters in this story—Anna, Dorothea, and Bairn—who started together, separated, then came together again, it was essentially Bairn's story. What did he have to come to grips with before he could move forward? Recall a time in your life when you were held captive by the past.
2. In what ways was Dorothea different after her time at Ephrata Cloister? What had the biggest influence on her?
3. Dorothea found something at Ephrata Cloister. How would you describe what she'd been missing?
4. What, if anything, did you admire about newcomer Henrik Newman? What did you find less than admirable in him?
5. Henrik Newman wasn't all bad, nor was he all good. What do you think motivated him? Have you ever known anyone like him?
6. Squivvers, the sailor, told Felix, "Good leaders don't grasp it. They live a life worthy of being followed." What does this story teach you about the importance of leadership, or lack of it?

7. Why did Anna decide to marry Henrik Newman? How did she view him?
8. In this day and age, with so many choices available, it might be hard to imagine the commitment Anna had to the survival of her church. Describe a time in your life when you felt a similar obligation—to your church, your community, or maybe even your family. How did your story play out?
9. "There is nothing without trouble," Anna told Felix. What are your thoughts about such a remark?
10. Bairn tells Felix a bedtime Bible story on the *Lady Luck* about the twelve spies that went into the Promised Land and came back with tales of giants, as well as evidence of fruitful abundance from the land. The giant stories, though, loomed larger. "Fear can be like that," Bairn said, "can take hold of a person." And then he realized he had let a giant in the Promised Land (metaphor!) strike fear in his own heart. What did he mean? What about you? What kind of giants keep you from your own Promised Land?
11. What surprised you most about the time period of the story? Could you imagine yourself living in it? Does anything in particular appeal to you about life in the New World of the eighteenth century? Maybe the vast wilderness, the untouched beauty?
12. Let's flip that around: name one or two things you learned that made you glad you're living in the twenty-first century. Say, for example, the common practice of bloodletting has been extinguished.
13. If you could write the next chapter in Anna and Bairn's life, what would it be?

Acknowledgments

A thank-you to Lindsey Ciraulo and Tad Fisher, my crackerjack team of first readers. They help me plug leaks and patch holes so my editor doesn't have to. Thank you, thank you!

I'm incredibly blessed by the team at Revell who take my manuscript, scrub and polish it, create a beautiful cover to slip it into, and then get it in the hands of readers: Andrea, Barb, Michele, Karen, Cheryl, Mary. You're all such extraordinary people! And a thank-you to my wonderful agent, Joyce Hart, who has the gift of encouragement.

I spent time walking in Philadelphia with Nick Cvetovic, found through the Travel Channel, who created an outstanding, customized tour focused on the city *prior* to the Revolution. Thank you for the excellent work you did on my behalf—including a sneak peek into an historical home in Elfreth's Alley.

Director Becky Gochnauer at the Hans Herr Haus in West Lampeter Township, Pennsylvania, was an invaluable resource—so helpful and so knowledgeable. The Hans Herr Haus, built in 1719, sparked my imagination of a young

1700s farm, carved out of the wilderness. And the Ephrata Cloister, in Ephrata, Pennsylvania, is definitely worth a visit. Don't miss the gift shop! Lots of unusual books you can't find elsewhere.

A thank-you to my faithful readers who asked for a sequel to *Anna's Crossing*. Originally, it was contracted and written as a stand alone, not a series. But I'm so glad you wanted more! You're the best. Just. The. Best.

Last but *never* least, my gratitude goes to the Almighty One. His providence never fails.

Historical Notes

Readers are often curious about how much of a story is fact and how much is fiction. While the characters in this story are made up, the wilderness setting, the time period, the hardships faced are based on historical research. I worked diligently to create a credible story, but any errors are my own blunders.

Penn's Woods in 1737 was a vastly unsettled wilderness. The fertile land, abundant with natural resources, had never been claimed, surveyed, or deeded. Immigrants seeking religious freedom and economic prosperity, largely German, along with Irish, Scots, Dutch, and others, swept into Philadelphia. The population of the city was swelling to 12,000. Rules for immigration changed constantly. In 1728, Mennonites filed a petition for the naturalization of those who, because of the dictates of their conscience, would not pledge allegiance to the Crown and thus could not become citizens. Here's how the naturalization document was adjusted: "promise and swear" was changed to "promise and solemnly declare." "Will be faithful and bear true allegiance" was changed to "will be true and faithful." "Majesty" was removed from the title of King George the second. "Abhor, detest and abjure" became "abhor, detest and renounce." "So help us God" was eliminated entirely. Interestingly, the signature of the Germantown printer Christoph Saur is on that document.

In 1737, Lancaster County encompassed a huge area. It wasn't until 1752 that it was divided up and a northeastern portion became Berks County. That would be the location, up the Schuylkill River, where the fictitious character Bishop Jacob Bauer in this novel had first settled.

The Ephrata Cloister was a commune in colonial Pennsylvania led by Conrad Beissel (known as Father Friedsam), a German Pietist immigrant who arrived in Pennsylvania in 1720 and became a Sabbatarian (a fancy way to say that he insisted on Saturday worship, not Sunday). A charismatic figure, Beissel attracted a group of followers who, in 1732, formed a commune on Cocalico Creek in Lancaster County, near the present town of Ephrata, Pennsylvania. The Ephrata Community became one of the most successful experiments in communal living in American history, with a significant contribution to the printing of German materials. By the way, it was true that Christoph Saur's wife left him and lived at the Ephrata Cloister for a period of time.

The newcomer's switcheroo with the land warrants was not entirely fictitious. After a warrant was applied for, the boundaries would be surveyed and the number of acres determined. Remember, this land had never been claimed, surveyed, or deeded. There were no hard-and-fast rules, except to file a claim one needed to mark the desired boundaries—with rocks in the ground or slashing the bark of a tree with a hatchet. Upon the final payment for the land, a patent deed was issued to the new landowner. As you can imagine, land warranting was an inexact process in the 1730s. And yet, by 1766, the land in Berks County was nearly fully claimed, and new arrivals of Amish families moved west to Lancaster and Mifflin Counties.

How likely was it for Anna's grandparents to sail across the ocean, in springtime, in such a seamless way? There were few crossings that went so smoothly. A few. Most were horrific. In fact, 1738 was dubbed The Year of the Destroying Angels due to overcrowded vessels, contagious diseases, and late autumn arrivals. I wanted Anna's grandparents to have a swift and smooth sailing on prosperous winds. Rare, very rare, though it did happen.

But then, that's the fun of being an author.

Resources

These books provided background materials that were helpful in trying to re-create an eighteenth-century Penn's Woods:

Beachy, Leroy, *Unser Leit: The Story of the Amish* (Millersburg, OH: Goodly Heritage Books, 2011).

Grove, Myrna, *The Path to America: From Switzerland to Lancaster County* (Morgantown, PA: Masthof Press, 2009).

Hostetler, Harvey, "Descendants of Barbara Hochstedler and Christian Stutzman," Gospel Book Store, Berlin, OH.

Isaacson, Walter, *Benjamin Franklin: An American Life* (New York: Simon & Schuster, 2003).

Kenny, Kevin, *Peaceable Kingdom Lost: The Paxton Boys and the Destruction of William Penn's Holy Experiment* (New York: Oxford University Press, 2009).

Larkin, Jack, *The Reshaping of Everyday Life 1790–1840* (New York: Harper Perennial, 1988).

McCullough, David, *1776* (New York: Simon & Schuster, 2005).

McCutcheon, Marc, *The Writer's Guide to Everyday Life in the 1800s* (Cincinnati, OH: Writer's Digest Books, 1993).

Silver, Peter, *Our Savage Neighbors: How Indian War Transformed Early America* (New York: W. W. Norton, 2008).

Wright, Louis B., *The Cultural Life of American Colonies* (New York: Dover Publications, 2002).

Suzanne Woods Fisher is the bestselling author of *The Imposter*, *The Quieting*, The Inn at Eagle Hill series, the Lancaster County Secrets series, and the Stoney Ridge Seasons series, as well as nonfiction books about the Amish, including *Amish Peace*. She is also the coauthor of an Amish children's series, The Adventures of Lily Lapp. Suzanne is a Carol Award winner for *The Search*, a Carol Award finalist for *The Choice*, and a Christy Award finalist for *The Waiting*. She lives in California. Learn more at www.suzannewoodsfisher.com and connect with Suzanne on Twitter @suzannewfisher.

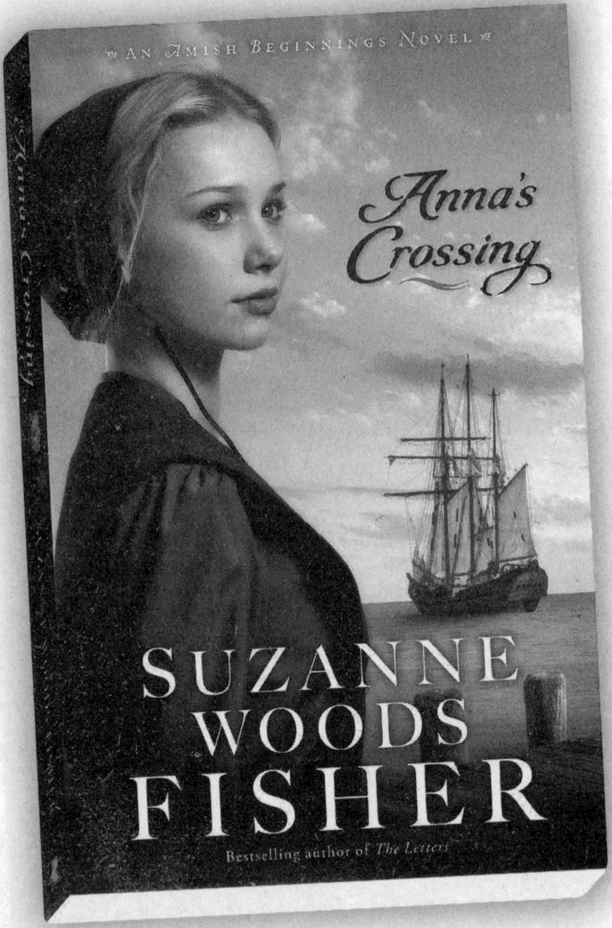

Don't Miss Any of The Bishop's Family

"Suzanne is an authority of the Plain folks. . . .
She always delivers a fantastic story with
interesting characters, all in a tightly woven plot."

—Beth Wiseman, bestselling author
of the Daughters of the Promise and the Land of Canaan series

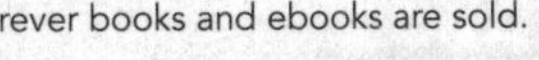

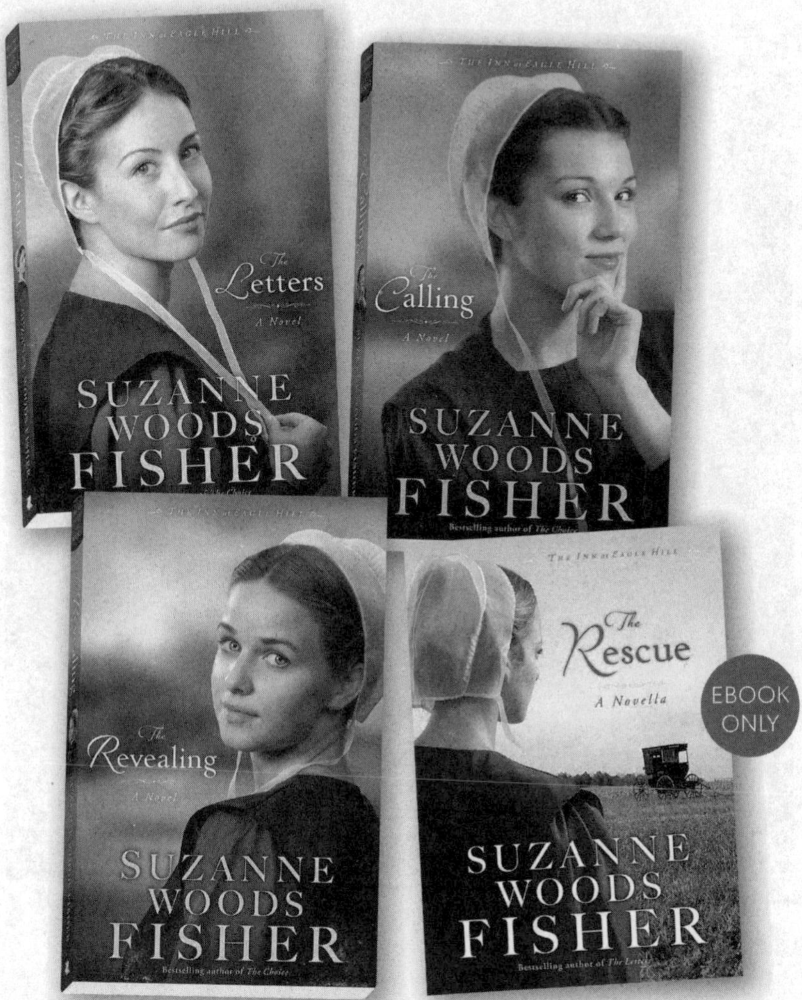